新概念英语（新版）辅导丛书

与《新概念英语》（新版）教材同步配套

新概念英语

同步能力拓展训练

北京书友佳苑教育咨询中心 编著

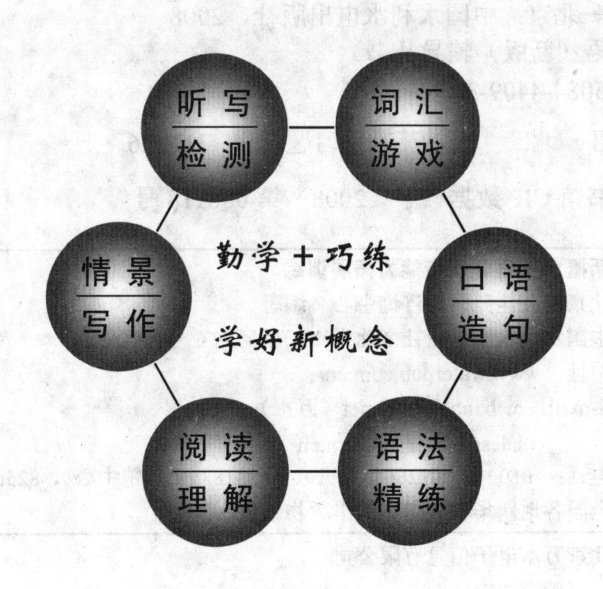

图书在版编目（CIP）数据

新概念英语2同步能力拓展训练 / 北京书友佳苑教育咨询中心编著. —北京：中国水利水电出版社，2008
（新概念英语（新版）辅导丛书）
ISBN 978-7-5084-4409-3

Ⅰ. 新… Ⅱ. 北… Ⅲ. 英语—习题 Ⅳ. H319.6

中国版本图书馆 CIP 数据核字（2008）第 008118 号

书 名	新概念英语2同步能力拓展训练
作 者	北京书友佳苑教育咨询中心 编著
出版 发行	中国水利水电出版社（北京市三里河路6号 100044） 网址：www.waterpub.com.cn E-mail：mchannel@263.net（万水） sales@waterpub.com.cn 电话：（010）63202266（总机）、68331835（营销中心）、82562819（万水）
经 售	全国各地新华书店和相关出版物销售网点
排 版	北京万水电子信息有限公司
印 刷	北京蓝空印刷厂
规 格	787mm×1092mm 16开本 15.25印张 350千字
版 次	2008年2月第1版 2008年2月第1次印刷
印 数	0001—5000册
定 价	26.00元（含MP3光盘）

凡购买我社图书，如有缺页、倒页、脱页的，本社营销中心负责调换

LOOK 致学习者

由英国著名英语教育专家路易·乔治·亚历山大教授与北京外国语大学何其莘教授联合编写的《新概念英语》教材，符合中国学生学习英语的特点。它侧重于听、说、读、写四种语言技能的综合训练；注重实际运用能力；语言活泼，趣味性强。自出版以来，《新概念英语》以其严密的体系性、严谨的科学性、超强的实用性、浓郁的趣味性深受广大英语学习者的青睐。

这套教材语言上最大的特点就是，往往看似平淡无奇的常用词汇，却准确而传神地表达了丰富的意象。亚历山大教授在课文的甄选和编排上表现出了深湛的功力和慧眼卓识。这些课文既具有文学性，又具有思想性，可谓雅俗共赏。文章的难度由浅入深，篇幅由短到长，层层递进，有条不紊，篇篇都是英语学习的典范之作。

为帮助广大英语学习者更好地学习《新概念英语》教材，我们特编写了《**新概念英语同步能力拓展训练**（1～4）》。本套书的编者都是多年从事一线教学的老师。他们经验丰富，对教材的语言点体系了如指掌，并对学习者在学习教材过程中的种种疑问非常熟悉。书中的很多知识点测试材料都是编者们在日常教学过程中反复使用和验证过的。这些测试材料不是用来单纯检测学习者某一阶段的学习水平的，而是通过对重要语言点的反复练习和不断强化，进一步帮助学习者熟练掌握和运用课文中出现的各类知识点，真正提高语言技能。

本套书着重巩固和测试的知识点分为六种类型，分别是：

1. **听写检测**：以单词和句子的听写为测试手段；
2. **词汇游戏**：通过趣味游戏的形式来检测单词；
3. **口语造句**：以补全对话或造句检测口语能力；
4. **语法精练**：以句型转换或补全句子检测语法；
5. **阅读理解**：阅读理解和完形填空的综合测试；
6. **情景写作**：全面检测学习者的命题写作能力。

上述这些拓展训练试题的题型多样，题量适中，并且与教材的内容同步，方便学习者灵活机动地安排学习进度，并根据同步拓展训练的结果，调整下一阶段的学习重点。我们建议学习者在使用本套书时，在学习完一个单元之后，先进行复习，再做拓展训练。

本套书特别设计了“听写”这种题型。听写是在具有一定英语语法和词汇的基础上进行的一种听力训练，是一项复杂的脑手相结合的活动。它不仅需要用耳朵去辨别声音信息，而且要求对经过耳朵输入大脑的信号进行处理，再通过手迅速准确地记录下来。写的过程同时也是复习巩固的过程，能进一步加深对语音内容的了解，在听的过程中把模糊的东西彻底搞明白。

专家证实，在短时间内，要测验出一个人的英语水平，听写就是最佳的手段。当听写的量超过一定的规模时，语言水平就会在不知不觉中获得提升。实践证明，听写是一项培养和测试学生语言能力的重要方法。

本套书所设计的听写练习包含两部分：单词听写和句子听写。根据中、高考听写试题的考试模式，书中的听写录音也做了相应的设计：

1．单词或句子的录音一共朗读五遍。

2．第一遍是连续朗读，学习者以听为主，不需要动手写。这一遍练习的目的是让学习者对于将要听写的内容有一个整体的了解，根据内容熟悉的程度，调整听写侧重点。

3．接下来，每个单词或句子都会分别朗读三遍。每次朗读之间均有时间间隔，用于学习者把听到的内容写下来。暂时写不下来的，可以先略过去。

4．最后还是一遍整体朗读。学习者可以边听录音，边检查自己刚才听写下来的内容，尽量把信息补全，不会写的单词可以通过读音先拼出来。

5．听写结束后，学习者需要对照本书最后面的单词录音答案及每个单元相应的课文，仔细检查，把错误之处标注出来，做进一步的重点复习。

本套书共包含四本，分别与《新概念英语》第1、2、3、4册教材相对应。每个级别均设计了36套同步拓展训练试题，分别与教材中的课文同步对应。具体对应如下：

1．《新概念英语1同步能力拓展训练》与《新概念英语》教材第1册同步配套

2．《新概念英语2同步能力拓展训练》与《新概念英语》教材第2册同步配套

3．《新概念英语3同步能力拓展训练》与《新概念英语》教材第3册同步配套

4．《新概念英语4同步能力拓展训练》与《新概念英语》教材第4册同步配套

参与本书编写的有宋黎、张艳敏、王海涛、陈丽辉、郭梅、殷晓芳、徐勤、时真妹、胡秀梅、顾玉梅、胡后伦、梁斐、米冬然、徐琤、王海涛、刘芳、王茜、胡芳芳、刘蕊、高国娟、武恒、张艳昌、胡后立、宋彩云、胡厚岭、闻人奕、卢洋和李云鹏等。

本套书既适合《新概念英语》自学者使用，也适合各类语言培训机构在《新概念英语》培训课堂上使用。书中在编写的过程中难免有疏漏之处，欢迎各位读者来信与我们交流和探讨。我们的E-mail是waterpress@126.com或yixuetong@126.com。

最后，祝所有《新概念英语》的学习者一帆风顺，学习快乐！

编者

2008年·北京

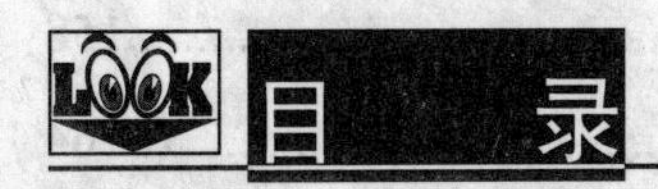

目　录

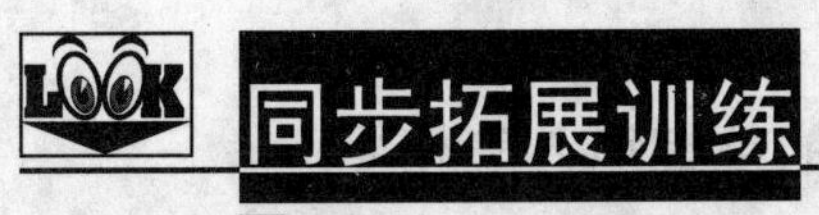

同步拓展训练 1

Lesson 1~3

听写检测——根据要求听写下列内容

Part A: 单词听写——听光盘录音，将听到的每个单词依次写在下面的横线上。

1.______ 2.______ 3.______
4.______ 5.______ 6.______
7.______ 8.______ 9.______
10.______ 11.______ 12.______
13.______ 14.______ 15.______
16.______ 17.______ 18.______
19.______ 20.______ 21.______
22.______ 23.______ 24.______
25.______ 26.______ 27.______
28.______ 29.______ 30.______
31.______ 32.______

Part B: 句子听写——听光盘录音，把课文内容听写在下面的横线上。

1.______
2.______
3.______
4.______
5.______
6.______
7.______
8.______
9.______
10.______

词汇游戏——根据汉语提示，将数字序号对应的单词填入表格中

横向提示		纵向提示	
	6. *n.*注意；9. *v.*到达 10. *n.*午餐时间 12. *n.*决定；15. *adj.*私人的 16. *adv.*大声地 17. *v.*重复；18. *adv.*生气地 20. *prep.*直到；23. *v.*容忍 25. *n.*姑，姨，婶，舅母 26. *n.*服务员，招待员 28. *v.*使索然无味；损坏 29. *v.*寄，送		1. *n.*演员；2. *adj.*公共的 3. *v.*教授；4. *n.*谈话 5. *adj.*友好的；7. *n.*明信片；8. *n.*事 11. *adv.*无礼地，粗鲁地 13. *adj.*唯一的，单个的 14. *n.*博物馆；16. *v.*借给 18. *adj.*生气的；19. *n.*戏 21. *n.*剧场，戏院；22. *n.*座位 24. *adv.*外面；26. *adj.*整个的 27. *v.*（铃或电话等）响

口语造句——根据要求完成下列内容

补全对话

A: You look worried, Peter.

B: I'm having trouble in __1__ English.

A: You said you like English. What's the __2__?

B: I can't get the __3__ right.

A: Well, Listening can help. Why __4__ you borrow the teacher's tapes? You can listen to them at home and repeat the sentences that are __5__ for you.

B: That's a good idea. But what __6__ all the new words? I __7__ a lot of new words.

A: You can always __8__ the new words in your notebook and study them at home. You can even study in the train or on the __9__ to school.

B: That might really __10__! Thanks a lot.

A: It's a pleasure.

语法精练——根据要求完成下列内容

根据句意，选用方框中所给词的适当形式填空。

can, do, join, can' t, like, be, club, swim, want, sing

1. My sister ______ sing. She is a good singer.
2. What can you______? I can dance…
3. What______ does he want to join?
4. Does she want to______ the art club?
5. He can play basketball, but he ______ play it very well.
6. I ______ playing the piano. I play it every day.
7. I like______ because it's interesting.
8. We______ two good musicians for our band.
9. He______ well, so he can be in our music band.
10. ______ you good with kids?

根据所给中文意思，完成句子。

11. 在晚上，我过去经常看电视或者和祖母聊天。

In the evening, I________ watch TV or ________with my grandmother.

12. 在过去的几年里你变化很大。

You have changed a lot ________the ____ ______years.

13. —你以前不很外向，是吗?

—是的，我不外向。

—You ______very outgoing, were you?

—______, I wasn't.

14. 你的生活好像发生了很大的变化。

It ________ that your life ________changed a________.

15. 我不知道怎样解这道题。

I don't know ________ ______work out the problem.

16. 不要担心太多，它会使你太紧张的。

Don't ____ _____things so much. It will make you______ ______.

17. Gina 过去经常憎恨考试，但现在她不担心考试了。

Gina_____ to____ tests but now she ______worry _____them.

18. 过去他常写信给朋友，现在他对发短信给朋友更感兴趣。

He____ _____ write to his friends. Now he is______ ______in _______ short _______to them.

阅读理解——根据要求完成下列内容

完形填空

My name is Bob. __1__ is my birthday. Dad and Mum __2__ me a big __3__. I like cakes, very much. On the table of the bedroom, you __4__ see my lovely cake. You can also __5__ my name on it. There are other things __6__ my birthday. They are apples, pears, __7__ bananas, but I'd __8__ to have something to drink now. My __9__ Bill and Sam are coming. I'd like to eat the food __10__ my friends.

1. A. It B. Today C. This D. That
2. A. get B. put C. find D. want
3. A. box B. apple C. cake D. book
4. A. don't B. can't C. do D. can

5.	A. find	B. put	C. look	D. know
6.	A. to	B. at	C. on	D. for
7.	A. or	B. and	C. but	D. with
8.	A. like	B. want	C. get	D. put
9.	A. sisters	B. brothers	C. teachers	D. friends
10.	A.with	B. and	C. for	D. at

阅读下面的文章，并选择正确答案。

Baseball is a very popular sport in the U.S.A. Many people enjoy this game. It is sometimes called "the most popular game" in the U. S. A. Many Americans think that it is the national sport.

Baseball is played by two teams of nine men each. Different men have different jobs when the team is on the field. Each team must try to score more points than the other team. A point is scored when one man hits the ball and then runs around the playing field to each of the four bases.

The men who play baseball must do two things well. First, they must hit the ball when it is their turn. If they can hit the ball well, they can help their team to win the game. Second, they must catch and throw the ball well. When their team is on the field, they can keep the other team from winning. These are the two abilities that a baseball player must have.

Of course, there are some good things about baseball. You don't have to be very intelligent to play baseball or watch it. You can easily understand what is happening on the field. Many Americans enjoy going to a baseball game during the summer months. The weather is warm and usually sunny, and it is a pleasure to sit outside for a few hours and watch a game. Baseball games do not usually cost much money. You can go to a baseball game for a very small amount of money, and still have a very good time.

1. Which of the following statements is TRUE?
   A. Baseball is played all over the U. S. A.
   B. Baseball is loved by young Americans.
   C. Baseball is less popular than football.
   D. Baseball is loved by every American.
2. There are altogether _________ players on the field in a baseball game.
   A. 17　　B. 18　　C.19　　D.20
3. A baseball player should _________.
   A. hit the ball well　　B. throw the ball well
   C. catch the ball well　　D. A, B and C
4. Which of the following statements is WRONG?

A. Baseball players are all very strong.

B. Baseball players have good eyesight.

C. Baseball players need to be very clever.

D. Baseball players need to run very fast.

5. All the following are told in the passage except that________.

A. a baseball player needs to run around the ground to score one point

B. every player on the field should both hit the ball and catch the ball

C. people enjoy playing baseball all the year round

D. tickets for a baseball match are usually not expensive

情景写作——根据要求完成下列内容

暑假就要到了，有些同学计划外出旅行。你都去过哪里呢？不妨向大家推荐一个你认为值得去的地方，并对该处进行简单的介绍。

Lesson 4~6

听写检测——根据要求听写下列内容

Part A: 单词听写——听光盘录音，将听到的每个单词依次写在下面的横线上。

1.______ 2.______ 3.______
4.______ 5.______ 6.______
7.______ 8.______ 9.______
10.______ 11.______ 12.______
13.______ 14.______ 15.______
16.______ 17.______ 18.______
19.______ 20.______ 21.______
22.______ 23.______ 24.______
25.______ 26.______ 27.______
28.______ 29.______ 30.______
31.______ 32.______

Part B: 句子听写——听光盘录音，把课文内容听写在下面的横线上。

1.______
2.______
3.______
4.______
5.______
6.______
7.______
8.______
9.______
10.______

词汇游戏——根据汉语提示，将数字序号对应的单词填入表格中

横向提示		纵向提示	
横向提示	2. *n.*乞丐；4. *n.*邻居 6. *n.*衣服口袋；7. *adj.*不同的 9. *n.*兄弟；11. *v.*越过 14. *n.*电话；15. *v.*唱歌 16. *n.*距离；20. *adv.*在国外 21. *n.*中心；25. *n.*分钟 26. *v.*敲；28. *n.*修车厂 29. *v.*搬家 30. *n.*月 31. *n.*要求，请求	纵向提示	1. *n.*澳大利亚；3. *adj.*令人兴奋的 5. *n.*地方，地点；8. *n.*商行，公司 10. *v.*接受，收到 12. *v.*参观，访问 13. *n.*食物；17. *n.*业务，服务 18. *n.*回报；19. *n.*一餐，一顿饭 22. *v.*携带，运送 23. *n.*信息 24. *n.*鸽子 27. *v.*拜访，光顾

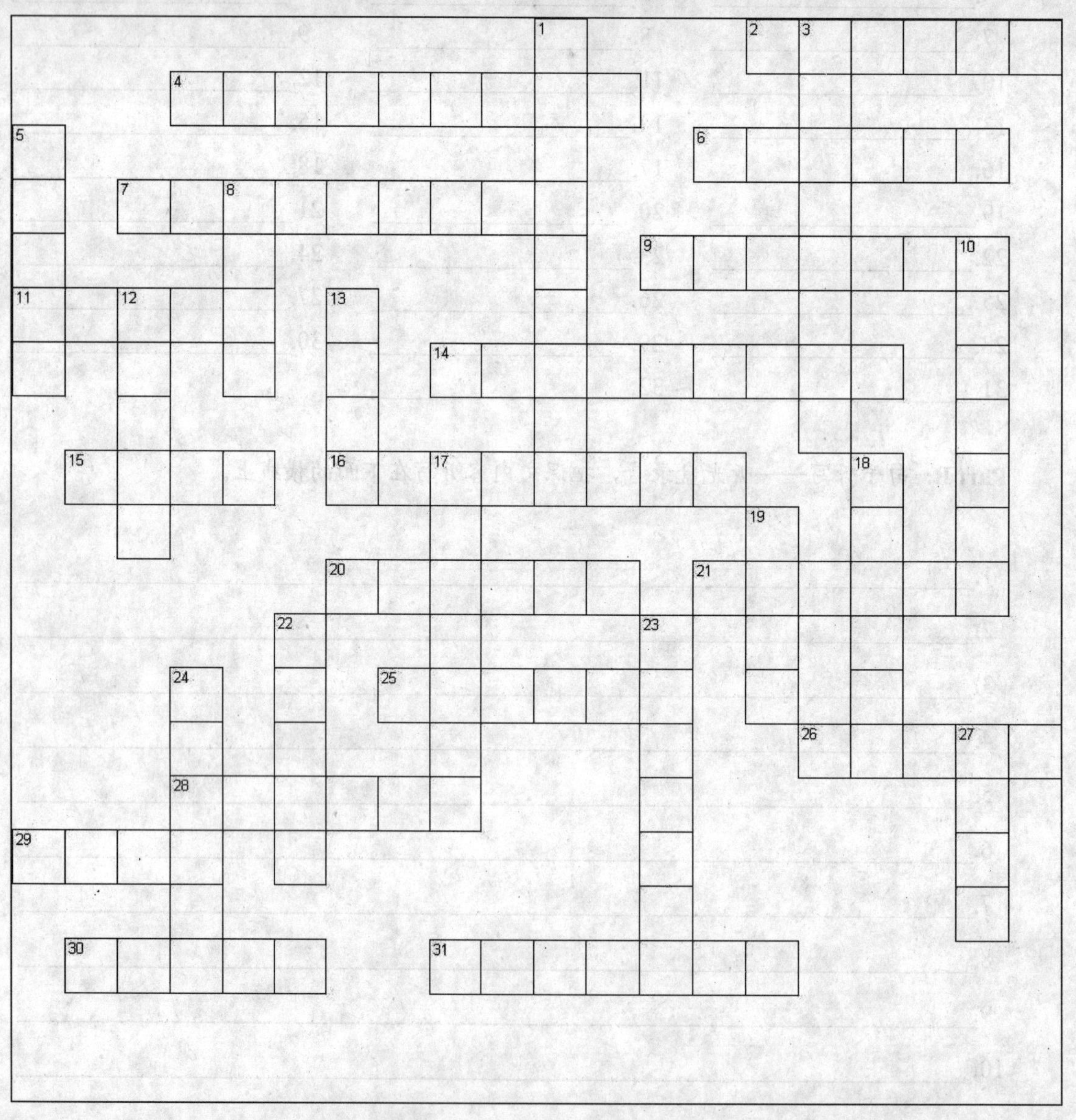

口语造句——根据要求完成下列内容

补全对话

Marie: Hello! May I speak to Karen?

Karen: Hello! This is Karen. How are you, Marie?

Marie: I' m fine. What__________________(do)?

Karem: Nothing much. I__________________(study) math. What about you?

Marie: I__________________(clean) my room.

Karen: Hey, do you want to__________________(go) to the movies?

Marie: That__________________(sound) boring.

Karen: I just call Lucy. She__________________(swim). Do you like__________(swim)?

Marie: Sure. We can swim in the school's swimming pool. When do you want to go?

Karen: Let's_______________(go) to the swimming pool now.

Marie: Great!

语法精练——根据要求完成下列内容

连词成句，注意句后标点。

1. musician, a, you, are

   ____?

2. call, Liz, 790-4230, please, at

   ____.

3. can, be, school, our, you, maybe, concert, in

   ____.

4. good, children, are, with, you

   ____?

5. play, guitar, I, the, can, but, can't, it, well, play, I

   ____.

6. want, we, good, singers, two, rock, band, for, our

   ____.

7. Jane, well, volleyball, play, can't

   ____.

8. club, you, do, what, want, join, to

____?

9. with, help, kids, swimming, can, you

____?

10. us, join, come, and

____.

根据所给中文意思，完成句子。

11. 这辆自行车肯定是我爸爸的。

The bike _____ _____ to my father.

12. 这件衬衫是谁的？肯定不是约翰的，对他来说这件衬衫太小了。

_____ shirt is this? It _____ _____ John's, it's too small _______ him.

13. 这个足球可能是李明的，因为他喜欢踢足球。

The football ______ be Li Ming's because he ______ playing football.

14. 他把笔掉在地上了。

He ______ the pen _____ the ground.

15. 他们看见一个男人在跑步，他可能为了锻炼。

They saw a man______, he _______ be running for exercise.

16. 昨晚，在我的梦中我在无尽的试卷中漂浮。

Last night, in my dream I was _______ in _____ _____ of papers.

17. 你不可能把一个假装睡觉的人叫醒。

You can' t _______ a person who ______ ______ to be ______.

18. 这本法语书一定是李平的，因为他是我们班唯一在学法语的人。

This French book _____ _____ Li Ping' s because he is the _____ one _____ studying French.

阅读理解——根据要求完成下列内容

完形填空

Kate __1__ from America. She's American. She __2__ English. She can also speak __3__ Chinese. She __4__ in Beijing now. She __5__ in a middle school. She __6__ classes __7__ weekdays. She often __8__ her mother go shopping __9__ Sundays. Her father __10__ in Beijing. He __11__ English. Her mother also __12__ in Beijing. They __13__ Chinese food, and __14__ like China and the Chinese people __15__.

1.	A. am	B. is	C. are
2.	A. speak	B. speaking	C. speaks
3.	A. little	B. many	C. a little
4.	A. is	B. am	C. are
5.	A. studies	B. is studying	C. studys
6.	A. have	B. is	C. has
7.	A. in	B. on	C.at
8.	A. helps	B. help	C. helping
9.	A. on	B. in	C. at
10.	A. am	B. is	C. are
11.	A. teach	B. teaching	C. teaches
12.	A. work	B. works	C. working
13.	A. like	B. likes	C. liking
14.	A. he	B. she	C. they
15.	A. very good	B. friendly	C. very much

阅读下面的文章，选择正确答案。

To me, life without music would not be exciting. I realize that this is not true for everybody. Many people get along quite well without going to concerts or listening to records. But music plays an important part in everyone's life, whether they realize it or not. Try to imagine, for example, what films or TV plays would be like without music. Would the feelings, the moving plot, and the greatest interests, be exciting or dramatic? I'm not sure about it.

Now, we have been speaking of music in its more common meaning-the kind of music we hear in the concert hall. But if we look at some parts of music more closely, we discover them in our everyday life too-in the rhythm of the sea, the melody of a bird in the woods and so on. So music surely has meaning for everyone, in some way or other. And, of course, it has special meaning for those who have spent all their lives working on playing or writing music.

It is well said, "Through music a child enters into a world of beauty, expresses himself from his heart, feels the joy of doing things alone, learns to take care of others, develops his mind and makes his body strong."

16. What does the writer say more about in the passage?

A. Life full of music　　B. Life without music

C. The importance of music　　D. The development of music

17. In the writer's opinion, if there is no music in films or TV plays,_________.

A. the cinema and theatre would be quiet

B. we would lose some of the audience

C. everything would be as exciting as before

D. it would be hard to imagine the result

18. What does the word "melody" mean in the passage?

A. Flying　　B. Looking　　C. Singing　　D. Living

19. Which of the follow is NOT true?

A. Life would be boring if there was no music.

B. Music surely has meaning for everyone, in some way or other.

C. Music is important for children during their growing up.

D. Anyone who doesn't listen to the music will be unhappy.

情景写作——根据要求完成下列内容

请阅读下面的短文，并完成两个任务。

My name is Zhang Peng. I like watching TV. I think watching TV is one of the most important activities of the day. TV brings the outside world closer to people's house. Watching TV can help me learn something new in the world. Watching English programs can improve my English. But my father thinks watching TV for a long time is bad for my eyes. He asks me to spend more time doing the homework. So I often argue with him about it. I feel unhappy.

A．请写出张鹏和他父亲的观点以及他的苦恼之处。

1. He likes ____________________

2. He thinks ____________________

3. His father thinks ____________________

4. He ____________________

B．请针对他所提到的问题阐述你的观点，并给出建议（40 words）。

____

____

____

Lesson 7~9

听写检测——根据要求听写下列内容

Part A: 单词听写——听光盘录音，将听到的每个单词依次写在下面的横线上。

1.______ 2.______ 3.______
4.______ 5.______ 6.______
7.______ 8.______ 9.______
10.______ 11.______ 12.______
13.______ 14.______ 15.______
16.______ 17.______ 18.______
19.______ 20.______ 21.______
22.______ 23.______ 24.______
25.______ 26.______ 27.______
28.______ 29.______ 30.______
31.______ 32.______

Part B: 句子听写——听光盘录音，把课文内容听写在下面的横线上。

1.______
2.______
3.______
4.______
5.______
6.______
7.______
8.______
9.______
10.______

词汇游戏——根据汉语提示，将数字序号对应的单词填入表格中

横向提示		纵向提示	
	1. v.笑；5. n.水池 7. n.飞机起落的场地 10. v.偷；11. n.沙子 14. n.小路，小径 15. adj.珍贵的；17. n.警戒，守卫 18. adj.有趣的；20. n.贼，小偷 22. n.建筑物；26. n.飞机 27. n.& v.欢迎；28. v.喊叫 29. adj.整齐的，整洁的 30. adj.木头的		2. n.机场；3. n.比赛，竞赛 4. adj.贵重的 6. n.石子；8. n.侦探 9. n.蔬菜；12. adj.美丽的 13. v.期待，等待 15. n.包裹；16. n.人群 19. v.聚集；21. n.指针 23. n.钻石；24. adj.主要的 25. v.拒绝 26. n.奖赏，奖品

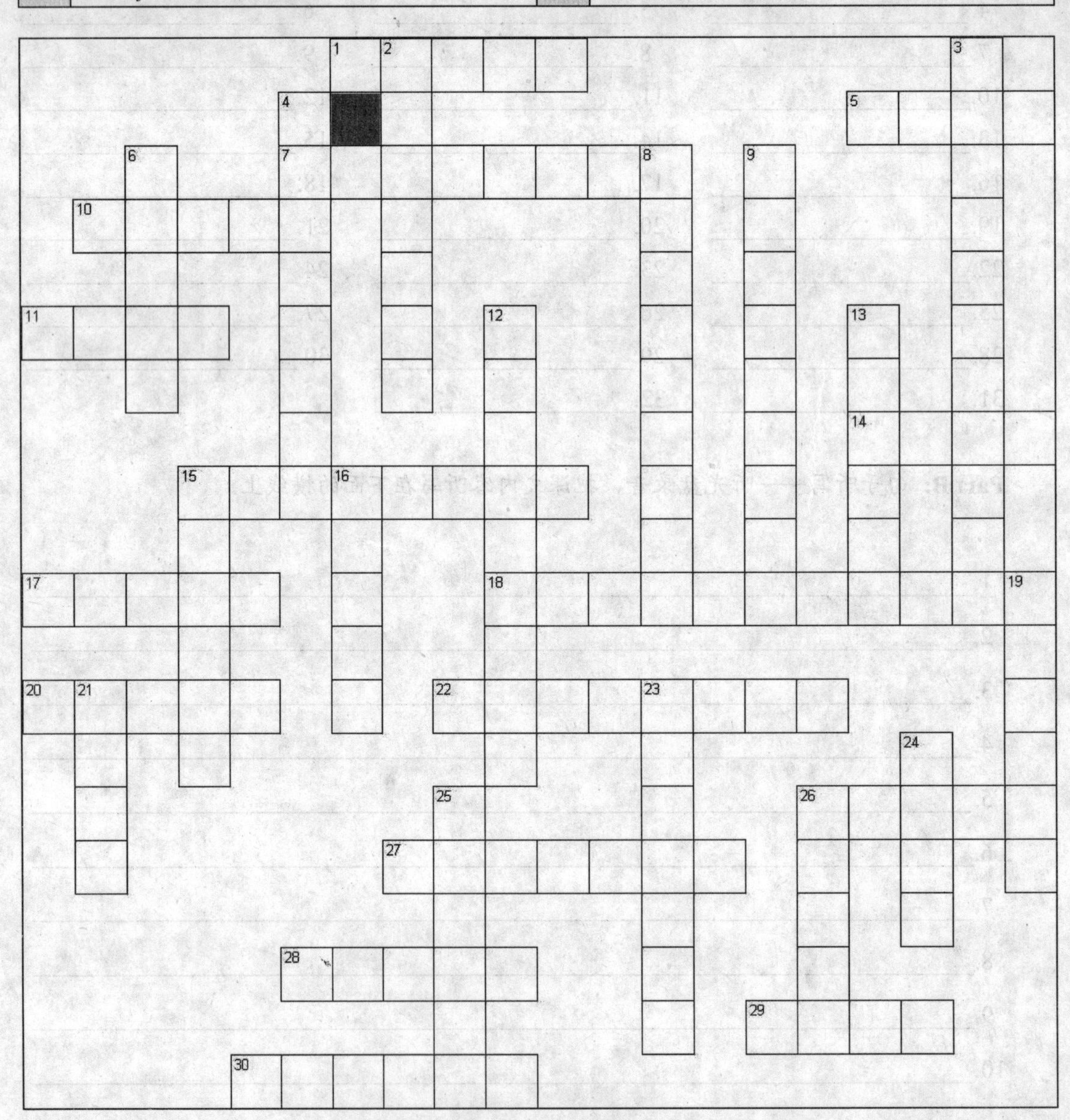

口语造句——根据要求完成下列内容

将下列句子排序成对话，把序号写在句子前面的横线上。

___ No, you look healthy. You look fine.

___ Well, you swim a lot, don't you?

___ Do I look kind of heavy?

___ That's good exercise. So you look fine.

___ But I'm a little heavy and I don't run.

___ Yes, I swim four times a week.

语法精练——根据要求完成下列内容

根据句意填写适当的词

1. The second day of the week is_____.
2. The third day of the week is _____.
3. The second month of the year is ______.
4. The ______month of the year is May.
5. There are seven days in a ______.
6. There are ______ months in a year.
7. There are twenty-four______ in a day.
8. The last month of the year is______.
9. I always have a party on ____ evening, so I get up late on Sunday morning.
10. The fourth day of a week is______.

根据句意，选用方框中所给的词填空。

What, Africa, Where, Why, them, because, see, grass

A: Let's __11__ the elephants.

B: __12__ do you like elephants?

A: __13__ they are very intelligent.

B: __14__ are they from?

A: They are from __15__.

B: And __16__ do they eat?

A: They eat __17__.

B: OK. Let's see __18__.

阅读理解——根据要求完成下列内容

看下面的表格，选择正确的答案。

Lucy's Timetable

	Monday	Tuesday	Wednesday	Thursday	Friday
08:00-08:45	English	History	English	Physics	Chinese
08:55-09-40	Chinese	Art	Chinese	Chinese	English
09:50-10:35	Math	English	History	Math	Music
10:45-11:30	P.E.	Geography	History	P.E.	Geography
11:30-13:30	Noon break				
13:30-14:15	Music	P.E.	P.E.	English	Self-study

1. Which lesson does Lucy have every weekday?

   A. math B. P.E. C. English

2. Lucy has a rest at noon for______.

   A. one hour

   B. two hours

   C. one and a half hours

3. How many music lessons does Lucy have in a week?______.

   A. one B. two C. three

4. The third class begins at ______in the morning.

   A. 9:50 B. 10:45 C. 8:55

5. When does Lucy have history?

   A. Tuesday and Wednesday.

   B. Tuesday and Friday.

   C. Wednesday and Thursday.

情景写作——根据要求完成下列内容

作为校刊的一名记者，Ren Xu 就如何提高英语水平采访了几位同学，但因为电脑病毒，他的采访记录被打乱了，请你帮他整理成正确的语序，写出句子，并把它们分别填在相应的横线上。

and magazines as many as you can	you can recite them
read English books	try to write about anything
for at least five minutes every day	you want in English every day
practice speaking English	listen to the English cassettes several times until

1）Listening skill: ______________________

2）Speaking skill: ______________________

3）Reading skill: ______________________

4）Writing skill: ______________________

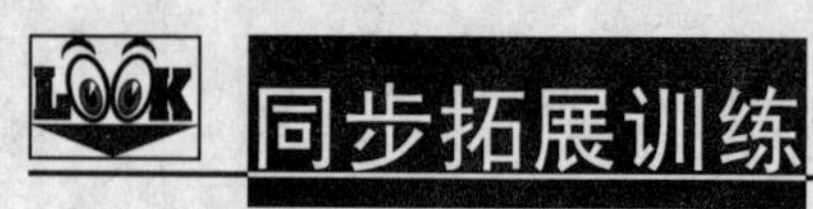

同步拓展训练 4

Lesson 10~12

听写检测——根据要求听写下列内容

Part A: 单词听写——听光盘录音，将听到的每个单词依次写在下面的横线上。

1.________	2.________	3.________
4.________	5.________	6.________
7.________	8.________	9.________
10.________	11.________	12.________
13.________	14.________	15.________
16.________	17.________	18.________
19.________	20.________	21.________
22.________	23.________	24.________
25.________	26.________	27.________
28.________	29.________	30.________
31.________	32.________	

Part B: 句子听写——听光盘录音，把课文内容听写在下面的横线上。

Lesson 10，Paragraph 1

1.____

2.____

3.____

4.____

5.____

6.____

7.____

8.____

9.____

10.____

词汇游戏——根据汉语提示，将数字序号对应的单词填入表格中

	横向提示		纵向提示
横向提示	3. *adj.*音乐的；5. *n.*运气，幸运 8. *n.*惊奇，惊喜 9. *n.*祖父；10. *v.*航行 11. *n.*船长；13. *n.*饭店 15. *v.*借，借入；16. *v.*应得到，值得 17. *v.*使不悦或生气，震惊 21. *n.*律师；22. *n.*爵士乐 23. *n.*工资；24. *v.*触摸 25. *n.*港口；26. *n.*琴键 27. *n.*银行	纵向提示	1. *n.*乐器；2. *adv.*立刻 4. *adj.*重要的；6. *n.*古钢琴 7. *v.*保持，保留 12. *adj.*著名的，出名的 14. *adv.*最近 18. *v.*允许，让 19. *adj.*自豪 20. *v.*损坏 23. *n.*（乐器的）弦 24. *n.*行为，举止

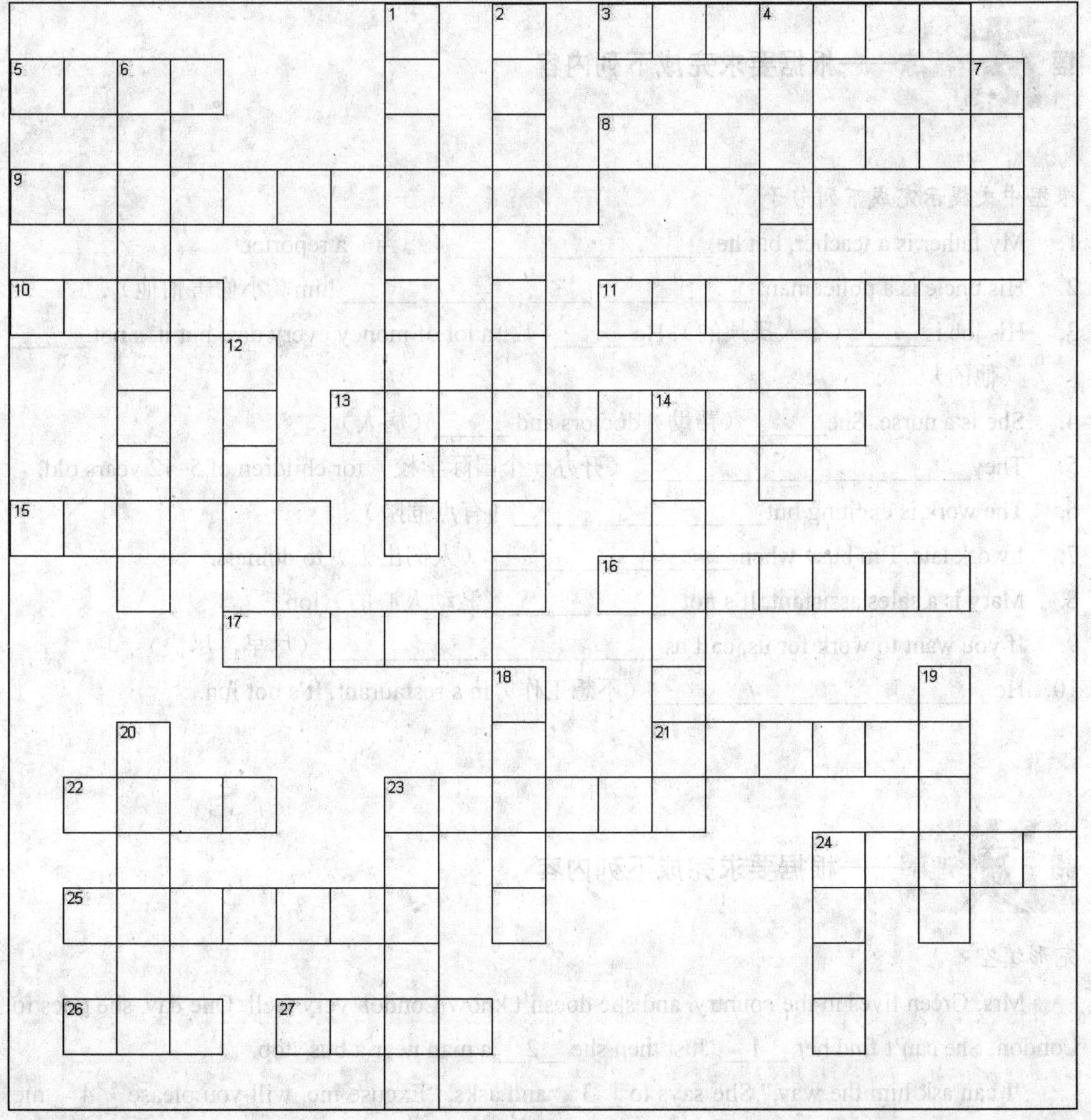

口语造句——根据要求完成下列内容

从右栏中找出与左栏各问句对应的答语

1. How do you get to school? A. About half an hour.
2. How far is it from your home to school? B. He walks.
3. How long does it take you to get there? C. I take the subway.
4. What do you think of the transportation here? D. About five kilometers.
5. Does he ride a bike or walk to school? E. It's not bad.

语法精练——根据要求完成下列内容

根据中文提示完成下列句子

1. My father is a teacher, but he ______ ______ ______（想当）a reporter.
2. His uncle is a policeman. ______ ______ ______ ______ ______him（小偷害怕他）.
3. His job is______（令人厌烦的）. He______（数）a lot of money every day, but it' s not______（他的）.
4. She is a nurse. She______（帮助）doctors and______（病人）.
5. They______ ______ ______ ______（开办一个国际学校）for children of 5~12 years old.
6. The work is exciting but______ ______ ______（有点危险）.
7. I work late. I'm busy when______ ______ ______（人们出去）to dinners.
8. Mary is a sales assistant. It's not ______ ______（激动人心的）job.
9. If you want to work for us, call us______ ______ ______ ______（尽早，尽快）.
10. He ______ ______ ______ ______（不想工作）in a restaurant. It's not fun.

阅读理解——根据要求完成下列内容

完形填空

Mrs. Green lives in the country, and she doesn't know London very well. One day, she goes to London. She can't find her __1__. Just then she __2__ a man near a bus stop.

"I can ask him the way," She says to __3__ and asks, "Excuse me, will you please __4__ me the way to King Street?" The man smiles with __5__ answer. He __6__ know English. He speaks Russian. He is a visitor. Then he __7__ his hand into his pocket, __8__ a piece of paper and lets her __9__ it. On the paper are these words, "Sorry, I __10__ English."

	A	B	C	D
1.	A. street	B. way	C. room	D. house
2.	A. looks at	B. watches	C. sees	D. looks
3.	A. herself	B. himself	C. itself	D. themselves
4.	A. speak	B. say	C. talk	D. tell
5.	A. not	B. an	C. no	D. any
6.	A. don't	B. doesn't	C. isn't	D. does
7.	A. puts	B. takes	C. carries	D. brings
8.	A. bring out	B. take out	C. takes out	D. takes away
9.	A. to see	B. look at	C. to look at	D. watches
10.	A. am not speak	B. don't speak	C. don't say	D. don't talk

阅读下面的文章，并选择正确答案。

Have you ever noticed an advertisement which says "Learn a foreign language in six weeks or your money back! From the first day your pronunciation will be excellent. Just send…" and so on? Of course, it never happens quite like that. The only language that is easy to learn is the mother language. And think how much practice that gets! Before the Second World War people usually learned a foreign language in order to read the literature（文学）of the country. Now speaking the foreign language is what most people want. Every year many millions of people start learning one. How do they do it?

Some people try at home, with books and tapes; some use radio or television programmes; others go to evening classes. If they use the language only two or three times a week, learning it will take a long time, like language learning at school. A few people try to learn a language fast by studying for six or more hours a day. It is clearly easier to learn the language in the country where it is spoken. However, most people cannot afford this, and for many people it is not necessary（必要）. They need the language in order to do their work better. For example, scientists and doctors mainly need to be able to read book and reports in the foreign language. Whether the language is learned quickly or slowly, it is hard work. Machines and good books will help, but they cannot do the students' work for them.

11. In the advertisement it is possible for a person to learn a foreign language______.

A. more than two months　　　　B. half a year

C. six months　　D. less than two months

12. Before the Second World War people learned a foreign language in order to______.

A. speak to each other　　B. listen to the radio

C. read something they didn't know　　D. write the literature of the country

13. The easiest way for us to learn a foreign language is__________.

A. using the language six or more hours a day

B. learning the language at school

C. studying the language in the foreign country

D. reading the foreign stories as many as possible

14. Most people now learn a foreign language to__________.

A. read books and reports in a foreign language

B. talk to foreign friends

C. go to the other country to learn a language well

D. try their best to work better

情景写作——根据要求完成下列内容

根据所给中文信息，用英文写出下周的安排。

星期	活动	时间/地点	备注
星期一	看电影	4:00p.m.海淀电影院	保持安静
星期二	数学测验	10:30a.m.教室	
星期三	排球赛 1-2 班	3:30 p.m.操场	
星期四	日本朋友参观我校	9:00a.m.	保持教室干净
星期五	参观北京电视台	2:00 p.m.	
星期六	郊游	7:00a.m.校门口集合	自带食品和饮料

Junior's Calendar（Nov. 11-17）

Week days	Activities	Time & Place	Notice
Monday		4:00p.m. Haidian Cinema	Keep quiet, please
		10:30a. m. in the classroom	
Wednesday	Class l VS Class 2		
Thursday	Japanese friends visit our school		
Friday			
Saturday	Field trip	at 7:00	

____

____

____

____

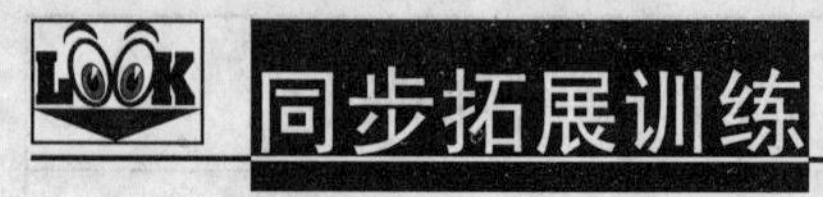

同步拓展训练 5

Lesson 13~15

听写检测——根据要求听写下列内容

Part A: 单词听写——听光盘录音，将听到的每个单词依次写在下面的横线上。

1.________ 2.________ 3.________
4.________ 5.________ 6.________
7.________ 8.________ 9.________
10.________ 11.________ 12.________
13.________ 14.________ 15.________
16.________ 17.________ 18.________
19.________ 20.________ 21.________
22.________ 23.________ 24.________
25.________ 26.________ 27.________
28.________ 29.________ 30.________
31.________ 32.________

Part B: 句子听写——听光盘录音，把课文内容听写在下面的横线上。

1.____
2.____
3.____
4.____
5.____
6.____
7.____
8.____
9.____
10.____

汇游戏——根据汉语提示，将数字序号对应的单词填入表格中

横向提示		纵向提示	
横向提示	1. *n.*商业，生意；5. *adj.*经历 6. *adj.*弱的；8. *n.*俱乐部 9. *v.*负担得起；10. *n.*语言 13. *v.*插话，打断 15. *n.*小组，团体 16. *n.*乡村，村庄；18. *adj.*困难的 20. *adj.*精神紧张的 24. *adv.*分离，分别地 25. *n.*搭便车；28. *v.*进入 29. *n.*场合	纵向提示	2. *n.*秘书；3. *v.*回答 4. *n.*演出 7. *adj.*有趣的，好笑的 11. *adj.*两者都不；12. *n.*南部，南 14. *prep.*在……期间 17. *n.*车站；19. *v.*感觉，觉得 21. *n.*薪水，工资；22. *v.*招手 23. *n.*停留，暂住 26. *n.*旅行；27. *n.*公司 30. *v.*到达

1 2 3 4 5 6 7 8 9 10 11 12 13 14 15 16 17 18 19 20 21 22 23 24 25 26 27 28 29 30

口语造句——根据要求完成下列内容

将下列句子排序成对话，把序号写在句子前面的横线上。

1 Hi, Mark. I want to have a class party. Will you help me organize it?

___ No, I don't think we should watch a video. Some students will be bored. Let's play party games.

___ Let's have it today after class.

___ Sure, Andrea, I can help you. So when shall we have the party?

___ Okay, Let's have it tomorrow.

___ Good idea. Can you organize the party games?

7 There's a test tomorrow. Students will leave early to study for their tests. Let's have it on the weekend.

___ No, today is too early. If we have it today, half the class won't come.

___ Sure, I can do that. And can you make some food for us?

___ Okay. Let's have it on Saturday afternoon. We can all meet and watch a video.

11 Yes, that's no problem.

语法精练——根据要求完成下列内容

根据句意，选用方框中所给的词填空。

clerk, waiter, hospital, fun, count, dangerous, store, difficult, reporter, thieves

1. Mr. Smith is a police officer. His job is ______.
2. Ms. Black is a bank ______.She is busy.
3. Peter is a______. He works in a restaurant.
4. Alice works in a______. She is a nurse.
5. He works at the TV station. He is a______.
6. I think an actor's job is______.
7. She is a sales assistant. She works in a______.
8. Is a doctor's job easy or______?
9. The ______are afraid of policemen.
10. I______ a lot of money. But it's not mine.

根据所给中文意思，完成句子。

11. 他最受人们喜爱的照片正在展览会上展出。

    Some of his ______ ______ photos are _____ _____ in the exhibition.

12. 树下的那位老人使我想起了我的祖父。

    The old man under the tree ______ ______ ______ my grandfather.

13. 我们不喜欢那些连歌词都唱不清楚的歌手。

    We don't like the singers _____ _____ _____ the words _____.

14. 我喜欢擅长演奏各种不同乐曲的音乐家。

    I like the musician _____ ____ good at _______ ______ _____ ______ music.

15. 无论你做什么，你一定不要忘记安全。

    _____ you _____, don't ________ the _______.

16. 虽然他很累，但他还是坚持工作。

    ______ he was tired, _____ still ______ ______ ______.

17. 正如你知道的，无论是谁都不能违反法律。

    _____ you ________, _____ you are, you shouldn't _____ the_____.

18. 快！电影已经开演大约十分钟了。

    Hurry up! The movie ______ ______ for ____ ____ ______.

阅读理解——根据要求完成下列内容

完形填空

Dick works in a factory. It is far __1__ his home. Every day he __2__ to work in the morning and back home in the evening. One day, he came home late and didn' t look __3__. His wife saw his __4__, and then I asked him, "Why aren't you happy? Are you not __5__, dear?"

"Yes, I'm quite well. But I'm very angry, __6__ the bus ticket was three pence last week. But today it is only two."

"That's __7__," his wife said. "The bus ticket is cheaper now. You __8__ save two pence every day."

But Dick said, "No, you're a fool. I walk to work and back home every day. __9__ I saved six pence every day, but now I have two pence __10__".

1. A. to　　B. at　　C. from　　D. away
2. A. rides　　B. drives　　C. runs　　D. walks

3. A. sorry B. happy C. strong D. ill
4. A. bag B. hand C. face D. bus
5. A. well B. hungry C. cold D. full
6. A. so B. or C. and D. because
7. A. bad B. wrong C. right D. good
8. A. can't B. mustn't C. can D. must
9. A. Next week B. Last week C. Yesterday D. Today
10. A. less B. more C. many D. much

阅读下面的文章，并选择正确答案。

There was a famous French writer. He was a man of great achievement（成就）. He said that one of his main achievements was his study of handwriting. He had spent much time on it and he often told his friends that he could tell a person's character（性格）from that person's handwriting.

One day, a woman brought him a page of a boy's handwriting. She said that she wanted to know what he thought of the boy's character.

He studied the handwriting carefully for a few minutes. Then he looked at the woman strangely（奇怪地）. The woman told him that the boy was not in her family and that he did not have to worry.

"Good!" said the writer, "Then I can tell you." He went on to say that he thought the boy was stupid and lazy. He added that the boy should be watched carefully, if not, he would bring harm to his family when he grew up.

"Isn't that strange?" said the woman, smiling. "Because this is a page from your own exercise book. You wrote it yourself when you were a boy."

11. It took the writer a lot of time__________.
    A. to read books B. to make friends
    C. to write books D. to study handwriting
12. From a person's __________,the writer could tell a person's character.
    A. pronunciation B. handwriting C. smiling face D. speech
13. The woman wanted to___________.
    A. know the write B. help the writer
    C. visit the writer D. test the writer
14. The writer was sure that the boy______.
    A. was not worth teaching B. would do good deeds for his family
    C. would do wrong to his family D. would work hard

15. From the story we know__________

A. the woman knew the writer very well

B. the writer knew the woman well

C. neither of them knew each other

D. both of them knew each other well

情景写作——根据要求完成下列内容

What will happen if you become a doctor (teacher, lawyer, policeman, athlete, singer, dancer…) in ten years? (at least 60 words)

____

____

____

____

____

____

Lesson 16~17

听写检测——根据要求听写下列内容

Part A: 单词听写——听光盘录音，将听到的每个单词依次写在下面的横线上。

1.______	2.______	3.______
4.______	5.______	6.______
7.______	8.______	9.______
10.______	11.______	12.______
13.______	14.______	15.______
16.______	17.______	18.______
19.______	20.______	21.______
22.______	23.______	24.______
25.______	26.______	27.______
28.______	29.______	30.______
31.______	32.______	

Part B: 句子听写——听光盘录音，把课文内容听写在下面的横线上。

1.______________________________

2.______________________________

3.______________________________

4.______________________________

5.______________________________

6.______________________________

7.______________________________

8.______________________________

9.______________________________

10.______________________________

词汇游戏——根据汉语提示，将数字序号对应的单词填入表格中

横向提示		纵向提示	
横向提示	4. *adv.*立刻，马上；5. *n.*小酒店 6. *n.*店主；8. *v.*停放（汽车） 10. *n.*提示；14. *n.*长筒袜 16. *adj.*鲜艳的 17. *n.*便条；18. *n.*交通 19. *v.*登场，扮演 20. *prep.*没有，不 21. *n.*账单；23. *prep.*在……旁边 25. *n.*短袜；27. *n.*地段 28. *n.*花园	纵向提示	1. *n.*交通违章罚款单 2. *v.*返回；3. *n.*注意，注意力 7. *adj.*错误的；9. *v.*回答 11. *v.*享受，欣赏；12. *n.*女演员 13. *v.*服从 15. *adj.*极坏的，可怕的 22. *adj.*幸运的 24. *n.*舞台 25. *n.*指示牌 26. *v.*无视，忘记

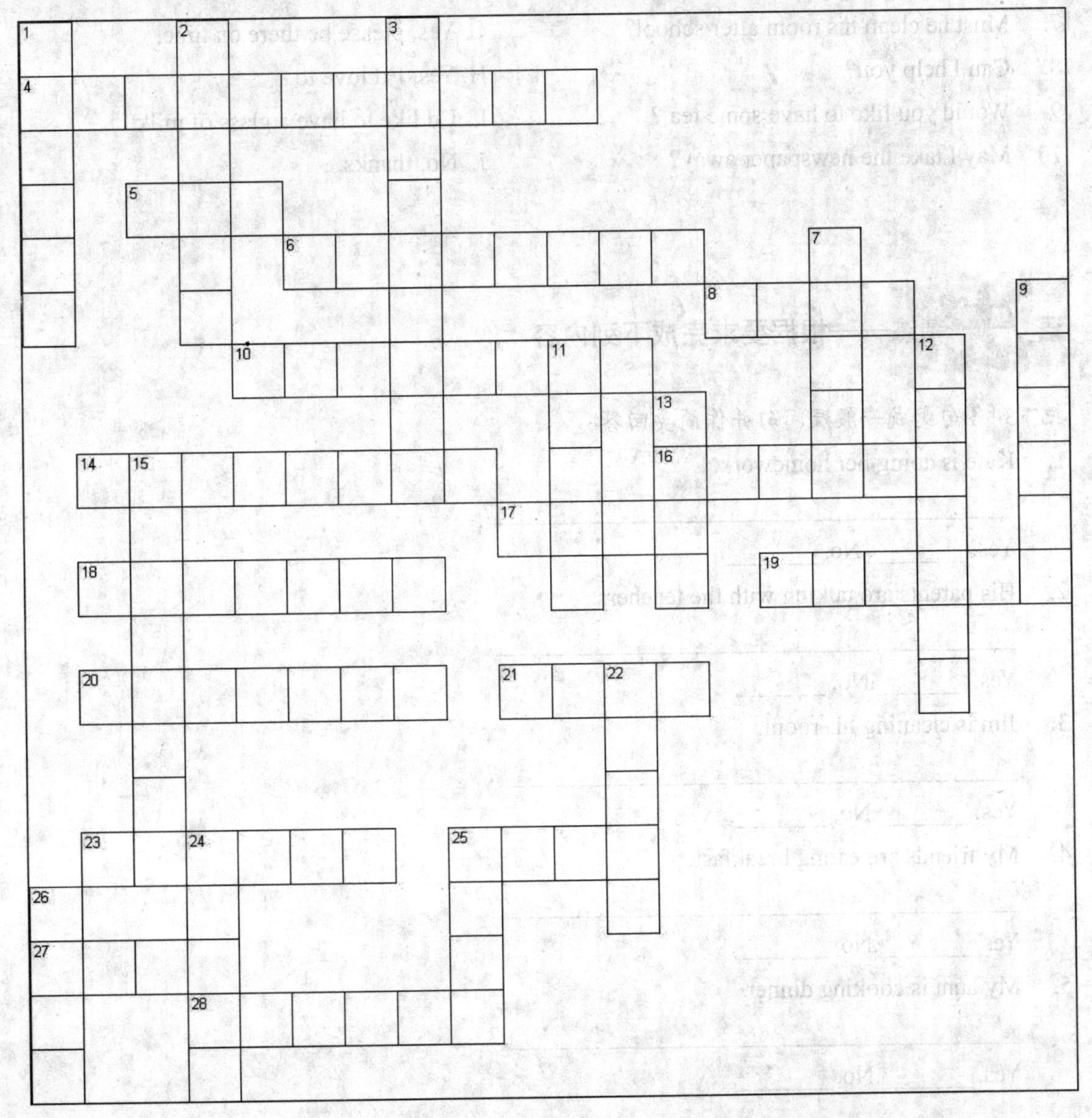

口语造句——根据要求完成下列内容

从右栏中找出与左栏各问句对应的答语

1. Could you wash your hands before dinner ?
2. Would you mind closing the windows ?
3. Could you please not put your bag here ?
4. Would you like to come for a walk ?
5. Shall we meet at the school gate?
6. May I have a sandwich?
7. Must he clean his room after school?
8. Can I help you?
9. Would you like to have some tea ?
10. May I take the newspaper away?

A. No, not at all.
B. Of course, you can.
C. Sure, I'm always washing them.
D. No, you mustn't.
E. Sorry. I'll put it in my desk.
F. No, he needn't.
G. Yes, please be there on time.
H. Yes, I'd love to.
I. I'd like to have a glass of milk.
J. No, thanks.

语法精练——根据要求完成下列内容

把下列各句变成一般疑问句并作简要回答

1. Kate is doing her homework.

   ____?

   Yes, _______. No, _______.

2. His parents are talking with the teachers.

   ____?

   Yes, _______.No, _______.

3. Jim is cleaning his room.

   ____?

   Yes, _______.No, _______.

4. My friends are eating breakfast.

   ____?

   Yes, _______.No, _______.

5. My aunt is cooking dinner.

   ____?

   Yes, _______.No, _______.

根据句意，选用方框中所给词的适当形式填空。

suggest, remind, Italy, potato, change, collect, hike, photograph, miss, gentle

6. Gu Changwei is one of the top ________in China.
7. Young people like going________ in the countryside or the mountain.
8. He likes ________coins and stamps.
9. Whatever you do, don't ________the concert.
10. We enjoy music that's quiet and________.
11. The music ________us of Brazilian dance music.
12. As the teacher said, we can't ________the result.
13. They will consider our________ later.
14. Eating more________ is good for your health.
15. I'd like French food instead of ________food.

阅读理解——根据要求完成下列内容

根据短文内容判断正误，正确写T，错误写F。

Look at the picture. Where are the children now? They are at the zoo. They are looking at the monkeys. The monkeys are in a large cage. Are the monkeys walking or jumping? They are jumping up and down in the cage. But one monkey is not jumping. It's sleeping. It is ill.

Where are the children now? The children are standing next to a small cage. What's in the small cage? There is a fox .What is the fox doing? The fox is walking in the cage. It's looking for something to eat. It wants to go out of the cage to play and walk.

Now the children are looking at the wolf. Is the wolf sleeping? No, it isn't. It is not sleeping at all. The wolf is eating. What is the wolf eating? It is eating meat. There is a bone in its mouth.

1. The children are in the zoo.
2. All the monkeys are jumping.
3. The ill monkey lives in a small cage.
4. The fox is looking for the meat.
5. The fox wants to go out of the cage to play and walk, but it can't.
6. The wolf is eating.

阅读下面的文章，并选择正确答案。

Sam likes fish very much. He often buys fish in the shop and takes it home. But when his wife sees the fish, she says to herself, "Good! Now I can ask my friends to have lunch, and we can eat this fish. They like fish very much."

So when Sam comes home in the evening, the fish is not there and his wife always says, "Oh, your cat eats it." And she gives Sam some bread for his supper. Sam gets very angry. He takes the cat and his wife to the shop near his house and weighs the cat. Then he turns to his wife and says, "My fish weighs one kilo. This cat weighs one, too. My cat is here, you see. Then where's my fish?"

7. Which sentence is right according to the text?

   A. Sam doesn't like eating fish at all.

   B. Sam often buys some fish for his cat.

   C. Sam's cat always eats the fish before he comes back.

   D. The friends of Sam's wife eat the fish.

8. What's the meaning of "comes home" in the sentence "so when Sam comes home"?

   A. goes home　　B. leaves home　　C. gets home　　D. at home

9. Does Sam take the cat and his wife to the shop near his home?

   A. Yes, he does.　　B. No, he doesn't.　　C. I don't know.　　D. I don't think so.

10. How much does the cat weigh?

    A. One kilo　　B. Two kilo

    C. Half a kilo　　D. One and a half kilo

11. Who gets very angry?

    A. Sam's wife　　B. Sam

    C. Sam's friends　　D. His wife's friends

I was getting fat. I work in an office and go there by car. I have good food, but I don't do enough exercise and that's how I get fat. My wife and I decided I had to do something about it. I don't have much time for exercise because life is very busy. There are not many sports which you can play at home either. Table tennis would be fine, but we don't have room large enough. Then I heard of a book of exercises for people like me. There are 5 different exercises. This is what you have to do.

1) Stand with your legs 15 centimeters apart. Point your arms above your head. Bend down to touch the ground between your feet. Reach up again, and so on. (2 minutes)

2) Lie on your back, flat on the ground with your arms at your sides. Sit up. Lie down again

and so on. (1 minute)

3) Lie on your front. Join your hands behind your back. Lift your legs and shoulders as far off the ground as possible. (1 minute)

4) Lie on your front. Lift your body off the ground so that your arms are straight. Only your hands and toes touch the ground. (1 minute)

5) Running on the spot. Lift your feet 10 centimeters off the ground. (5 minutes)

Each of the exercises is done as many times as possible. The exercises get more difficult stage by stage. For women they are different. If you don't get much exercise, you'll enjoy them.

12. Life is very busy, so I__________.

A. was getting fat　　B. don't have any time

C. don't have much time for exercises　　D. work in an office

13. The book of exercises is for people who__________.

A. walk to work every day

B. don't have large room in their house

C. like getting a lot of exercises

D. want to spend a short time on exercise every day

14. People take only __________ to do exercises.

A. a long time　　B. ten minutes every day

C. a lot of money　　D. five minutes every day

15. The first exercise is __________ than the last.

A. more difficult　　B. more expensive　　C. easier　　D. cheaper

16. The exercise will help people to__________.

A. get fat　　B. enjoy themselves

C. be kept fat　　D. stop getting fat

情景写作——根据要求完成下列内容

暑假你要去夏令营两周，但家里的花及小狗没人照料，请你写一封电子邮件给你的堂姐Lucy，请她帮忙照看。

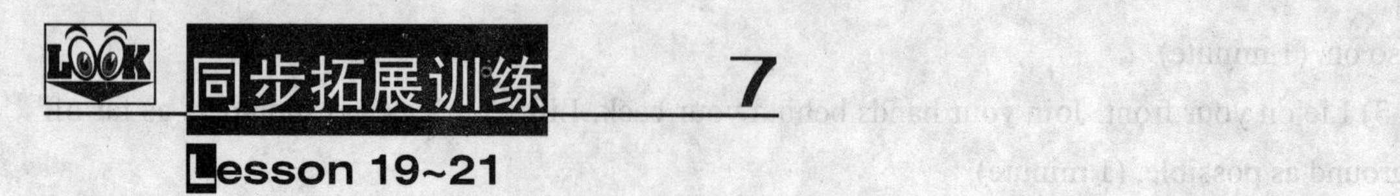

听写检测——根据要求听写下列内容

Part A: 单词听写——听光盘录音，将听到的每个单词依次写在下面的横线上。

1.______ 2.______ 3.______
4.______ 5.______ 6.______
7.______ 8.______ 9.______
10.______ 11.______ 12.______
13.______ 14.______ 15.______
16.______ 17.______ 18.______
19.______ 20.______ 21.______
22.______ 23.______ 24.______
25.______ 26.______ 27.______
28.______ 29.______ 30.______
31.______ 32.______

Part B: 句子听写——听光盘录音，把课文内容听写在下面的横线上。

1.______
2.______
3.______
4.______
5.______
6.______
7.______
8.______
9.______
10.______

词汇游戏——根据汉语提示，将数字序号对应的单词填入表格中

横向提示	纵向提示
3. *n.*垃圾，废物；9. *n.*表演 10. *adv.*的确，当然；11. *n.*量 13. *n.*钓鱼人，渔民 16. *n.*浪费 18. *adv.*大概，或许 21. *n.*星期三 22. *n.*令人遗憾的事 24. *v.*抓到 25. *v.*匆忙 27. *adv.*悲哀地，丧气地	1. *adj.*坚定的；2. *n.*飞机 4. *adj.*感兴趣的；5. *v.*大声说 6. *adj.*特别喜爱的 7. *n.*靴子；8. *v.*意识到 12. *adj.*重要的，重大的 14. *n.*原因；15. *adj.*不幸的 16. *v.*担心，烦恼；17. *v.*提供，出价 19. *v.*退回；20. *v.*花费，消耗 23. *v.*赶紧，匆忙 26. *adj.*发疯

1 2 3 4 5 6 7 8 9 10 11 12 13 14 15 16 17 18 19 20 21 22 23 24 25 26 27

口语造句——根据要求完成下列内容

补全对话

Jim: Hey, Sally! I didn't see you over the weekend.

Sally: No, I ____1____ home.

Jim: Why?

Sally: Well, I ____2____ lots of things to do.

Jim: Like what?

Sally: Well, I ____3____ my room. And I ____4____ my homework.

Jim: You did? Not much fun, huh?

Sally: Well, ____5____ wasn't too bad on Saturday. I ____6____to the library. How ___7___ you? What ____8____ you do?

Jim: Well, I ____9____ soccer on Saturday morning ___10___ Saturday afternoon, I ____11____ to a movie. And on Sunday night, I visited my friend's house.

Sally: Wow! You ____12____ fun.

Jim: Yeah, I had fun. ____13____ I didn't do my homework, so school this morning ____14____ fun!

语法精练——根据要求完成下列内容

连词成句，注意句后标点。

1. like, weather, do, cold, you

____?

2. an, place, what, interesting, is, it

____!

3. weather, was, there, how, the

____?

4. is, how, going, you, with, it

____?

5. of, taking, we, pyramids, photos, are, the

____.

6. looking, at, years, five, I'm, history, thousand, history, of

____.

7. is, a, good, having, everyone, time

____.

8. cold, is, how, weather, the

____!

9. Paris, cool, is, now, it, in

____?

10. windy, the, is, cold, weather, and

____.

根据句意，选用方框中所给词的适当形式填空。

home, call up, fix up, work out, put off, project, hand out, give away, run out of, clean up

11. The boy often helps ________ advertisements in front of the supermarket.
12. The strategies that they came up with ________ fine.
13. The car can't start, because it ________ the gas.
14. Never ________ till tomorrow what you can do today.
15. Mr Smith is a kind man. He ________ most of his money to charities.
16. The living room is too dirty. You should ________ it ________.
17. Please ________ me ________ when you get to Hong Kong.
18. Can you help me ________ the broken bike?
19. We all want to help those ________ children.
20. Everyone would like to join the school volunteer ________.

阅读理解——根据要求完成下列内容

根据对话内容填写表格

Lucy: Oh dear, it's cold today, isn't it?

Jim: Oh, do you think it's cold, Lucy? I think it's quite warm today.

Lucy: That's because you're wearing warm clothes, Jim!

Lily: Yes, it's not really warm today at all, is it?

Li Lei: Don't you like this time of year? It's spring time now. I think that spring is the best time of the year.

Jim: Do you, Li Lei? Why?

Li Lei: Because winter is over! What about you, Lucy? Which is your favourite season?

Lucy: Oh, I love summer best. I love summer because I enjoy swimming.

Lily: Yes. Lucy likes swimming a lot. But I like skating more than swimming. So I like winter best. I really enjoy skating in winter. Winter is my favourite season! What about you, Jim?

Jim: Oh, my favourite time of the year is autumn.

Lily: Why do you like autumn best, Jim?

Jim: Because it's not too hot, and not too cold!

Name	Favourite season	Why?
Lucy:	Summer	She enjoys swimming.
Lily	1	2
Jim	3	4
Li Lei	Spring	5

完形填空

When you are invited to a meal in Thailand（泰国）, the words of the invitation mean "come and eat rice". In fact, nearly all Thai dishes are __6__ with rice, which grows there very easily __7__ the climate is warm and there is much rain.

The food that is served is __8__ cut into pieces, so there is no need to use knives and forks but, instead, special spoons and forks are used. The Thais __9__ to eat with their hands and now there are still some people who eat this way. There is a special __10__ of doing it. First they wash their __11__ hands in a bowl of water, they only eat with their right hands. They are careful not to let the food __12__ the palms of their hands. After the meal, the __13__ are again carefully washed.

The meal usually has several different dishes. They are all hot. They are served in bowls which everyone shares, __14__ each person has their own bowl of __15__. As Thailand has a long coastline, it is not surprising that fish and shellfish play an important part in Thai cooking.

6. A. eaten B. used C. smelled D. tasted
7. A. when B. if C. because D. so
8. A. never B. perhaps C. hardly D. always
9. A. went B. had C. wanted D. used
10. A. reason B. way C. idea D. result
11. A. dirty B. right C. left D. big

12. A. touch	B. catch	C. feel	D. drop
13. A. forks	B. spoons	C. hands	D. bowls
14. A. because	B. though	C. since	D. until
15. A. fish	B. rice	C. water	D. shellfish

情景写作——根据要求完成下列内容

你喜欢拥有什么样的朋友？请至少写出 5 个句子来描述你和你最好的朋友之间的相同点和不同点。

I like to have friends who are ____

____

____

____

同步拓展训练 8

Lesson 22~24

听写检测——根据要求听写下列内容

Part A: 单词听写——听光盘录音，将听到的每个单词依次写在下面的横线上。

1.______ 2.______ 3.______
4.______ 5.______ 6.______
7.______ 8.______ 9.______
10.______ 11.______ 12.______
13.______ 14.______ 15.______
16.______ 17.______ 18.______
19.______ 20.______ 21.______
22.______ 23.______ 24.______
25.______ 26.______ 27.______
28.______ 29.______ 30.______
31.______ 32.______

Part B: 句子听写——听光盘录音，把课文内容听写在下面的横线上。

1.______
2.______
3.______
4.______
5.______
6.______
7.______
8.______
9.______
10.______

词汇游戏——根据汉语提示，将数字序号对应的单词填入表格中

横向提示		纵向提示	
	5. *adv.*有规律地；6. *n.*地区 10. *v.*旅行；11. *v.*打断，打扰 13. *v.*完成 16. *adj.*外面的，外界的 18. *n.*惊奇；19. *adj.*奇怪的 24. *v.*决定；26. *n.*地址 27. *v.*包含，内装 28. *v.*出发，开始，着手 29. *v.*收到；30. *v.*扔，抛 31. *adj.*可爱的		1. *v.*花费；2. *n.*年龄 3. *adj.*表示同情的 4. *adj.*新式的，与以往不同的 7. *v.*抱怨；8. *v.*做梦，梦想 9. *v.*敲；12. *n.*诚实 14. *n.*信封；15. *adj.*陌生的，奇怪的 17. *adj.*很坏的，邪恶的 20. *n.*海峡；21. *adj.*不安 22. *n.*经理；23. *v.*暂住 25. *v.*进入

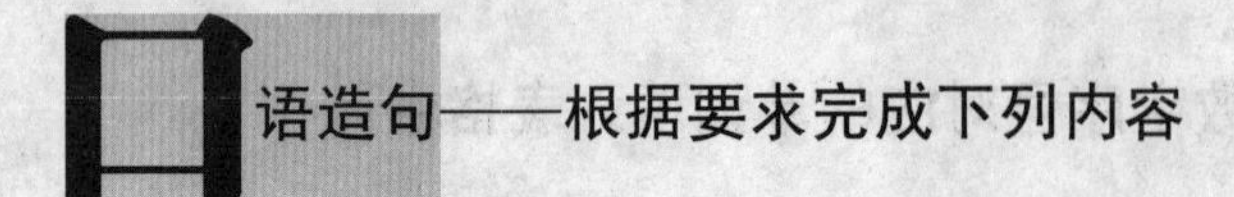

口语造句——根据要求完成下列内容

从右栏中找出与左栏各问句对应的答语

1. How often does Tom drink milk?
2. How many hours does Jim sleep?
3. How often does your brother exercise?
4. How long can you keep the books?
5. How much is the radio?

A. About six hours.
B. It's $48.
C. Never, He doesn't like it at all.
D. Two weeks.
E. Every day. He likes sports very much.

语法精练——根据要求完成下列内容

连词成句，注意句后标点。

1. tell, the, post office, way, me, you, could, to, the

   ____?

2. cousin, my, like, milk, doesn't, all, at

   ____.

3. like, pizza, you, on, your, would, what

   ____?

4. classical, CDs, I, find, can, where, the

   ____?

5. the, library, and, he, to, some, did, went, reading

   ____.

根据所给中文意思，完成句子。

6. 格林夫妇去过两次悉尼。

   Mr. and Mrs. Green ______ _______to Sydney________.

7. 你想到哪里去度假？

   Where _____ you _______ to go _______vacation?

8. 我喜欢天气总是很温暖的地方。

   I like ___ _____ the _____ is always warm.

9. 不要打算在新加坡开车。

   Don't______ _____ ______ a car in_____.

10. 她正为到夏威夷旅行而存钱。

She______ ______ ______ for her trip to Hawaii.

11. 你能给我提供有关度假场所的信息吗？

Could you ______ me ________ some information about vacation_____?

12. 布朗夫妇打算去海滨做冲浪运动，他们要离开两个星期。

The Browns are going to the beach for____. They will____ ____ for two weeks

13. 今年冬天他们全家想去中国南部的某个地方去旅游。

Their family want to_____ ______ ______this winter somewhere______ ______ ______ ______.

14. 我正在考虑寒假里参观桂林，那里的气候总是很温暖。

During the winter vacation I_____ _____ _______Guilin, where it is always warm.

15. 每年的这个时候西安相当冷，你如果去看碑林，最好（在包裹里）装上暖和的衣服。

Xi'an is rather cold______ _______ ______ ______. You'd _______ _______warm clothes if you visit the Forest of Steles.

阅读理解——根据要求完成下列内容

完形填空

When you wave to a friend, you are using sign language. When you smile at someone, you mean to be __1__. When you put one finger in front of your __2__, you mean "Be quiet." Yet, people in different countries may use different sign languages.

Once an Englishman was in Italy. He could speak __3__ Italian. One day while he was walking in the street, he felt __4__ and went into a restaurant. When the waiter came, the Englishman __5__ his mouth, put his fingers into it and took them out again and moved his lips. In this way, he __6__ to say, "Bring me something to eat." But the waiter brought him a lot of things to __7__. First tea, then coffee, then milk, but no food. The Englishman was __8__ that he was not able to tell the waiter he was hungry. He was __9__ to leave the restaurant when another man came in and put his hands on his stomach. And this sign was __10__ enough for the waiter. In a few minutes, the waiter brought him a large plate of bread and mean. At last the Englishman had his meal in the same way.

	A	B	C	D
1.	A. nice	B. friendly	C. fine	D. well
2.	A. eye	B. hand	C. mouth	D. arm
3.	A. a little	B. few	C. a few	D. little
4.	A. hungry	B. tired	C. sad	D. worried
5.	A. washed	B. opened	C. closed	D. touched
6.	A. dared	B. meant	C. had	D. decided
7.	A. eat	B. play	C. carry	D. drink
8.	A. happy	B. glad	C. sorry	D. afraid
9.	A. quick	B. slow	C. ready	D. quiet
10.	A. good	B. bad	C. bright	D. wrong

根据短文内容判断正误，正确写 T，错误写 F。

Dear Jimmy,

I just came back from Mexico and I had a wonderful time. I'd go back next week, if I could! I love big cities. I'd love to visit Moscow next, but it's too far away. It takes more than sixteen hours to fly there.

Someday I hope to visit England, too. I've always wanted to see what London looks like. My sister Joan is fine. She didn't go with me to Mexico. She says she'd love to visit Alaska with me someday, but I don't know there are no big cities there, are there? Write to me soon.

Best wishes,

Tim

11. Tim had a wonderful time in Mexico.
12. Tim has been to London before.
13. It takes sixteen hours to fly to Moscow.
14. Joan would like to go to Alaska in the future.
15. Tim will go to visit Alaska someday with his sister.

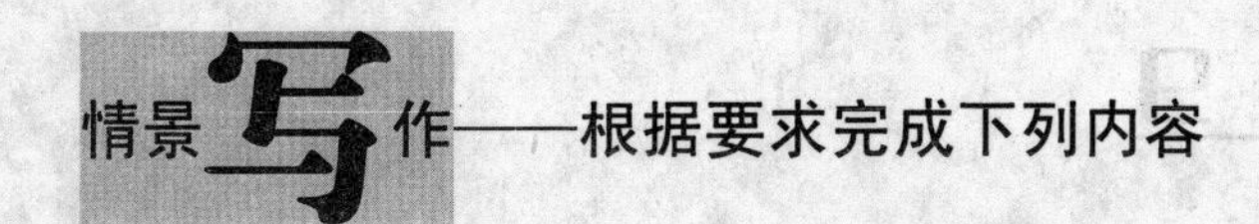

用表格中所给的词和信息完成调查报告

The best	Name	Reason
Radio station	Beijing Music 97. 4 FM	It plays the most interesting music.
Supermarket	Pricesmart	It has the best quality things.
Movie theatre	Chang'an theater	It has the friendliest service.

We made a survey and this is what we learned. ____
____
____
____

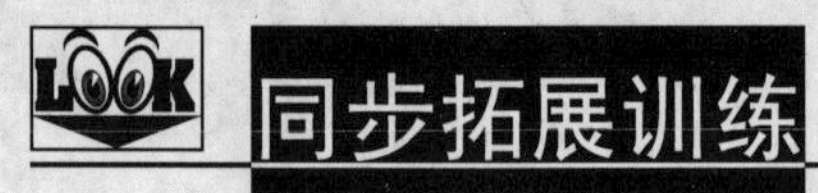

同步拓展训练 9

Lesson 25~27

听写检测——根据要求听写下列内容

Part A: 单词听写——听光盘录音，将听到的每个单词依次写在下面的横线上。

1.________ 2.________ 3.________
4.________ 5.________ 6.________
7.________ 8.________ 9.________
10.________ 11.________ 12.________
13.________ 14.________ 15.________
16.________ 17.________ 18.________
19.________ 20.________ 21.________
22.________ 23.________ 24.________
25.________ 26.________ 27.________
28.________ 29.________ 30.________
31.________ 32.________

Part B: 句子听写——听光盘录音，把课文内容听写在下面的横线上。

1.________________________________
2.________________________________
3.________________________________
4.________________________________
5.________________________________
6.________________________________
7.________________________________
8.________________________________
9.________________________________
10.________________________________

词汇游戏——根据汉语提示，将数字序号对应的单词填入表格中

横向提示		纵向提示	
	2. v.注意到；5. n.搬运工 6. n.帐篷；11. n.铁路 12. adj.舒适的，安逸的 16. n.图案；17. n.窗帘，幕布 18. v.爬行 20. adv.香甜地，深入地 22. conj.是否 23. adv.正好 25. n.田地，田野 26. v.蜿蜒		1. v.鉴赏；3. n.评论家 4. n.小溪；7. adv.批评地 8. n.外国人；9. v.假装 10. adj.极好的；13. n.材料 14. adv.大量地 15. pron.几个 19. v.画；20. v.闻起来，闻到 21. v.跳跃，跳起 22. v.感到奇怪 24. v.悬挂；25. v.形成

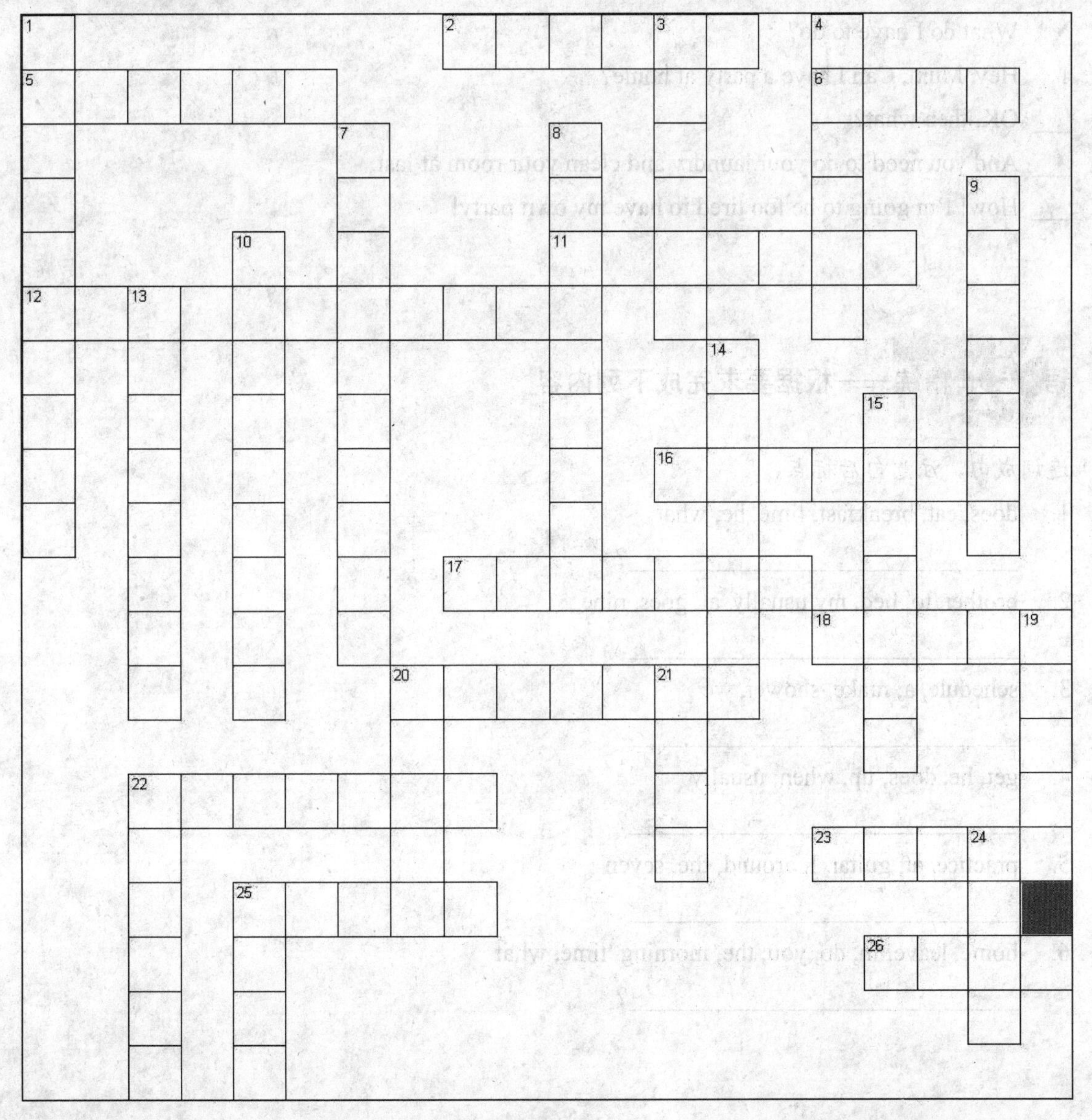

口语造句——根据要求完成下列内容

将下列句子排序成对话，把序号写在句子前面的横线上。

___ Sure, you can. But you have to do some chores first.

7 Yeah, I can do that.

___ Thanks, Mum!

___ I'll help you. And I'll go to the store for drinks and snacks.

___ Well, first you clean the kitchen.

6 Then you could take out the trash.

___ What do I have to do?

1 Hey, Mum, Can I have a party at home?

___ OK, then what?

___ And you need to do your laundry and clean your room at last.

___ How! I'm going to be too tired to have my own party!

语法精练——根据要求完成下列内容

连词成句，注意句后标点。

1. does, eat, breakfast, time, he, what

   ________________________________?

2. brother, to, bed, my usually, at, goes, nine

   ________________________________.

3. schedule, a, make, shower, we

   ________________________________.

4. get, he, does, up, when, usually

   ________________________________?

5. practice, at, guitar, I, around, the, seven

   ________________________________.

6. home, leave, in, do, you, the, morning, time, what

   ________________________________?

根据所给中文意思，完成句子。

7. 你今天做了多久作业了？

How ______ ______ you been ________ your homework today?

8. 我们去过两次长城了。

We ______ ______ ______ the Great Wall ______.

9. 我该为我妈妈的生日买些什么呢？

What ______ I ______ my mother _______ her birthday?

10. 李先生在这所学校工作已经三年了。

Mr. Li ______ ______ in this school _______ 3 years.

11. 你介意我坐在你旁边吗？不，一点儿也不。

Would you ______ ______ beside you? No, _______ ______ ______.

12. 她不喜欢游泳，是吗？不，她喜欢。

She ______ like ______, ______ she ? ______ ,she ______.

13. 他从没去过海南，我也没去过。

He ______ never ______ to Hainan, ______ ______ ______.

阅读理解——根据要求完成下列内容

根据短文内容判断正误，正确写 T，错误写 F。

Nothing was going right for Dr. Turner at the hospital. He made a mistake while operating on a patient. He felt sure he was no longer trusted and decided to change his job. One day he learned from the paper that a doctor was looking for a partner. The doctor, whose name was Johnson, lived in Thorby , a small town in the north of England.

A few days later Dr. Turner went to Thorby, and arrived at Dr. Johnson's home early in the afternoon. Though old and a little deaf, Dr. Johnson still had a good brain. He kept talking to the visitor about the town and its people. When they turned to the question of partnership, it was already seven in the evening. Dr. Johnson invited Dr. Turner to have dinner with him in a restaurant before catching the train back to London. Dr. Turner noticed that Dr. Johnson was fond of good food and expensive wines. They had an excellent meal. When the bill was brought, Dr. Johnson felt in his pocket. "Oh, dear," he said. "I've forgotten my money." "That's all right," Dr. Turner said. "I'll pay the bill." As he did so, he began to wonder whether Dr. Johnson was worthy of trust.

1. Dr. Turner decided to leave his present job because he had never been trusted.

2. The two doctors spent most of the afternoon talking about things of no importance to Dr. Turner.
3. The story suggests that Dr. Johnson did not like Dr. Turner.
4. The words did so in the last sentence mean said those words.
5. The two doctors will soon be partners.

阅读下面的文章，并选择正确答案。

A bag is useful and the word "bag" is useful too. It gives us some interesting phrases. One is "to let the cat out of the bag". It is the same as "to tell a secret". There's an old interesting story about it.

Long ago, when people sold things in big cloth bags, a woman asked a man for a pig. The man held up his cloth bag. There seemed to be a little pig in it. The woman asked to see it. When the man opened the cloth bag, a big black cat ran out. Not a pig! The man's secret was out and everyone knew it.

Now when someone lets out a secret, he "lets the cat out of the bag". And that is the story of where the interesting phrase came from.

6. The phrase "to let the cat out of the bag" come from________.
   A. a woman and a pig B. a man and a cat
   C. a pig and a cat D. an old interesting story
7. The woman wanted to buy_________.
   A. a cloth bag B. a little pig
   C. a black cat D. a bag and a pig
8. The man knew there was____in his cloth bag.
   A. a bag B. a pig C. a cat D. nothing
9. At the end of the second passage "…everyone knew it", "it" refers to________.
   A. there was a pig in the man' s bag B. the woman bought a cat
   C. the cloth bag D. the man's secret
10. John "let the cat out of the bag" means he________.
   A. makes everyone know a secret B. puts the cat away from the bag
   C. buys a cat in the bag D. sells the cat in the bag

情景写作——根据要求完成下列内容

阅读下面的表格，完成下列两项任务。

	Tom	Tim
Different	1.76 meters	1.74 meters
	130 pounds	135 pounds
	always gets 100 in math exams	always fails math exams
	collects stamps	collects coins
	pen pal's name: Tony	pen pal's name: Mark
Same	both have pen pals, both love collecting things	

A. 根据表格内容完成下列句子

1. ______ is taller than ______.
2. Tim is five pounds ______ than Tom.
3. In math, Tom ______________Tim.

B. Tom 和 Tim 经常与他们的笔友联系，彼此交流爱好与收藏等。Tom 收到了笔友 Tony 的电子邮件，请仿照下面的短文替 Tim 给他的笔友写一封电子邮件。

> Dear Tom,
>
> Thank you for sending me the stamps while you were on vacation in South Africa. I love them very much. I've been collecting stamps for three years. Now I have more than 100 stamps from different countries. I hope that I can show you my stamps some day.
>
> Yours,
>
> Tony

____

____

____

____

____

Lesson 28~30

听写检测——根据要求听写下列内容

Part A: 单词听写——听光盘录音，将听到的每个单词依次写在下面的横线上。

1.________ 2.________ 3.________
4.________ 5.________ 6.________
7.________ 8.________ 9.________
10.________ 11.________ 12.________
13.________ 14.________ 15.________
16.________ 17.________ 18.________
19.________ 20.________ 21.________
22.________ 23.________ 24.________
25.________ 26.________ 27.________
28.________ 29.________ 30.________
31.________ 32.________

Part B: 句子听写——听光盘录音，把课文内容听写在下面的横线上。

1.________________
2.________________
3.________________
4.________________
5.________________
6.________________
7.________________
8.________________
9.________________
10.________________

词汇游戏——根据汉语提示，将数字序号对应的单词填入表格中

横向提示	纵向提示
2. *n.*公寓房；5. *prep.*朝，向 7. *adj.*孤独的，寂寞的 8. *v.*穿过；9. *n.*眼界，视域 10. *v.*废弃；12. *n.*商人 14. *n.*麻烦；16. *n.*楼顶 19. *v.*踢；20. *n.*车库 22. *adv.*几乎；23. *n.*石头 25. *adj.*丑陋的，难看的 27. *n.*神话故事；28. *v.*停放汽车（等） 29. *n.*水球	1. *n.*乘客，旅客；3. *adj.*古代的，古老的 4. *adj.*不平常的；6. *n.*场合，机会 11. *n.*出租汽车 12. *n.*一座大楼 13. *n.*服务；15. *n.*结果，效果 17. *v.*着陆 18. *adj.*罕见的 21. *v.*耕地 24. *n.*主人，所有者 26. *adj.*偏僻的，人迹罕至的

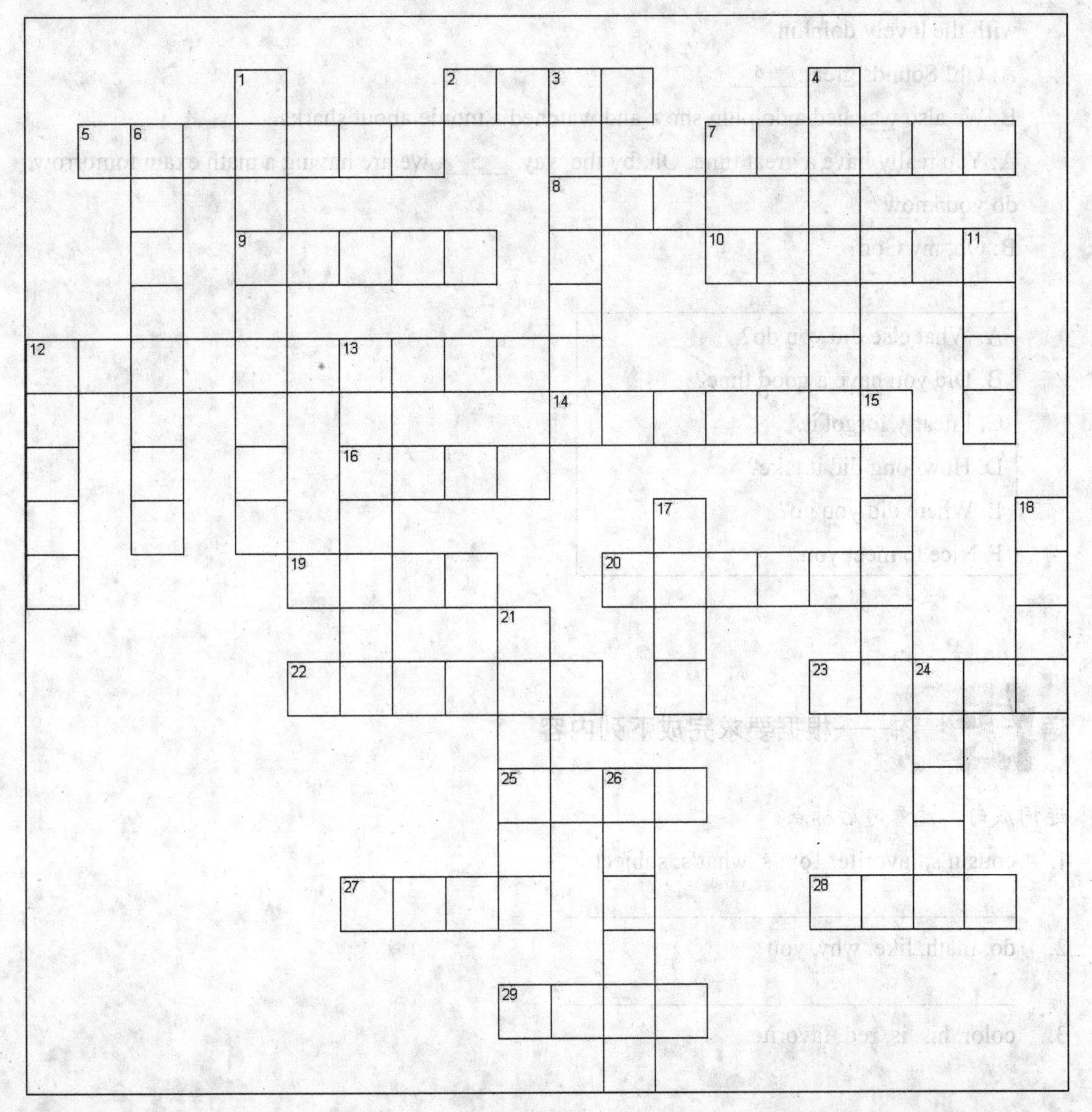

口语造句——根据要求完成下列内容

根据情景，用方框中所给的句子补全对话。

A: __1__.

B: Nice to meet you, too.

A : 1 called you yesterday, but you weren't in. __2__.

B: I went to the aquarium with my mother and sister.

A: __3__.

B: Yes, of course. We bought some souvenirs and what's more important is that I took a photo with the lovely dolphin.

A: Oh! Sounds great. __4__.

B: We also watched a dolphin show and watched a movie about sharks.

A: You really have a great time. Oh, by the way, __5__, we are having a math exam tomorrow, do you know?

B: Oh, my God!

A. What else did you do?
B. Did you have a good time?
C. I nearly forgot it.
D. How long did it take?
E. Where did you go?
F. Nice to meet you.

语法精练——根据要求完成下列内容

连词成句，注意句后标点。

1. cousin's, favorite, Tom's, what's, subject

   ________________________________?

2. do, math, like, why, you

   ________________________________?

3. color, his, is, red, favorite

   ________________________________.

4. is, your, teacher, who, science

______________________________?

5. get, does, he, up, when, usually

______________________________?

根据所给中文意思，完成句子。

6. 你能告诉我在哪里能兑换钱吗？

Could you tell me where I ______ ______ money?

7. 打扰了，请问怎么才能到达科学博物馆？

Excuse me, could you tell me ______ I ______ ______ ______ the Science Museum?

8. 实际上，英语和美语有许多不同点。

In ________, there are ______ ______ ______ American English ______ Britain English.

9. 当我看到他时，他正躺在海滩上看书。

When I ______ ______, he ______ ______ ______ the beach ______.

10. 他问我地球是否绕着太阳转。

He asked me ______ the earth ______ ______ the sun.

11. 孩子们对动画片的兴趣比成年人更浓。

Kids are showing ______ in ______ ______ ______ ______ adults.

12. 她经常制定大计划，却从未实施过。

She often ______ ______ ______ that never happen.

13. 那是一个闲逛的好地方吗？

Is that a good place ______ ______ ______?

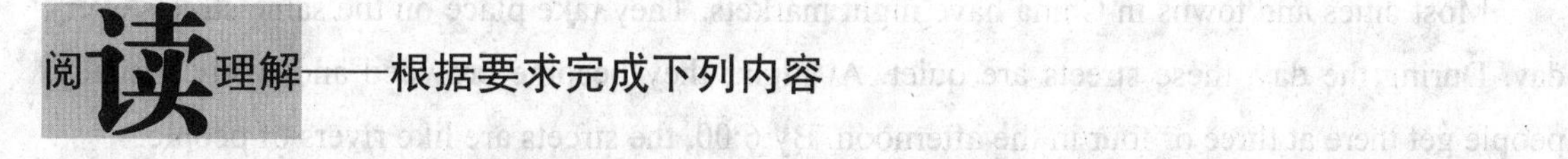

阅读理解——根据要求完成下列内容

阅读下面的文章，并选择正确答案。

Modern life is impossible without travelling. The fastest way of travelling is by plane. With a modern airline you can travel in one day to places which it took a month or more to get to a hundred years ago.

Travelling by train is slower than by plane, but it has its advantages. You can see the country you are travelling through. Modern trains have comfortable seats and dining-cars. They make even the longest journey enjoyable.

Some people like to travel by sea when possible. There are large liners（大客轮）and river boats. You can visit many other countries and different parts of your country on them. Ships are not so fast as trains or planes, but travelling by sea is a very pleasant way to spend a holiday.

Many people like to travel by car. You can make your own timetable. You can travel three or four hundred miles or only fifty or one hundred miles a day, just as you like. You can stop wherever you wish where there is something interesting to see, at a good restaurant where you can enjoy a good meal, or at a hotel to spend the night. That is why travelling by car is popular, while people usually take a train or a plane when they are travelling on business.

1. From the passage, we know that the fastest way of travelling is________.

   A. by train B. by sea C. by plane D. by car

2. If we travel by car, we can________.

   A. make the longest journey enjoyable

   B. travel to a very far place in several minutes

   C. make our own timetable

   D. travel only fifty or one hundred miles a day

3. The underlined（划线的）word They in the passage refers to ______.

   A. modern trains in the country B. comfortable seats and dining-cars

   C. the travellers on the modern trains D. the slower ways of travelling

4. When people travel on business, they usually take________.

   A. a plane or a car B. a car or a boat

   C. a boat or a train D. a train or a plane

5. How many ways of travelling are mentioned in the passage?

   A. Four. B. Three. C. Two. D. Six.

Most cities and towns in China have night markets. They take place on the same streets every day. During the day, these streets are quiet. At night, they become crowded and lively. Usually, people get there at three or four in the afternoon. By 6:00, the streets are like rivers of people.

Night markets are fun places to shop. Sellers open small booths, or they place their things on mats on the street. You can buy clothes, shoes, and many other things. If you think the price is too high, you can bargain with the seller.

You can also buy lots of delicious food. When you are just a little hungry, you can buy a snack. When you're really hungry, you can sit down for a meal. Smelly tofu is popular, but it really smells bad!

There are also games to play. In one game, you throw plastic rings around the top of a bottle. In another game, you shoot balloons with a toy gun. If you are lucky, you can win a prize. Do you like to play these games? Do you ever win anything?

The best thing is, everything at night markets is cheap! You don't need a lot of money to have a great time.

6. When you go to the night markets, ________.
   A. you can see a lot of people by six o' clock
   B. you can buy a lot of things at six o' clock
   C. you must get there at three or four p. m.
   D. you may eat all kinds of food during a day
7. If you think the price is too high at night market, you______.
   A. can call the police   B. can't do anything
   C. can bargain with the seller   D. can shout at the seller
8. You can ________at the night markets when you are just a little hungry.
   A. buy some food   B. eat only smelly tofu
   C. put your things on the street   D. eat everything
9. The text tells us________.
   A. about cities and towns
   B. you can buy everything at the markets
   C. about night markets in most cities and towns in China
   D. people can eat something at the night markets

情景写作——根据要求完成下列内容

根据表格所给的信息，写出语法正确、意思连贯的英语短文。

Name	Age	Hobby	Plan
Tom	26	soccer	to be a P.E. teacher
Lisa	22	music	to hold a concert

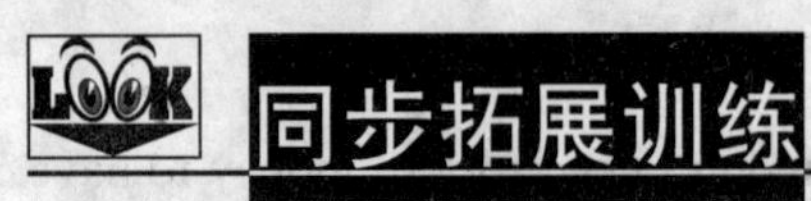

同步拓展训练 11

Lesson 31~33

听写检测——根据要求听写下列内容

Part A: 单词听写——听光盘录音，将听到的每个单词依次写在下面的横线上。

1.______	2.______	3.______
4.______	5.______	6.______
7.______	8.______	9.______
10.______	11.______	12.______
13.______	14.______	15.______
16.______	17.______	18.______
19.______	20.______	21.______
22.______	23.______	24.______
25.______	26.______	27.______
28.______	29.______	30.______
31.______	32.______	

Part B: 句子听写——听光盘录音，把课文内容听写在下面的横线上。

1.______

2.______

3.______

4.______

5.______

6.______

7.______

8.______

9.______

10.______

词汇游戏——根据汉语提示，将数字序号对应的单词填入表格中

横向提示		纵向提示	
横向提示	1. *n.*峭壁；5. *adj.*昂贵的 9. *n.*海岸；11. *n.*车间 14. *v.*包裹；15. *v.*解释，叙述 16. *n.*孙子；20. *n.*物品，东西 21. *n.*暴风雨 22. *prep.*向，朝；接近 25. *v.*雇佣 26. *n.*帮手，助手 29. *adj.*诚实的，正直的 30. *n.*黑暗	纵向提示	2. *n.*灯光；3. *n.*自行车 4. *n.*诱惑；6. *n.*海岸 7. *n.*公司；8. *n.*医院 10. *n.*成功；12. *v.*挣扎 13. *adv.*在前面 17. *adv.*仅仅 18. *n.*工厂；19. *v.*退休 23. *v.*逮捕；24. *v.*积蓄 27. *n.*岩石，礁石 28. *adv.*曾经，以前

口语造句——根据要求完成下列内容

根据情景，用方框中所给的句子补全对话。

A: Excuse me. Could you please tell me where the nearest museum is?

B: Well, it's a bit far. You can go along the street, then take the first turning on the right, walk on and you'll find one there. __1__

A: Oh, thanks. __2__

B: It should be open now. It opens at 8:00 am.

A: Good. __3__

B: Which bus? I don't know. You may ask the policeman over there. __4__

A: OK. By the way, where's the nearest McDonald's, do you know?

B: Right behind you. See that sign.

A: Oh, thanks a lot.

B: __5__.

A. And can you tell me which bus I should take?
B. Do you know at what time it opens?
C. He must know that.
D. You're welcome.
E. What's wrong with you?
F. You can't miss it.
G. Let me help you.

语法精练——根据要求完成下列内容

连词成句，注意句后标点。

1. on weekends, do, usually, you, what, do

   ____?

2. often, the movies, he, to, goes, on Sunday

   ____.

3. shop, month, a, they, twice

____.

4. watch TV, Mr. Li, often, how, does

____?

5. you, exercise, often, do, how

____?

6. should, milk , every, we, drink, day

____.

7. at least, sleep, teenagers, for, hours, should, eight, night, every

____.

根据所给中文意思，完成句子。

8. 让孩子们对学习感兴趣是很重要的。

It's ________ to get children ______ _______ their studies.

9. 从前这儿曾有所医院。

There _______ _______ _______ a hospital here.

10. 如果你有个约会，请按时到达。

If you have______ _____, please _____ there _____ ______.

11. 我们需要了解一些餐桌礼仪。

We____ _______ ________ something about______ _____.

12. 家长和老师应当使用不同的方式、方法来帮助孩子们。

Parents and teachers _____ _____ _____ _____ to help the students.

13. 你最好不要事先不打电话就去拜访朋友。

You'd better _____ _____ a friend's house _______ _______ first.

14. 外国朋友们正逐渐习惯于在中国生活。

The foreign friends are ________ used to ________ in China.

15. 他们特意花费心思让我们感觉轻松。

They ______ _______ _______ their way _____ ______us ______ at home.

阅读理解——根据要求完成下列内容

完形填空

I've never been late for school, but yesterday I came very close. My alarm clock didn't __1__ And by the time I woke up, my father had already __2__ into the bathroom and had to wait for him

__3__. I had to really rush. I took a quick shower, and had some breakfast, and then __4__ to the bus stop. Unfortunately, by the time I got there, the bus had __5__ left. I started walking, but I knew I couldn't get to school __6__ time. Luckily, my friend Tony and his dad came __7__ in his dad's car and they __8__ me a ride. When I got to school, the final bell __9__. I __10__ made it to my class.

1.	A. go off	B. turn off	C. go on	D. turn on
2.	A.been	B. go	C. gone	D. went
3.	A. to come out	B. coming inside	C. to go outside	D. getting into
4.	A. runoff	B. walked	C. walk	D. ran off
5.	A. never	B. ever	C. nearly	D. already
6.	A.by	B. at	C. for	D. on
7.	A.on	B. by	C. close	D. here
8.	A.get	B. gave	C. give	D. got
9.	A. was ringing	B. rang	C. rung	D. had rung
10.	A. just only	B. only	C. only just	D. just

阅读下面的文章，并选择正确答案。

Can dolphins talk? May be they can't talk with words, but they talk with sounds.

Dolphins travel in a group. We call a group of fish a "school". They don't study but they travel together. Dolphins are mammals, not fish, but they swim together in a school.

Dolphins talk to other dolphins in the school. They give information. They-tell when they are happy or sad or afraid. They say welcome when a dolphin comes back to the school. They talk when they play.

They make a few sounds above water. They make many more sounds under water. People can't hear these sounds because they are very very high. Scientists make tapes of the sounds and study them.

Sometimes people catch a dolphin for a large aquarium. People watch the dolphins in a show. Dolphins don't like to be away from their school. In the aquarium, they are sad and lonely. There are many stories about dolphins. They can help people. Sometimes they save somebody's life. Dolphin meat is good but people don't like to kill them. They say that dolphins bring good luck. Many people believe this.

11. Dolphins can talk with________.

A. sounds　　B. words　　C. language　　D. action

12. Dolphins ________ be in their school.

A. don't like to　　B. like to　　C. liking　　D. likes

13. Dolphins always bring________ .

A. sadness　　B. wishes　　C. bad luck　　D. good luck

14. Dolphins make ________ sounds above water.

A. more　　B. many　　C. a few　　D. much

15. Which of the following is true?

A. Dolphin meat is good, so people like to kill them.

B. Sometimes dolphins save somebody's life.

C. Dolphins make a few sounds under water.

D. People can hear these sounds from under water.

情景写作——根据要求完成下列内容

请给音乐节目主持人写一封信，告诉他你是一名中学生，你喜欢这个节目，特别是英语歌曲。因为你不但从英语歌里学了很多单词，同时也消除了疲劳。最后提出希望能得到 My Heart Will Go On 这首歌的歌词。

Dear Sir,

____

____

____

____

____

____

____

____

Yours sincerely

XXX

同步拓展训练 12

Lesson 34~36

听写检测——根据要求听写下列内容

Part A: 单词听写——听光盘录音，将听到的每个单词依次写在下面的横线上。

1.________ 2.________ 3.________
4.________ 5.________ 6.________
7.________ 8.________ 9.________
10.________ 11.________ 12.________
13.________ 14.________ 15.________
16.________ 17.________ 18.________
19.________ 20.________ 21.________
22.________ 23.________ 24.________
25.________ 26.________ 27.________
28.________ 29.________ 30.________
31.________ 32.________

Part B: 句子听写——听光盘录音，把课文内容听写在下面的横线上。

1.________________
2.________________
3.________________
4.________________
5.________________
6.________________
7.________________
8.________________
9.________________
10.________________

词汇游戏——根据汉语提示，将数字序号对应的单词填入表格中

横向提示		纵向提示	
	1. *adj.*愉快的，开心的 5. *v.*行动；8. *n.*害怕 9. *v.*认可，认出 11. *v.*冲；12. *v.*收到，接到 13. *v.*逮捕；15. *adv.*焦急地 17. *adj.*固体的，硬的 19. *adv.*很快，不久 21. *n.*（警察）局 22. *v.*期待，期望 24. *n.*记录；25. *n.*小偷，贼		2. *n.*游泳运动员 3. *v.*成功；4. *adj.*令人兴奋的 5. *adv.*以后；6. *adv.*径直 7. *v.*后悔；8. *adv.*非常 10. *n.*一段时间；14. *adj.*撞坏的 16. *adj.*地方的，当地的 17. *v.*偷，偷窃；18. *v.*损害，伤害 19. *adj.*微笑的；20. *v.*打算 21. *adj.*强壮的 23. *adv.*相当，非常

1 2 3 4 5 6 7 8 9 10 11 12 13 14 15 16 17 18 19 20 21 22 23 24 25

口语造句——根据要求完成下列内容

将下列句子排序成对话，把序号写在句子前面的横线上。

___ Thanks a lot, A friend in need is a friend indeed.

___ A headache? You shouldn't go to work.

1 Are you OK?

8 That sounds good. But who can help me to finish the work?

___ Yes, I guess so.

___ But I have lots of work to finish.

___ No, I am not. I have a headache.

___ Don't worry. Sam and I will finish the work instead.

5 Well, don't you think you have a headache because you are stressed out.

___ So you should stay home and listen to some music to relax.

语法精练——根据要求完成下列内容

下列各句中各有一处有错，请指出并改正。

1. It's an interesting work.
   A B C D
2. What does she wants to be?
   A B C D
3. People call we nurses "angels in white".
   A B C D
4. He is reporter. He works at a TV station.
   A B C D
5. Jim is an actor. He have to work in the evenings.
   A B C D

根据句意，用方框中所给词的适当形式填空。

become, mislead, set up, show, move, thank, hurry up, write down, spend, make

6. At times, people are ________ by the advertisements.
7. Customers usually enjoy ________ more time eating in a quiet place.

8. The teacher told us that the moon ________around the earth.
9. Fast food is ________popular all over the world.
10. The Government is considering ________more shopping malls for the sake of convenience of the people.
11. The smile on the teacher's face ______he is pleased with his students.
12. Could you pass me a pen? I'd like to ________the phone number.
13. The old woman was very ________to us for our help.
14. We like loud music, it ______us energetic.
15. We have to ________so that we can catch the last train.

阅读理解——根据要求完成下列内容

阅读下面的文章，并选择正确答案。

In many English homes people eat four meals a day. They have breakfast at any time from seven to nine in the morning. They eat porridge eggs or bread and drink tea or coffee at breakfast. Lunch comes at one o'clock. Afternoon tea is from four to five in the afternoon and dinner is about half past seven. First they have soup, then they have meat or fish with vegetables. After that they eat some other things, like bananas, apples or oranges. But not all English people eat like that. Some of them have their dinner in the middle of the day. Their meals are breakfast, dinner, tea and supper and all these meals are very simple.

1. Many English people have ______meals a day.
   A. two B. three C. four D. five
2. People may have _____for their breakfast according to the passage.
   A. tea and eggs B. hamburgers and tea C. coffee and salad D. eggs and fish
3. People have lunch at__________.
   A. any time B. nine C. five D. one
4. People don't have _______for their dinner.
   A. bananas and apples B. soup and meat C. meat and fish D. porridge
5. Most Englishmen have dinner__________.
   A. at one's o'colck B. at any time C. at D. in the evening

完形填空

The world is divided into two important parts. One half of the world is rich and __6__ half is poor. In the poor part, a lot of people never get __7__. In the rich part, a lot of people eat too much. In one part, children are hungry and in the other, a lot of people are __8__ and have to go on diets or __9__ some exercises in order to lose weight. For example, a dog or a cat in North America __10__ than a child in the poorer countries.

The poor countries have some difficult problems. Sometimes the land is too poor __11__. The land can be got or made better, but a lot of things must be done __12__. The people must be __13__ and water must be __14__.

But rich countries have problems, too. They are not always pleasant places to live in. Sometimes the air is too dirty to breathe and the rivers are too dirty to swim in or to __15__. The roads and streets __16__ people and buses. Cars usually move slowly. Noise is __17__. A lot of people do not have houses to live in. Some things will have to be done about these problems. The air and the rivers must be __18__, and more houses will have __19__. But these can't be done easily.

6. A. other B. another C. the other D. others
7. A. to eat enough B. enough eat C. to enough eat D. enough to eat
8. A. fattest B. as fat as C. thinner and thinner D. fatter and fatter
9. A.make B. do C. join D. take part in
10. A. eat better B. eats better C. eat more D. happier
11. A. to grow something on B. to grow anything C. to grow anything on D. to grow something
12. A. at first B. then C. at last D. first
13. A. taught B. taken C. spent D. come
14. A. founded B. drunk C. found D. found out
15. A. take from B. take water from C. drink D. drink it
16. A. full of B. are full of C. filled with D. have many
17. A. terrible B. badly C. difficult D. frighten
18. A. change B. become C. turned into D. cleaned
19. A. to build B. to built C. to be built D. be built

情景写作——根据要求完成下列内容

Write a letter to a friend of yours to tell him or her about your school report card. (at least 80 words)

Report Card
Name: ________
Math—hard-working
English—good at speaking
History—can do better
Science—lazy student

____

____

____

____

____

____

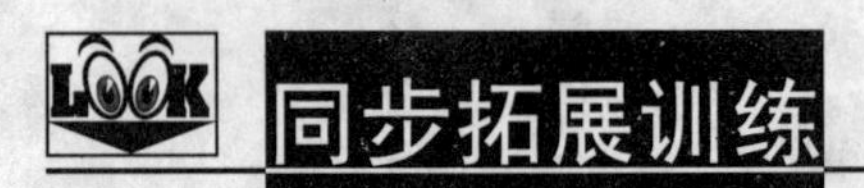

同步拓展训练 13

Lesson 37~39

听写检测——根据要求听写下列内容

Part A: 单词听写——听光盘录音，将听到的每个单词依次写在下面的横线上。

1.________	2.________	3.________
4.________	5.________	6.________
7.________	8.________	9.________
10.________	11.________	12.________
13.________	14.________	15.________
16.________	17.________	18.________
19.________	20.________	21.________
22.________	23.________	24.________
25.________	26.________	27.________
28.________	29.________	30.________
31.________	32.________	

Part B: 句子听写——听光盘录音，把课文内容听写在下面的横线上。

1.____

2.____

3.____

4.____

5.____

6.____

7.____

8.____

9.____

10.____

词汇游戏——根据汉语提示，将数字序号对应的单词填入表格中

横向提示	纵向提示
4. *adv.*不断地；5. *v.*抱怨 7. *n.*震动，打击；8. *adv.*刺骨地 10. *adv.*忧虑地，不安地 11. *n.*亲戚；12. *adj.*巨大的 15. *adj.*下一个 16. *adj.*奥林匹克的 17. *n.*阳光；21. *n.*（电话的）交换台 23. *n.*打电话的人；26. *v.*返回 27. *n.*病人；28. *v.*召开 29. *adj.*独自的	1. *n.*政府；2. *adj.*成功的 3. *v.*询问，打听；6. *n.*手术 9. *adj.*某个 13. *v.*完成，完善 14. *adj.*巨大的；17. *n.*标准 18. *adj.*特别的，特殊的 19. *prep.*除了；20. *n.*国家 22. *n.*首都 24. *v.*退休 25. *v.*做梦

口语造句——根据要求完成下列内容

根据情景，用方框中所给的句子补全对话。

A: I want to get good grades. ___1___

B: Maybe you could attend after-school class on weekends.

A: ___2___ I have to do my homework on weekends.

B: Well, you could ask your friends for help.

A: ___3___

B: You should say "sorry" to your friend.

A: OK. ___4___

B: I think you shouldn't play computer games or watch TV any more.

A: ___5___ I'll study harder and harder from now on.

A. But I argued with my best friend yesterday. B. That's a good idea. C. I don't have enough time. D. What should I do? E. I'll try to apologize to her.

语法精练——根据要求完成下列内容

根据句意，用方框中所给词的适当形式填空。

good, careful, heavy, brightly, strongly, well, heavily, bright, carefully, strong

1. Her English is very______. She can speak English very______.
2. Last night there was ______rain. It rained______ all night.
3. Listen! It's blowing______.
   Yes. It's a very______ wind.
4. Look at the ______sun. It always shines ______at this time of year.
5. Oh, how______ he's writing! He is always______ like that.

根据所给中文意思，完成句子。

6. 我同意你的观点，这个工作根本不适合她。

   I _______ _______ your opinion that she is not _______ for the job.

7. 请支持我们的教育事业。

   Please _______ our country's _______.

8. 谁能为伊拉克妇女儿童提供衣食住所呢？

   Who can _______ the Iraqi women and children _______ food, clothes and houses?

9. 废塑料能够被回收利用。

   The _______ and _______ plastics can be _______.

10. 虽然野生动物可能会给人类带来一些疾病，但它们应该被关爱。

    _______ wild animals may _______ some diseases to human beings, they _______ _______ _______ by us.

11. 如今熊猫的居住地（栖息地）越来越少了。

    Today there are _______ and _______ _______ for pandas.

12. 过去有大量的海牛，但是据发现它们现在正濒临灭绝。

    There _______ _______ _______ many manatees, but now it _______ _______ they are _______.

13. 每只海牛平均大约有10英尺长，重大约1000磅。

    The average manatee is about _______ _______ _______ and it _______ about 1,000 _______.

阅读理解——根据要求完成下列内容

阅读下面的文章，并选择正确答案。

Everyone knows Egypt is famous for its pyramids. But do you know that Cairo is a cat city? Last summer I visited Cairo. It was really hot. I saw cats almost everywhere. Pyramids have cats. offices and hospitals have cats. Cats are also in the hotels and restaurants. Cats appear in the cinema, too. To my surprise, even an airplane have one.

There are some singing cats in concert halls. They are famous throughout the city. Once an actor was holding his pet, a dying cat, in his arms on the stage. Another cat walked around the dying cat. The cat listened to the music and looked at the dying cat, crying sadly. At first people laughed at him. A few minutes later people began to cry.

1. There are many______ in Egypt.

   A. pyramids　　B. cats　　C. both A and B

2. According to the author, you can find cats______.

   A. in restaurants and aircrafts　　B. everywhere

   C. in concert halls and hospitals

3. Why are the cats in concert halls famous? ______

   A. Because there are too many cats.　　B. Because the cats can sing.

   C. Because the cats can be actors.

4. People in the concert hall ______after listening to the cat's crying.

   A. couldn't help crying　　B. couldn't help laughing

   C. couldn't help singing

5. Which of the following is the best title of the passage?

   A. Singing Cats　　B. Cats in Egypt　　C. Cats Everywhere

完形填空

Miss Brown __6__ up early in the morning. If her sister did not wake her up, she would often be late for, her classes. One day a lecture was going to be given by a famous artist at nine o'clock. Her sister was __7__. She set her alarm clock for half past seven. This should __8__ her plenty of time to get ready and __9__ early enough for a good seat. She was determined to __10__ there in time. She would never forgive herself for __11__ the lecture. She had been admiring the artist's work since she was a child.

The next morning, she slept through the alarm bell and woke up at half past eight. She was not used to rushing and everything went __12__. At last, she was ready, and rushed out to catch a bus. She jumped on the first one. She looked at her watch, but it was not there. She must have forgotten to put it on in her rush. When she arrived at the university, she __13__ to the lecture hall. She was surprised to find that the doors were locked. She looked round to find someone, and saw a clock. It said half past seven. "I can't understand it." She cried out. "Nobody's here and the clock is __14__!" Then she suddenly remembered. Her alarm clock had stopped the day before and she must __15__ to reset the hands. "This is the first time I'll hear the __16__ of a lecture." She said to __17__, laughing.

6. A. enjoyed getting　　B. did not like getting　　C. loved getting　　D. wanted to get

7. A. asleep　　B. at home　　C. sleeping　　D. away

8. A.take　　B. give　　C. spend　　D. pay

9. A. arrive　　B. reach　　C. get　　D. get to

10.	A.be	B. stay	C. come	D. stand
11.	A. losing	B. listen to	C. hearing	D. missing
12.	A. wrong	B. well	C. away	D. out
13.	A. walking	B. moved	C. hurried	D. jumped
14.	A.slow	B. fast	C. right	D. quick
15.	A. be forgotten	B. has forgotten	C. have forgotten	D. forget
16.	A. end	B. beginning	C hall	D. middle part
17.	A. him	B. himself	C. her	D. herself

情景写作——根据要求完成下列内容

目前在中国有不少孩子生活困难，学习条件差，有的甚至上不了学……作为北京的一名中学生，你打算为他们做哪些事情？

必须用到复合句，可以参考下列词语和句型。

life, difficult, not enough books, so poor that… (too…to), as a middle school student, I'm going to…I should…I would…I'd better…

____

____

____

____

____

____

____

同步拓展训练 14

Lesson 40~42

听写检测——根据要求听写下列内容。

Part A: 单词听写——听光盘录音，将听到的每个单词依次写在下面的横线上。

1.________ 2.________ 3.________
4.________ 5.________ 6.________
7.________ 8.________ 9.________
10.________ 11.________ 12.________
13.________ 14.________ 15.________
16.________ 17.________ 18.________
19.________ 20.________ 21.________
22.________ 23.________ 24.________
25.________ 26.________ 27.________
28.________ 29.________ 30.________
31.________ 32.________

Part B: 句子听写——听光盘录音，把课文内容听写在下面的横线上。

1.________________
2.________________
3.________________
4.________________
5.________________
6.________________
7.________________
8.________________
9.________________
10.________________

词汇游戏——根据汉语提示，将数字序号对应的单词填入表格中

横向提示		纵向提示	
横向提示	3. *v.*后悔，遗憾 4. *n.*灯塔 8. *n.*（吹奏的）管乐器 9. *n.*动作；14. *n.*一瞥 15. *n.*会话，交谈；17. *adv.*突然地 20. *n.*蛇 26. *adj.*印度的 27. *n.*镜子 28. *adj.*现代的 29. *prep.*在旁边	纵向提示	1. *n.*差别；2. *n.*孔 3. *adj.*无礼的；5. *adj.*可怕的，糟糕的 6. *n.*女主人；7. *adj.*精通音乐的 10. *adv.*显然地；11. *v.*继续 12. *adj.*不笑的，严肃的 13. *n.*绝望；16. *n.*地球 18. *v.*跳舞；19. *v.*提醒 21. *adv.*往国外，海外 22. *n.*曲调；23. *v.*评说 24. *n.*市场，集市；25. *adj.*紧身的

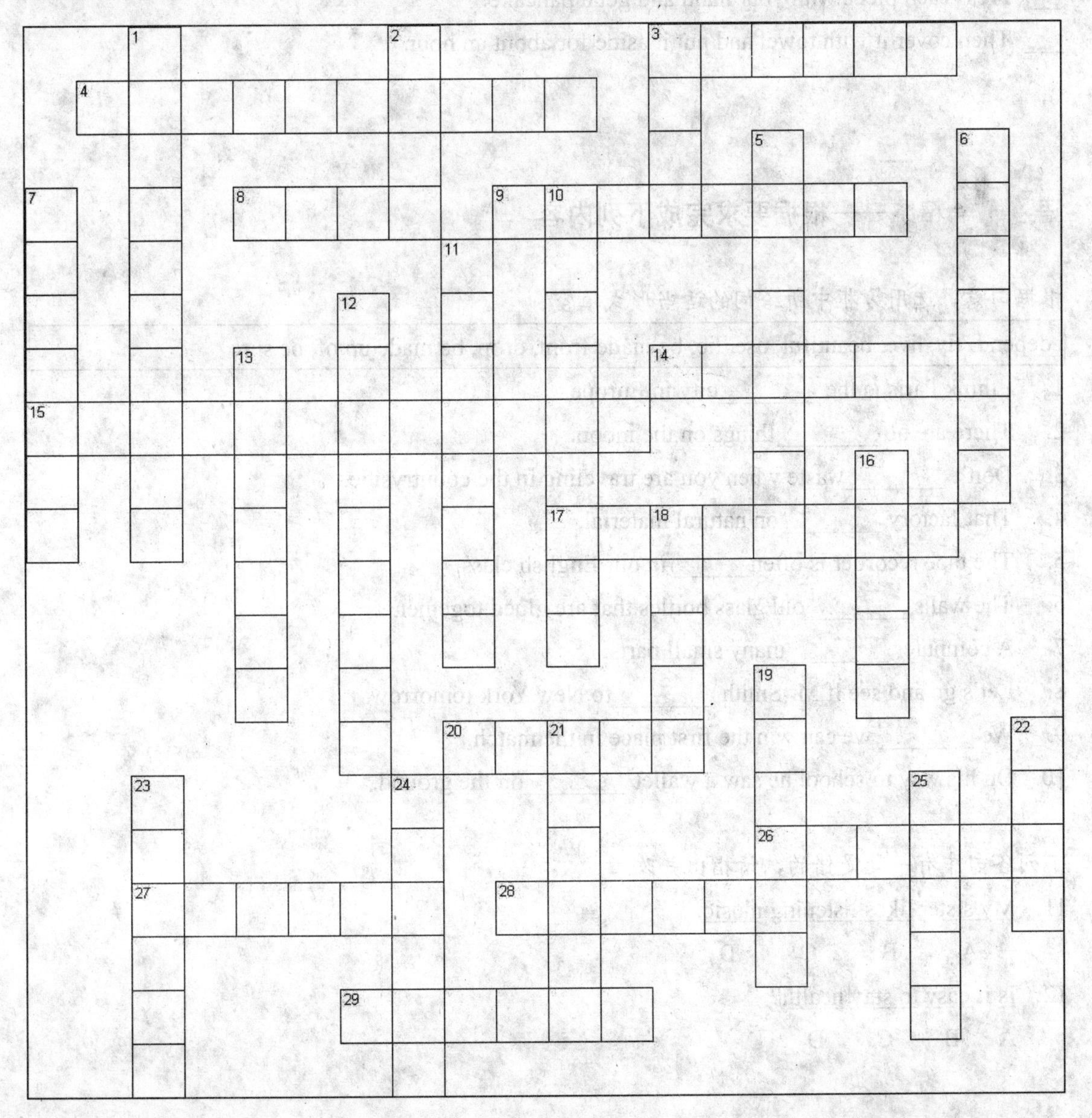

口语造句——根据要求完成下列内容

将下列句子排序成对话，把序号写在句子前面的横线上。

___ Next scatter(撒)some dry flour on the board, knead(揉)and roll it into a sausage-like dough.
___ Finally, you should hold the pancake with your palm and put the filling in the center.
___ Wrap it into half-moon shapes and seal the edges.
___ Then cut it into small pieces.
___ Make water and flour into soft dough（面团）.
___ Press each piece with your hand and get a pancake.
___ Then cover it with towel and put it aside for about an hour.

语法精练——根据要求完成下列内容

根据句意，选用方框中所给词的适当形式填空。

depend, fly, live, beautiful, use, lie, be made from, drop, be made up of, be sure

1. I think Paris is the ________city in Europe.
2. There are no ________things on the moon.
3. Don't ________waste when you are traveling in the countryside.
4. That factory ________on natural material.
5. The tape recorder is often______ in our English class.
6. The walls ________old glass bottles that are glued together.
7. A computer ________many small parts.
8. Let's go and see if Mr Smith ________to New York tomorrow.
9. We ________we can win the first place in the match.
10. On his way to school he saw a wallet ________on the ground.

下列各句中有一处是错的，请指出并改正。

11. My sister likes listening music.
    A B C D
12. Is it easy to stay health?
    A B C D

13. You real need to see the dentist.
    A B C D

14. Is your speaking improve?
    A B C D

15. Eat too much is bad for your health.
    A B C D

阅读理解——根据要求完成下列内容

阅读下面的文章，并选择正确答案。

In most parts of the world, many students help their schools make less pollution. They join "environment clubs". In an environment club, people work together to make our environment clean.

Here are some things students often do.

No-garbage lunches. How much do you throw away after lunch? Environment clubs ask students to bring their lunches in bags that can be used again. Every week they will choose the classes that make the least garbage and report them to the whole school!

No-car day. On a no-car day, nobody comes to school in a car—not the students and not the teachers! Cars give pollution to our air, so remember.

Walk, jump, bike or run.

Use your legs! It's lots of fun!

Turn off the water! Did you know that some toilets can waste twenty to forty ml of water an hour? In a year, that would fill a small river! In environment clubs, students mend those broken toilets.

We love our environment. Let's work together to make it clean.

1. Environment clubs ask students ________.
   A. to run to school every day　　B. to take exercise every day
   C. not to forget to take cars　　D. not to throw away lunch bags

2. From the passage we know the students usually have lunch ________.
   A. at school　　B. in shops　　C. in clubs　　D. at home

3. On a no-car day, ________ will take a car to school.
   A. both students and teachers　　B. only students
   C. neither students nor teachers　　D. only teachers

4. The writer wrote the passage to ask students to________.

A. clean schools
B. make less pollution
C. join clubs
D. help teachers

完形填空

About 70,000,000 Americans are trying to lose weight. That is almost 1 out of every 3 people in the United States. Some people eat __5__ food and they hardly have any fats or sweets. Others do running, exercise with machines, take medicines, or even have operations. __6__ you can see losing weight is __7__ work. Why do so many people in the United States want to lose weight?

Many people in the United States worry about their figure? For many people, looking nice also means to be __8__ Other people worry about their health as many doctors say overweight is not good.

Most people want to find a faster and __9__ way to take off fat, and books of this kind are very popular. These books tell people how to lose weight. Each year a lot of new books like these are __10__. Each one says it can easily help people take fat away.

Losing weight can be __11__. Some overweight people go to health centers, like La Costa in California. Men and women pay several hundred dollars a day at these health centers. People live there for one week or two, taking exercises, eating different foods. Meals there may be just a little. All this works for losing weight. __12__ 4 days on the programme, one woman called Mrs. Warren lost 5 pounds (2. 27kg). At $ 400 a day, she spent $ 320 to lose each pound. But she said she was still __13__ to do so.

Health centers, books, medicines, operations, running and exercise machines all need a lot of money. So in the United States, losing weight may mean losing __14__ too.

5. A. less B. more C. nice D. fast
6. A. For B. So C. Or D. And
7. A. good B. useful C. hard D. easy
8. A. high B. short C. thin D. fat
9. A. dearer B. harder C. shorter D. easier
10. A. taken B. given C. written D. copied
11. A. cheap B. expensive C. easy D. safe
12. A. Before B. In C. After D. At
13. A. sorry B. angry C. sad D. glad
14. A. health B. time C. food D. money

情景写作——根据要求完成下列内容

根据下面提供的情景，续写一段文字。

注意：词数不少于 30。

Xu Chen is a Junior school student, who usually goes to school by bike. He lives far from the school.

It was an cold, dark and snowy morning. Lin Hao arrived at the school early. At the entrance to the classroom building, he saw Xu Chen without his bike. So Lin Hao asked him why he didn't come to school by bike.

If you are Xu Chen, please tell Lin Hao why.

____

____

____

____

____

____

____

Lesson 43~45

听写检测——根据要求听写下列内容

Part A: 单词听写——听光盘录音，将听到的每个单词依次写在下面的横线上。

1.______ 2.______ 3.______
4.______ 5.______ 6.______
7.______ 8.______ 9.______
10.______ 11.______ 12.______
13.______ 14.______ 15.______
16.______ 17.______ 18.______
19.______ 20.______ 21.______
22.______ 23.______ 24.______
25.______ 26.______ 27.______
28.______ 29.______ 30.______
31.______ 32.______

Part B: 句子听写——听光盘录音，把课文内容听写在下面的横线上。

1.______
2.______
3.______
4.______
5.______
6.______
7.______
8.______
9.______
10.______

词汇游戏——根据汉语提示，将数字序号对应的单词填入表格中

横向提示		纵向提示	
	4. *n.*（常用复数）内有的物品 5. *n.*野餐；7. *n.*呼吸 8. *adv.*顺利地；9. *n.*（地球的）极 10. *n.*探险家；15. *n.*飞行 18. *n.*存款；20. *n.*森林 21. *n.*袋子 22. *n.*危险，冒险 23. *n.*飞机；25. *v.*命令 26. *n.*平原 27. *v.*似乎，好像		1. *n.*所有；2. *v.*修理 3. *n.*村民 4. *n.*良心，道德心 6. *v.*处于；9. *n.*地点 11. 百分之……；12. *adj.*无尽的 13. *n.*皮夹，钱夹；14. *n.*边缘 16. *adj.*无罪的，不亏心的 17. *n.*山，山脉；18. *adj.*严重的 19. *n.*带，皮带 24. *v.*坠毁

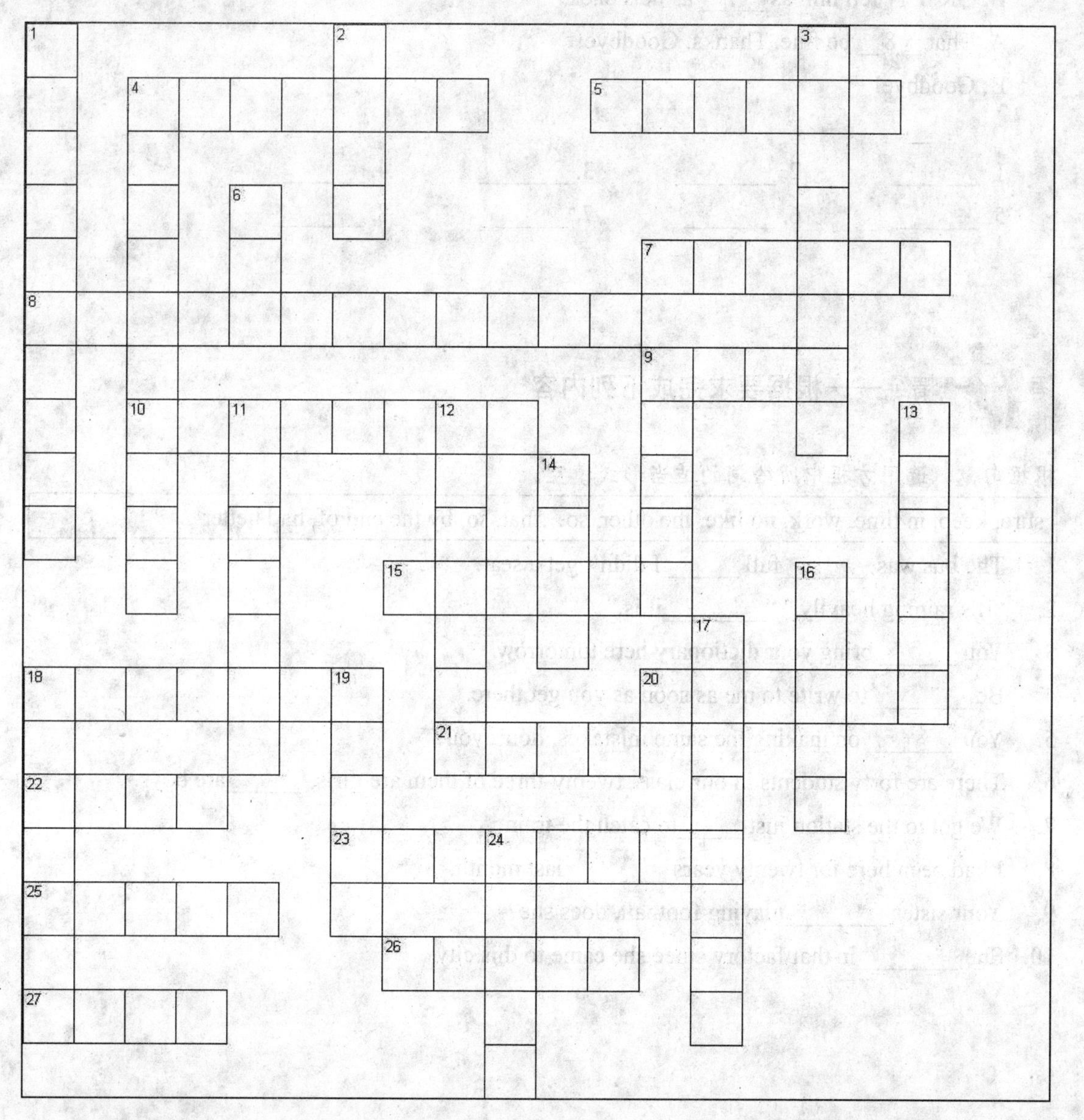

口语造句——根据要求完成下列内容

补全对话

A: Hello! __1__ is Ms. Jordan. Can I __2__ to Mr. Jordan, please?

B: Yes. Please __3__ on for a moment.

I m sorry, he left a moment ago. Can I __4__ a message?

A: Please tell him __5__ I __6__ go to Shanghai on business tomorrow.

Please ask him to phone me back.

B: OK. I'11 tell him as __7__ as he's back.

A: That __8__ be fine. Thanks. Goodbye!

B: Goodbye!

1. ________ 2. ________ 3. ________ 4. ________

5. ________ 6. ________ 7. ________ 8. ________

语法精练——根据要求完成下列内容

根据句意，选用方框中所给词的适当形式填空。

sure, keep, in time, work, no like, the other, so…that, so, by the end of, had better

1. The bus was ________full ______I didn't get a seat.
2. "It's raining heavily." "________it is."
3. You ______ bring your dictionary here tomorrow.
4. Be________ to write to me as soon as you get there.
5. You _______ on making the same mistakes, don't you?
6. There are forty students in our class, twenty-three of them are girls, ______are boys.
7. We got to the station just _____to catch the train.
8. I had been here for twenty years ________last month.
9. Your sister ________playing football, does she?
10. She ________in that factory since she came to this city.

根据所给中文意思，完成句子。

11. 今天我感到不舒服，我大概感冒了。

Today I _______ _______. Maybe I _______ _______ _______.

12. 他头痛，嗓子痛，他得去看病。

He _______ a _______ and a _______ _______. He has to _______ a _______.

13. 她感到压力很大，因为她英语口语没长进。

She is _______ _______ because her speaking English _______ _______.

14. 听说你已康复，我们都很高兴。

We are _______ to _______ that you are _______ now.

15. 多吃蔬菜和水果对你的健康有好处。

_______ a lot of vegetables and fruits _______ good _______ your _______.

16. 搞得太累会使你得病的。

Getting _______ _______ will _______ you _______.

17. 我想他不健康，因为他几乎不锻炼。

I _______ think he is kind of _______. Because he _______ _______ _______.

18. 良好的饮食和锻炼能帮助我们学得更多更好。

Good food and exercise _______ _______ to _______ _______ and _______.

19. 我妈让我每天喝牛奶，她说这对我的健康有好处。

My mother wants me _______ _______ _______ every day. She says it's _______ _______ my _______.

20. 我们每 40 分钟休息一次。

We have a rest _______ _______ _______.

阅读理解——根据要求完成下列内容

根据短文内容判断正误，正确写 T，错误写 F。

When Mr. Young was twenty-one, he began to work in a post office in a small town. His wife died three years ago and he lives there alone. Next month he'll be sixty and he'll retire. He's often ill and no body can take care of him. His daughter hopes that he will move to London to live with her. He thought it a good idea and agreed with her.

One Sunday morning Mr. Young began to pack his things. He was going to sell most of them but wanted to take an old easy chair with him. His mother left it to him and his wife died on it. And he of ten sits on it when he's free. But it was too big and he couldn't find anything to pack it.

Suddenly he remembered one of his friends had bought a fridge. So he drove his car to ask for the packing box.

His friend was glad to help him. He helped him to tie the packing box on top of his car. Then he left. On his way home, a car drove before his. The driver stopped his car on the side of the road and shouted to him. "You've lost your fridge, sir."

1. Mr. Young has worked in the post office for about 21 years.
2. The word "retire" in the story means "stop working and stay at home. "
3. Mr. Young agreed with his daughter because he could live a happy life in the capital.
4. Mr. Young wanted to take the easy chair to London because he liked it better than any other thing.
5. Mr. Young didn't know he had lost his fridge.

完形填空

Mr. White works in an office. He liked reading in bed when he was at school. It was bad for to know about it his __6__ and now he is near sight. But he wouldn't want __7__ to know about it and he never wears a pair of glasses, It often __8__ him some trouble.

One winter morning he was sent to a village school on business. He __9__ a bus at a stop in a small town. Then he had to walk there. The road to the village wasn't smooth. He fell over some times and it __10__ his clothes dirty. __11__ he got to the village. Suddenly it began to blow and it got colder. He was looking for the school while his __12__ was blown off. He began to run after it but he couldn't get it. He couldn't understand why his hat ran into a house as if it had __13__. And he ran into the house, __14__.

A woman stopped him and shouted angrily, "__15__ are you running after my hen for ?"

6.	A. ears	B. nose	C. month	D. eyes
7.	A. anybody else	B. nobody	C. woman	D. somebody
8.	A. follows	B. takes	C. brings	D. carries
9.	A. took off	B. got off	C. got on	D. came on
10.	A. let	B. made	C. gave	D. felt
11.	A. At first	B. At home	C. At times	D. At last
12.	A. clothes	B. bag	C. hat	D. glasses
13.	A. legs	B. hands	C. shoes	D. arms
14.	A. always	B. also	C. either	D. too
15.	A. What	B. Why	C. Which	D. Who

情景写作——根据要求完成下列内容

人们在生活中难免会有抱怨或要求，如果你遇到这样的情况，怎么才能有礼貌地表示你的抱怨或要求呢？

请用下面的语言结构表达你的抱怨或要求。

语言结构	抱怨或要求
Would you mind ___________ Could you please ___________ Please ___________ Would you please ___________	A. not smoke here B. not make so much noise C. not play football in the street D. turn down the radio E. get up early

1. ____
2. ____
3. ____
4. ____
5. ____

同步拓展训练 16

Lesson 46~48

听写检测——根据要求听写下列内容

Part A: 单词听写——听光盘录音，将听到的每个单词依次写在下面的横线上。

1.________	2.________	3.________
4.________	5.________	6.________
7.________	8.________	9.________
10.________	11.________	12.________
13.________	14.________	15.________
16.________	17.________	18.________
19.________	20.________	21.________
22.________	23.________	24.________
25.________	26.________	27.________
28.________	29.________	30.________
31.________	32.________	

Part B: 句子听写——听光盘录音，把课文内容听写在下面的横线上。

1.____

2.____

3.____

4.____

5.____

6.____

7.____

8.____

9.____

10.____

词汇游戏——根据汉语提示，将数字序号对应的单词填入表格中

横向提示	纵向提示
1. *v.*点头；3. *v.*发现 6. *v.*暗示；8. *n.*家具 10. *v.*使惊讶；12. *n.*威士忌酒 14. *n.*货物，商品；15. *v.*（鬼）来访，闹鬼 17. *n.*收藏品，收集品；19. *v.*包含 22. *n.*管子 24. *v.*承认 25. *n.*管子 26. *adj.*羊毛的 27. *v.*卸（货）	2. *v.*发生；3. *v.*发现 4. *n.*问题；5. *adv.*同时 7. *adj.*贪杯的；9. *adj.*不可能的 11. *adv.*非常，极其；12. *adj.*木制的 13. *v.*收集 16. *v.*接受 18. *v.*关在（狭小的空间里） 20. *adj.*正常的，通常的 21. *v.*摇动 23. *v.*拔

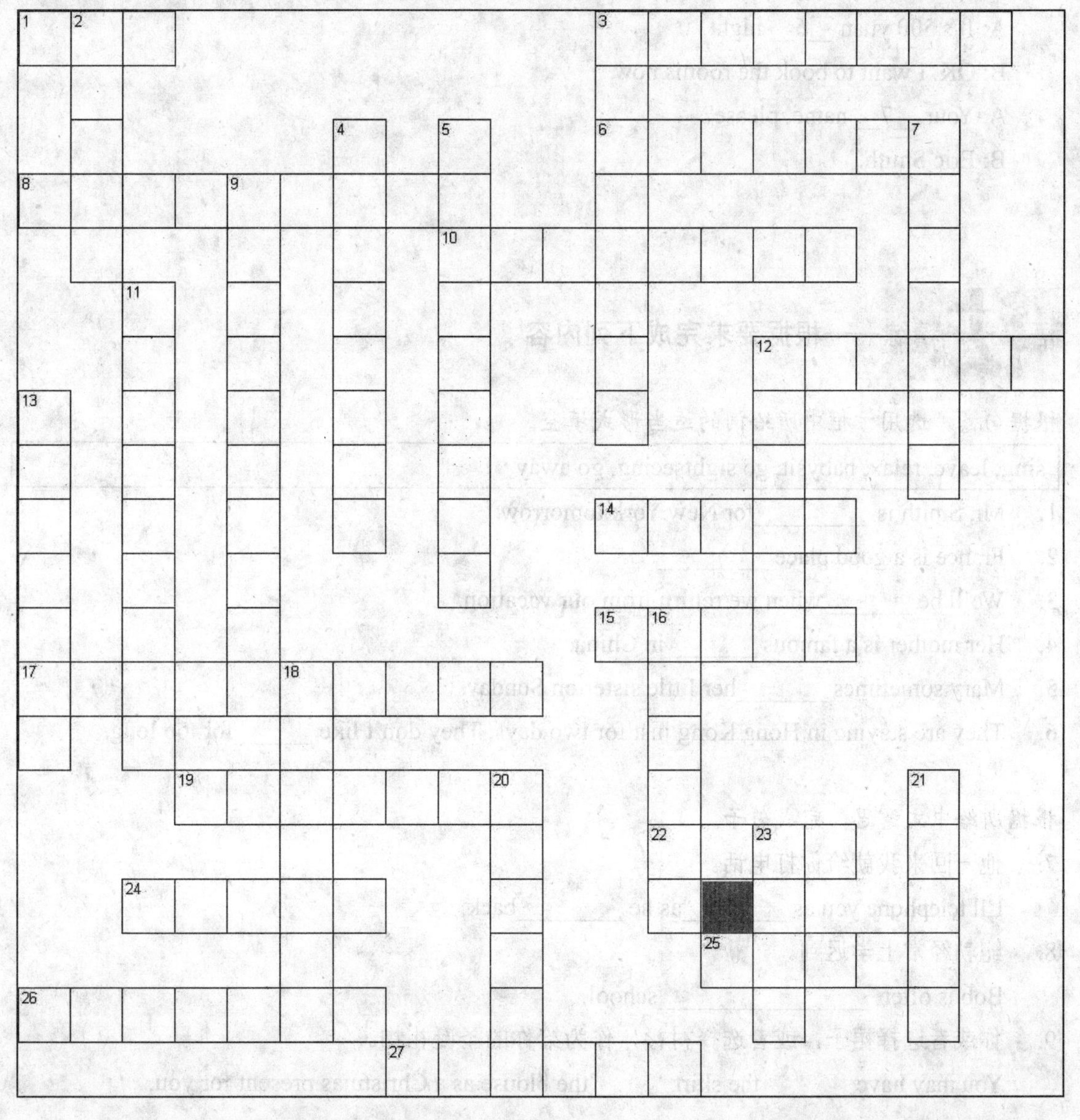

口语造句——根据要求完成下列内容

补全对话（一空一词）

A: Hello! New Century Hotel. Can I help you?

B: Yes.I'd like to __1__ two rooms next week.

A: Could you please tell me how __2__ nights you will stay?

B: Three nights. __3__ Monday to Wednesday.

A: Do you need __4__ rooms or double?

B: Two double rooms, please. __5__ the price of a double room ?

A: It's 500 yuan __6__ night.

B: OK. I want to book the rooms now.

A: Your __7__ name, please?

B: Eric Smith.

语法精练——根据要求完成下列内容

根据句意，选用方框中所给词的适当形式填空。

sing, leave, relax, babysit, go sightseeing, go away

1. Mr. Smith is ________ for New York tomorrow.
2. France is a good place________.
3. We'll be _______ when we return from our vacation.
4. Her mother is a famous _______ in China.
5. Mary sometimes _______ her little sister on Sunday.
6. They are staying in Hong Kong just for two days. They don't like ______ for too long.

根据所给中文意思，完成句子。

7. 他一回来我就给你打电话。

   I'll telephone you as ________ as he ________ back.
8. 鲍勃经常上学迟到。

   Bob is often ________ ________ school.
9. 你或者选择裙子，或者选择衬衫，作为给你的圣诞礼物。

   You may have _______ the skirt ______ the blouse as a Christmas present for you.

10. 数学和科学一样重要。

Maths is ________important ________science.

11. 把英语学好，对我们来说很有好处。

________is good for us ________learn English well.

12. 使用信用卡在网上购物的人应小心谨慎。

People ________ ________credit cards to buy things online ________ ________very careful.

13. 是团队精神使我们成功了。

It was team work________ ________ ________.

14. 当我到达学校时，我意识到自己把作业忘在家里了。

When I got to school, I ______that I ________ ______my homework at home.

阅读理解——根据要求完成下列内容

完形填空

Kate is against __1__ a new zoo in their town. Zoos are terrible __2__ for animals to live. She has visited a lot of zoos __3__ her life, and she has never seen one she liked or one that was suitable __4__ animals to live in. Just last week, she visited a zoo and couldn't believe what she __5__.The animals are kept in tiny __6__ and can __7__ move at all. However, Alice thinks zoos are very important places. They are like living __8__ for young people. They provide homes __9__ many endangered animals, and help to educate __10__ about caring for them.

1.	A. to build	B. building	C. build	D. built
2.	A. places	B. cinemas	C. houses	D. schools
3.	A. on	B. at	C. in	D. over
4.	A. of	B. for	C. to	D. on
5.	A. thought	B. liked	C. had	D. saw
6.	A. rooms	B. cars	C. boxes	D. cages
7.	A. nearly	B. mostly	C. hardly	D. almost
8.	A. textbooks	B. magazines	C. newspapers	D. CDs
9.	A. for	B. of	C. with	D. to
10	A. the children	B. the students	C. the foreigners	D. the public

根据短文内容判断正误，正确写 T，错误写 F。

An old man visited a new doctor. He was very young.

"I don't feel well, doctor," he said. "Please find out what's wrong with me."

"Take off your clothes and lie on the bed," the young doctor said, "I'll examine you."

The old man took off his clothes and lay down on the bed, and the young doctor examined However, he couldn't find anything wrong with the old man.

He listened to his heart, He looked into his throat. He examined every part of him.

At last he said, "I'm sorry, but I can't find anything wrong with you. You're as healthy as I am."

"That's very strange," the old man said, "because I feel really bad."

"Come back tomorrow and see me again if you don't feel better." the young doctor said. "I'll examine you again."

"All right, doctor." the old man said.

Slowly, he stood up and put on his clothes. Then he walked out of the hospital.

A few seconds later, the doctor's nurse ran in.

"Doctor! Doctor!" she cried. "That man you said was healthy has just died outside the door."

The doctor thought quickly.

"Then turn the body around so that people will think he was coming in." he said.

11. The doctor was new and he was young.
12. The old man felt bad.
13. The doctor found something wrong with the old man.
14. The old man died inside the door.
15. The doctor wanted anyone to know that he had examined the old man.

情景写作——根据要求完成下列内容

根据中文意思写一封意思连贯、符合逻辑、不少于 50 词的书信。

你叫李刚，你的澳洲网友 Gerry 今年暑假打算来中国学汉语。你得知你们学校将于 7 月 20 日举办为期六周的“暑假汉语口语培训班”，请将此消息以及相关上课时间、地点、学费等写信告诉他。

提示词语：course, by the way, look forward to

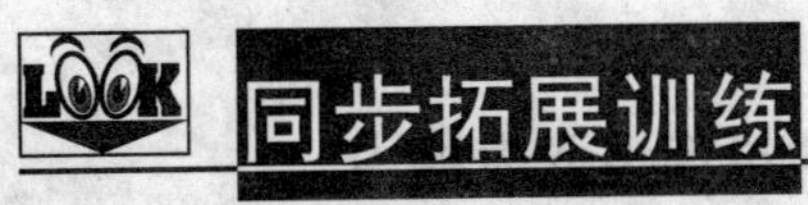

同步拓展训练 17

Lesson 49~51

听写检测——根据要求听写下列内容

Part A: 单词听写——听光盘录音，将听到的每个单词依次写在下面的横线上。

1.________ 2.________ 3.________
4.________ 5.________ 6.________
7.________ 8.________ 9.________
10.________ 11.________ 12.________
13.________ 14.________ 15.________
16.________ 17.________ 18.________
19.________ 20.________ 21.________
22.________ 23.________ 24.________
25.________ 26.________ 27.________
28.________ 29.________ 30.________
31.________ 32.________

Part B: 句子听写——听光盘录音，把课文内容听写在下面的横线上。

1.________
2.________
3.________
4.________
5.________
6.________
7.________
8.________
9.________
10.________

词汇游戏——根据汉语提示，将数字序号对应的单词填入表格中

横向提示		纵向提示	
横向提示	3. *n.*售票员；7. *v.*给奖赏 8. *adv.*偶尔地；9. *adv.*匆忙地 13. *v.*扫视；14. *adv.*内疚地 17. *v.*使尴尬；19. *adv.*迅速地 21. *adj.*没有受伤的 23. *adj.*严格的 26. *v.*碰碎，摔碎 28. *n.*节食 29. *n.*美德 30. *adj.*骄傲的	纵向提示	1. *adv.*奇迹般地；2. *n.*弹簧 3. *n.*乡下地方；4. *n.*报偿 5. *n.*旅行；6. *n.*院子 10. *adj.*真正的；11. *n.*远足 12. *v.*风吹；15. *n.*床垫 16. *n.*主人；18. *n.*一阵风 20. *adv.*最近；22. *adj.*厌烦的 24. *v.*节省，节约 25. *v.*扫，刮 27. *n.*景色

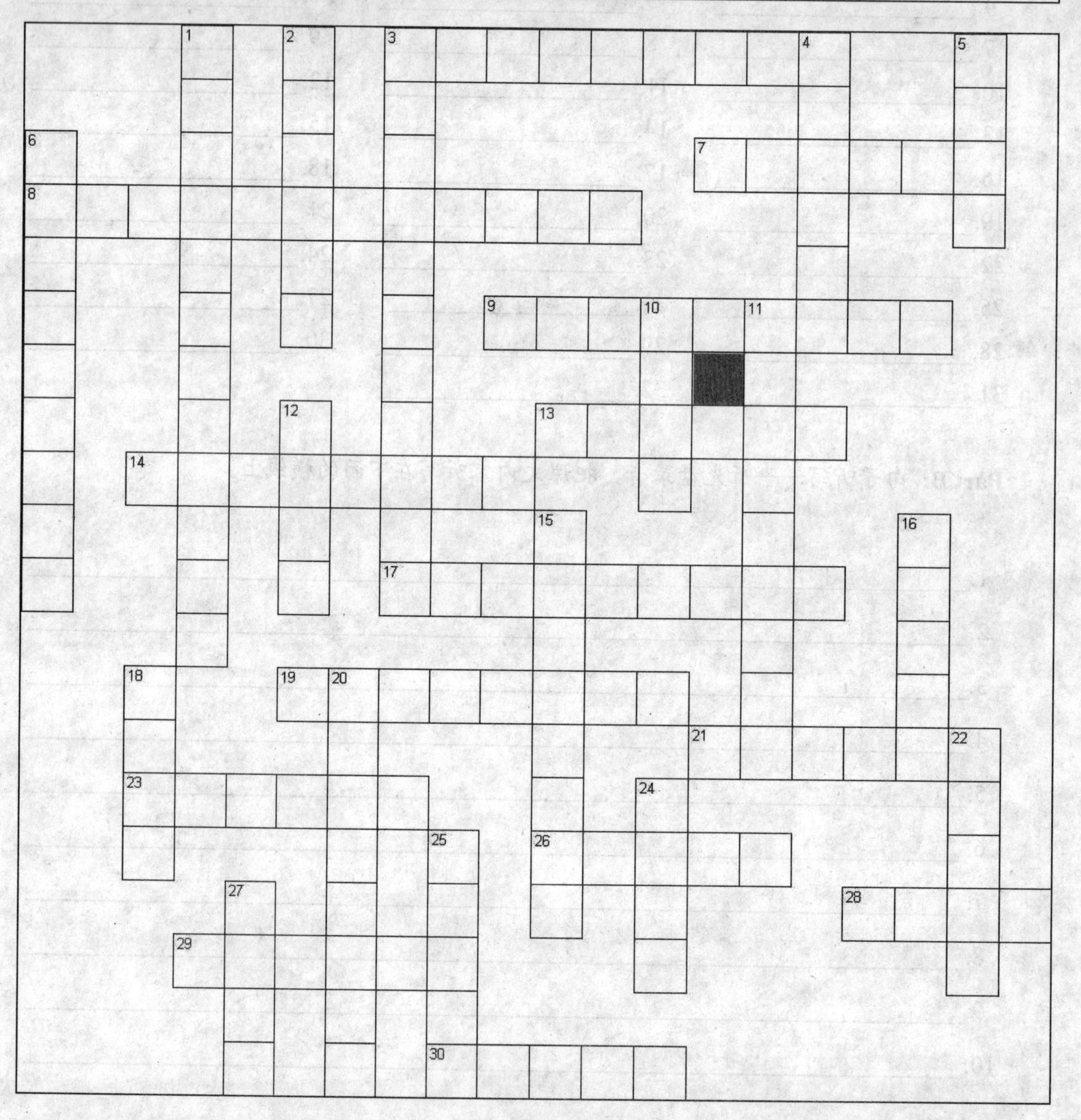

口语造句——根据要求完成下列内容

根据情景，用方框中所给的句子补全对话。

A: Excuse me. Could you please tell me where the nearest museum is?

B: Well, it's a bit far. You can go along the street, then take the first turning on the right. Walk on and you'll find one there. __1__

A: Oh, thanks. __2__

B: It should be open now, It opens at 8:00 am.

A: Good. __3__

B: Which bus? I don't know. You may ask the policeman over there. __4__

A: OK. By the way, where's the nearest McDonald's, do you know?

B: Right behind you. See that sign?

A: Oh, thanks a lot.

B: __5__.

A. And can you tell me which bus I should take?
B. Do you know at what time it opens?
C. He must know that.
D. You're welcome.
E. What's wrong with you?
F. You can't miss it.
G. Let me help you.

语法精练——根据要求完成下列内容

根据句意，选用方框中所给词的适当形式填空。

be sure, not hear, collect water, chat, give, water, win, take…away, grow up, write

1. Did your grandfather have to ______ from the village well when he was a kid.
2. She ________ to find out the secret.
3. I'm sorry. I ________ you clearly. Could you please say it again.
4. Do you know if she _______ the plants yet?
5. I can't find today's newspaper. Maybe somebody _______ it _______.

6. Tom says he wants to be a musician when he ________.
7. He did the best of all. He ________ an award.
8. They are interested in ________ on the Net, for it can make them know each other well.
9. The old man ________ ten articles for the newspaper since he retired.
10. One of the members in the band ________ an award for his hit CD this year.

连词成句，注意句后标点。

11. you, what, for, are, vacation, doing

____?

12. they,when, going, are

____?

13. with, he, going, who, is

____?

14. there you, long, staying how, are

____?

15. weather, there, is, the, how

____?

16. like, there, what, it, is

____?

阅读理解——根据要求完成下列内容

完形填空

It is interesting to visit another country, but sometimes there are problems when we don't know the __1__ very well. It may be __2__ to talk with the people there. We may not know how to use the telephone in the country we are visiting. We may not know how to buy the __3__ we need. In a __4__ country, we might not know where to eat or what to order in a __5__. It is not easy to decide how __6__ to tip waiters or taxi drivers. When we need help, we might not know how to ask for help. It is not pleasant to have an experience __7__ that. __8__ a short time, however, we learn what to do and what to __9__. We learn to enjoy life in another country, and then we may be __10__ to leave.

1. A. people B. country C. language D. words
2. A. easy B. difficult C. happy D. tired

3. A. things B. shopping C. something D. anything
4. A. strange B. known C. native D. new
5. A. school B. shop C. restauramt D. hospital
6. A. often B. many C. soon D. much
7. A. as B. for C. like D. with
8. A. Before B. After C. For D. In
9. A. speak B. talk C. tell D. say
10. A. sorry B. glad C. worried D. interested

阅读下面的文章，并选择正确答案。

Here are two cars. They may someday take the place of today's big cars. If we use such cars in the future, there will be less pollution in the air. There will be more space for parking cars in cities, and the streets will be less crowded. Three such cars can park in the space that is needed for one of today's cars.

The little cars will be very cheap. They will be very safe, too, because these little cars can go at a speed of only 65 kilometres per hour.

The cars of the future will be fine for getting around a city, but they will not be useful for long trips. If the car is powered by electricity, it will have two batteries-one battery for the motor and the other for the lights, signals, etc. If the little cars run on gasoline, they will go 450 kilometres before they need to stop for more gasoline.

If big cars are still used along with the small ones, we must build two sets of roads, one for the big, fast cars and the other for the small, slower ones.

11. If we use these little cars in the future, ________.
A. there will be no pollution in the air
B. there will be less pollution in the air
C. there will be a little more pollution in the air
D. there will little pollution in the air

12. In the space for one of today's cars we will be able to park________.
A. three such small cars B. two such small cars
C. four such small cars D. two such big cars

13. The cars of the future will be fine________.
A. for long trips B. for getting around a city
C. for both short and long trips D. for getting into the country

14. If small cars are used along with today's big ones, we must build_______.

A. a new set of wide roads
B. lots of gasoline stations
C. two sets of different roads
D. two sets of the same road

情景写作——根据要求完成下列内容

昨天下了雪，路非常滑。在放学回家的路上，你看见了一件令你感动的事。一个骑自行车的人撞倒了一名学生，你认为他们会吵架吗？

生词：光滑的 slippery；出乎意料 unexpectedly；吵架 quarrel

词数：80 词左右

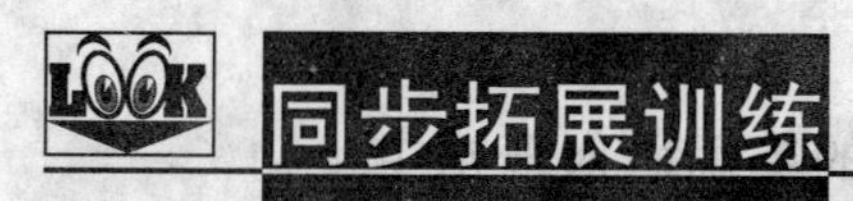

同步拓展训练 18

Lesson 52~54

听写检测——根据要求听写下列内容

Part A: 单词听写——听光盘录音，将听到的每个单词依次写在下面的横线上。

1.________ 2.________ 3.________
4.________ 5.________ 6.________
7.________ 8.________ 9.________
10.________ 11.________ 12.________
13.________ 14.________ 15.________
16.________ 17.________ 18.________
19.________ 20.________ 21.________
22.________ 23.________ 24.________
25.________ 26.________ 27.________
28.________ 29.________ 30.________
31.________ 32.________

Part B: 句子听写——听光盘录音，把课文内容听写在下面的横线上。

1.________________________________
2.________________________________
3.________________________________
4.________________________________
5.________________________________
6.________________________________
7.________________________________
8.________________________________
9.________________________________
10.________________________________

词汇游戏——根据汉语提示，将数字序号对应的单词填入表格中

横向提示	纵向提示
1. *v.*抓住；4. *adj.*恼人的 5. *adj.*带电的，充电的 9. *n.*英寸；10. *adv.* 暂时地 11. *n.*乱七八糟 13. *n.*谜；14. *v.*混合，搅拌 17. *v.*说服，劝说；22. *v.*检查 24. *adj.*粘的 25. *n.*消防队员 26. *v.*解决 27. *n.*门把手	1. *n.*空间；2. *adv.* 意外地，偶然地 3. *n.*书架；4. *adv.*实际上 6. *v.*认出，听出；7. *v.*失望，泄气 8. *n.*手指；12. *v.*签字 15. *v.*引起；*n.*原因 16. *n.*电话的话筒；17. *n.*面糊 18. *v.*挂号邮寄；19. *n.*尸体，残骸 20. *n.*馅饼；21. *n.*伏特（电压单位） 23. *n.*电线 24. *n.*电火花

1 2 3 4 5 6 7 8 9 10 11 12 13 14 15 16 17 18 19 20 21 22 23 24 25 26 27

口语造句——根据要求完成下列内容

补全对话（每空一词）

It's four o'clock in the afternoon. Liu Ying is at the library. She's going to borrow some books. She's speaking to the assistant.

Liu Ying: Good afternoon!

Assistant: Good afternoon! Can I __1__ you?

Liu Ying: Do you have From Earth to Moon?

Assistant: Let me __2__. Ah, __3__ it is.

Liu Ying: Thank you. How long may I __4__ it ?

Assistant: Two weeks.

Liu Ying: Can I keep it a little __5__?

Assistant: Yes, you can. But you must come and __6__ it if you can't finish it __7__ time.

Liu Ying: Must I __8__ the book back for that?

Assistant: Yes, you must. And you mustn't __9__ it to others.

Liu Ying: All right, I won't. May I look at some of the new books?

Assistant: __10__. They are over there.

1.________ 2. ________ 3. ________ 4. ________ 5. ________
6. ________ 7. ________ 8. ________ 9. ________ 10.________

语法精练——根据要求完成下列内容

根据所给中文意思，完成句子。

1. Mary is a good girl. She is very________（友好的）.
2. I think elephants are____________________（有点懒）.
3. Mr. Brown wants to be a police officer. He thinks it's________________（一份令人激动的工作）.
4. She often __________（去购物）on Sunday. But last Sunday she________（去看了电影）.
5. Tom _________（去游泳）over the weekend. But Tom's sister_______ （学习）for the math test.
6. I'd like a _____（中号）pizza with some__________________（蘑菇和奶酪）on it.

7. ______________________（她最喜欢的歌手）is Madonna.
8. Thieves______________________（害怕）policemen.

下列各句中有一处是错的，请指出并改正。

9. He leaves to school at seven every day.
   A B C D
10. The bus rides usually takes 20 minutes.
   A B C D
11. That must be more fun than take a train.
   A B C D
12. How long does it take you get there from home?
   A B C D
13. If it snows, I take a taxi.
   A B C D

阅读理解——根据要求完成下列内容

阅读下面的文章，并选择正确答案。

What is it? Sometimes it is long. Sometimes it is round. There may be only one. There may be more of them than you can count. Now you can guess what it is. It is a line.

Sometimes a line is straight. Some lines are side by side. They never meet. Train tracks are like these lines. Some lines do meet. They cross each other. Streets are like lines that cross each other.

When lines change, new shapes are made. Sometimes a line is curved. Curved lines may boss each other. Curved lines may be side by side. Curved lines may be closed. A circle is one kind of closed curve.

Look about you. Can you find straight lines and curved lines? Can you find lines that cross and lines that do not cross?

1. Which of the following is a closed curved line?
   A.+ B. = C. ~~ D. O
2. We can know from the passage that _______.
   A. all lines are straight and long B. all lines look like train tracks

C. lines are used by man in many ways　　　　D. lines are very unusual in our life

3. What happens when lines change?

A. New shapes are made.　　　　B. Streets have to cross each other.

C. They get crossed.　　　　D. They never meet.

If you are going away this year or just thinking about it, take a good look at the Usit Globeplotter.

As usual, it's full of information, interesting ideas on where to go, and great fares to get you there. Fares that get you there directly, or let you take the long way round, travel insurance you can afford, information on where to go and how to get there, maps and guide books to help you see it all.

If there are ten or more travelings, we'll make a special group booking and help you plan your journey, If your band or theatre group are planning a trip, Akts-our special travel service for performing artists is ready to help.

Usit can help while you are abroad too-we have offices in Britain, France Belgium, Greece, Germany, and the USA. And our sister offices in fifty countries around the world, all members of the International Student Travel Union are there to help too.

If you're under 26 or a full-time student within this age, traveling on a budget, and you want it to take you as far as possible, start your trip at your nearest Usit office.

4. Usit can give you a lot of_________.

A. information　　B. guide books　　C. insurance　　D. all of the above

5. According to the passage, Usit is_________.

A. a theatre group of young people

B. a traveling department in different countries

C. a union of youth and student travel

D. an office which organizes activities for students

6. Usit gives services for_________.

A. any student　　　　B. people younger than 26

C. all travelers　　　　D. people of all ages

7. What's the meaning of the words "sister offices"?

A. Offices of other organizations associated with Usit.

B. Offices which are run by girl students and teachers.

C. Other departments in different countries.

D. Other groups of Usit in the cities.

8. Which of the following is True?

A. Usit can help you make a plan for your study.

B. Usit can help you find a job in a big city.

C. Usit can make special service for touring artists.

D. Usit can make a double-decker booking.

情景写作——根据要求完成下列内容

根据以下内容提示写一篇 80 词左右的英语日记。

1. 时间：12 月 3 号，星期天
2. 天气：晴
3. 在商店购物时遇到一对美国夫妇，他们想买一部照相机，但与售货员语言不通。
4. 我帮助他们，他们对我表示感谢。
5. 我很高兴自己能用英语交谈了。

听写检测——根据要求听写下列内容

Part A: 单词听写——听光盘录音，将听到的每个单词依次写在下面的横线上。

1.________ 2.________ 3.________
4.________ 5.________ 6.________
7.________ 8.________ 9.________
10.________ 11.________ 12.________
13.________ 14.________ 15.________
16.________ 17.________ 18.________
19.________ 20.________ 21.________
22.________ 23.________ 24.________
25.________ 26.________ 27.________
28.________ 29.________ 30.________
31.________ 32.________

Part B: 句子听写——听光盘录音，把课文内容听写在下面的横线上。

1.________________________________
2.________________________________
3.________________________________
4.________________________________
5.________________________________
6.________________________________
7.________________________________
8.________________________________
9.________________________________
10.________________________________

词汇游戏——根据汉语提示，将数字序号对应的单词填入表格中

横向提示		纵向提示	
横向提示	5. *v.*探测；8. *adj.*漂亮的，美观的 11. *adj.*有信心的；13. *n.*海盗 14. *n.*激动，兴奋 16. *n.*行李箱 18. *adj.*毫无价值的 21. *n.*裘皮 25. *v.*发明 26. *n.*爆炸，轰响 27. *v.*疾驶 28. *n.*轮子	纵向提示	1. *n.*入口；2. *n.*海岸 3. *n.*泥土；4. *n.* 探测器 6. *adj.*热切的，热情的 7. *n.*牛仔裤；8. *v.*犹豫，迟疑 9. *adv.*下坡；10. *adv.* 轻蔑地 12. *n.*太太，夫人；15. *adv.*彻底地 17. *n.*跑道，行程；19. *n.*财宝 20. *v.*接待（顾客）；22. *v.*惩罚 23. *n.*价值 24. *adv.*最后

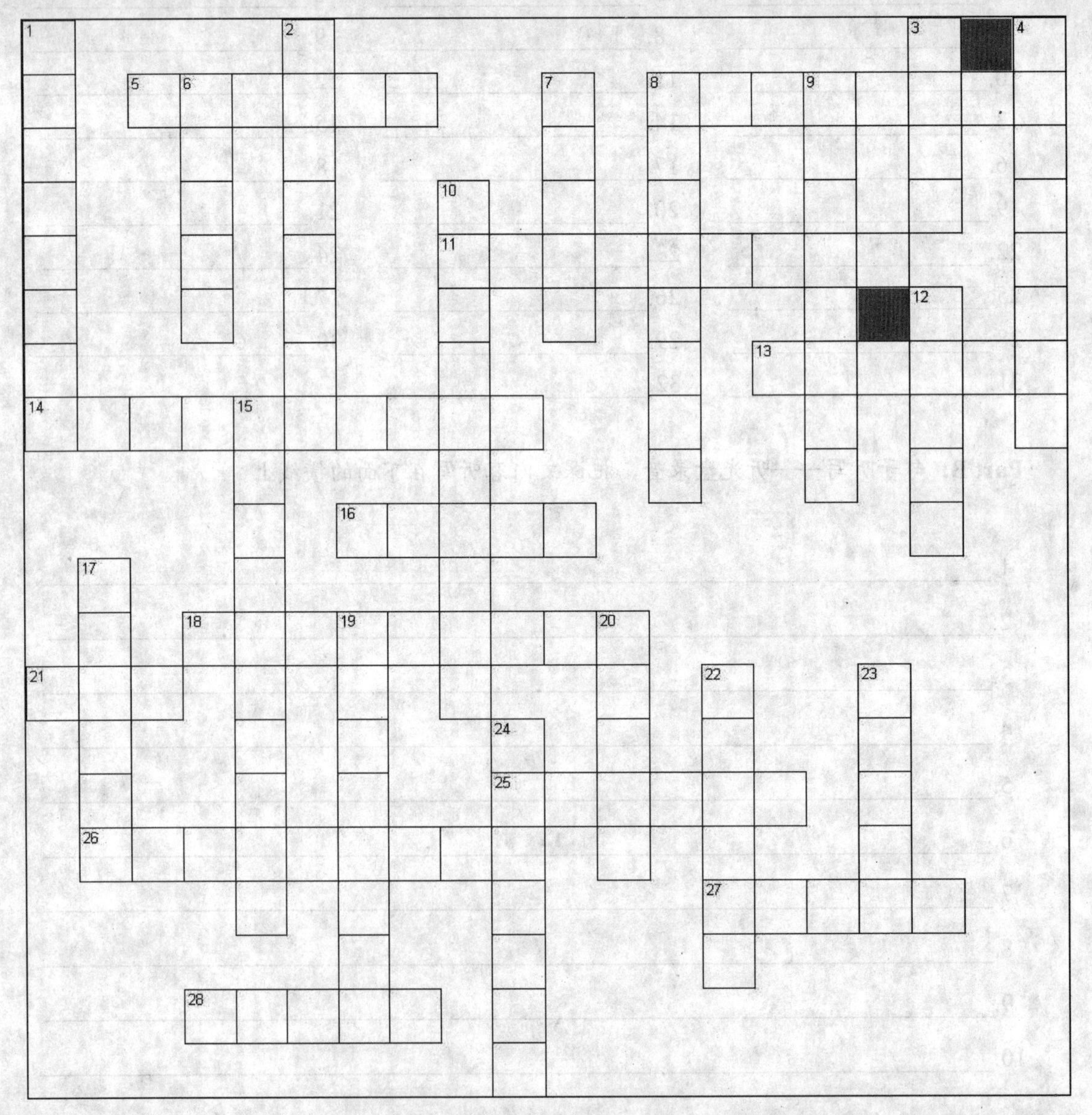

口语造句——根据要求完成下列内容

补全对话

A: Have you __1__ to the Great Wall?

B: Yes, of course.

A: Do you know __2__ it was __3__ ?

B: It was first built during the Warring States Period（战国时期）. Later Qin Shihuang linked the walls together.

A: __4__ was it __5__ for?

B: It was used for fighting against enemies and __6__ homeland.

A: __7__ is it so famous?

B: It is because the Great Wall is __8__ of __9__ greatest wonder of world history. Today the Great Wall attracts tourist from __10__ over the country.

1. ______ 2. ______ 3. ______ 4. ______ 5. ______

6. ______ 7. ______ 8. ______ 9. ______ 10. ______

语法精练——根据要求完成下列内容

根据句意，选用方框中所给词的适当形式填空。

result, oneself, exercise, have buy, health, want, although, keep, drink

1. We often go to book shops _______ some books.
2. My grandparents like ______ tea very much.
3. The _______ for "go to the movies" are interesting.
4. I exercise every day, so I'm pretty _______.
5. We are old enough to look after ______.
6. Do you _______ a healthy lifestyle?
7. I'm not good at English, _______ I try to read it every day.
8. She's unhealthy because She hardly ever _______.
9. I don't like milk at all, but my parent _______ me to drink it every day.
10. What do you do to ___ you in good health?

根据所给中文意思，完成句子。

11. 你有今晚的电影票吗？

Have you ______ any ______ ______ tonight's film?

12. 他过去是位军人，现在是位经理。

He ______ to ______ a soldier. Now he is a manager.

13. 我的业余爱好是集邮。

My ______ is to ______ stamps.

14. 你出过国吗？我出过国，仅仅一次。

Have you ever ______ ______? Yes, just ______.

15. 咱们在电脑上查查谁借了这本书。

Let's find who ______ ______ this book ______ the computer.

16. 你能查明是谁把录像带拿走的吗？

Can you find ______ who ______ ______ the video tape ?

阅读理解——根据要求完成下列内容

完形填空

The telephone rang. Mrs. Johnson went to __1__ it. To her great joy, it was Besty, her good friend. They got to talk. Without thinking Mrs Johnson __2__ Besty to come and __3__ with her and her husband that evening. __4__ a quarter to six, Mr. Johnson came back home. He found his wife anxious.

"What's the matter, dear?" he asked.

"I've __5__ a terrible mistake, Jim." she said, "I've asked Besty to come and have dinner with us this evening."

"Well, that's __6__ to get upset about," Jim said. "We should have a good time together. We haven't seen her for __7__"

"But I've just found there's hardly __8__ food in the house." said Mrs. Johnson. "You didn't __9__ to buy some beef? I asked you to get some on your way home three days ago."

"Oh, dear!" said Jim. In no time he was __10__ the house. He found a piece of beef in the boot of the car. It had been there for the past three days.

1.	A. call	B. answer	C. do	D. make
2.	A. called	B. told	C. let	D. asked
3.	A. have a talk	B. go to the cinema	C. have dinner	D. to take a walk

4.	A. At	B. On	C. In	D . For
5.	A. taken	B. done	C. made	D. brought
6.	A. something	B. nothing	C. anything	D. everything
7.	A. hours	B. years	C. seasons	D. moments
8.	A. some	B. many	C. little	D. any
9.	A. forget	B. think	C. ask	D. need
10.	A. to	B. from	C. out of	D. into

阅读下面的文章，并选择正确答案。

Every people uses its own special words to show its ideas and feelings. Some of these expressions are commonly used for many years. Others are popular for just a short time. One such American expression is "Where's the beef?". It is used when something is not as good as it is said to be. In the early 1980s "Where' s the beef? " was one of the most popular expressions in the United States. It seemed as if everyone was using it at the time.

Beef, of course, is the meat from a cow, and no food is more popular in America than a hamburger made from beef. In the 1960s a businessman named Ray Kroc began building small restaurants that sold hamburgers at a low price. Kroc called his restaurant "McDonald's". Ray Kroc became one of the richest businessmen in America.

Other business people watched his success. Some of them opened their own hamburger restaurants. One company called "Wendy's" said its hamburgers were bigger than those sold by McDonald's or anyone else. The Wendy's Company began to use the expression "Where's the beef?" to make people know that Wendy's hamburgers were the biggest. The Wendy's television advertisement showed three old women eating hamburgers. The bread that covered the meat was very big, but inside there was only a bit of meat. One of the women said she would not eat a hamburger with such a little piece of beef. "Where's the beef?" she shouted in a funny way. The advertisement for Wendy's hamburger restaurants was a success. As we said, it seemed everyone began using the expression "Where's the beef?"

11. ________started McDonald' s restaurant.

A. Ray Kroc　　B. McDonald

C. Wendy　　D. Three old women

12. Other people wanted to open hamburger restaurants because they thought______.

A. they could sell hamburgers at a low price

B. hamburgers were easy to make

C. beef was very popular in America

D. they could make a lot of money

13. Wendy's made the expression known to everybody________.

A. with many old women eating hamburgers

B. by a television advertisement

C. while selling bread with a bit of meat in it

D. at the McDonald's restaurant

14. We can learn from the passage that the expression "Where's the beef? " means________.

A. the beef in hamburgers is not as much as it is said to be

B. the hamburgers are not as good as they are said to be

C. something is not so good as one says.

D. Wendy's is the biggest

15. The advertisement for Wendy's hamburger restaurants was________.

A. a success　　B. foolish　　C. false　　D. failing

情景写作——根据要求完成下列内容

根据中文大意，写出意思连贯、符合逻辑，且不少于80词的短文。所给英文提示词语供选用。

你一定外出旅游过吧！你怎么去的？住在哪里？看到了什么？感受如何？请记叙一次你的旅游经历。

提示词语： take a trip to, by..., stay

同步拓展训练 20

Lesson 58~60

听写检测——根据要求听写下列内容

Part A: 单词听写——听光盘录音，将听到的每个单词依次写在下面的横线上。

1.______ 2.______ 3.______
4.______ 5.______ 6.______
7.______ 8.______ 9.______
10.______ 11.______ 12.______
13.______ 14.______ 15.______
16.______ 17.______ 18.______
19.______ 20.______ 21.______
22.______ 23.______ 24.______
25.______ 26.______ 27.______
28.______ 29.______ 30.______
31.______ 32.______

Part B: 句子听写——听光盘录音，把课文内容听写在下面的横线上。

1.______
2.______
3.______
4.______
5.______
6.______
7.______
8.______
9.______
10.______

词汇游戏——根据汉语提示，将数字序号对应的单词填入表格中

横向提示	纵向提示
1. *v.*增加；2. *n.*名声 6. *v.*种植；7. *v.*养成 8. *v.*狗叫；9. *n.*福份，福气 11. *n.*专家；14. *v.*抱怨 15. *n.*来源；17. *n.*亲属 18. *v.*按，压；19. *adj.*极小的 20. *v.*以……为其后果 21. *adj.*可恨的；22. *n.*门闩 25. *n.*收入 26. *n.*教堂	1. *adv.* 不耐烦地；3. *n.*未来，前途 4. *n.*集市；5. *n.*习惯 6. *n.*脚爪；7. *n.*伪装 10. *v.*提及，提到；12. *v.*拆掉，取下 13. *n.*受害者，牺牲品 14. *n.*水晶 16. *adj.*坏的 18. *v.*拥有 23. *n.*树干 24. *n.*教区牧师

1 2 3 4 5 6 7 8 9 10 11 12 13 14 15 16 17 18 19 20 21 22 23 24 25 26

口语造句——根据要求完成下列内容

补全对话（一空一词）

A: My father has bought an apple tree. Could you help me to plant it, please?

B: Certainly. __1__ shall we plant it?

A: In the garden.

B: __2__ shall we do, now?

A: __3__ a hole. OK?

B:OK! I __4__ the hole, and you __5__ a stick into the earth. Is the hole large __6__?

A: Yes, now put the tree in the hole. Hold it __7__. I'll put the earth __8__ in the hole again.

B: Put it down hard with my foot, right?

A: Yes, now let's __9__ the tree to the top of the stick.

B: What's that for?

A: __10__ it straight.

1.________ 2. ________ 3. ________ 4. ________ 5. ________

6. ________ 7. ________ 8. ________ 9. ________ 10. ________

语法精练——根据要求完成下列内容

根据句意，选用方框中所给词的适当形式填空。

babysit, listen to, really, science test, help, discuss

1. Look. The students ________their teacher.
2. He can't go to the movie. He is ________busy.
3. She always ________her little sister.
4. We have to study for our________.
5. They ________us clean the classroom yesterday.
6. Can you came over ________the science report?

根据所给中文意思，完成句子。

7. 下星期天下午，你能和我一起去听音乐会吗？

________you ________ to the______ ________ ________next Sunday afternoon?

8. 谢谢你告诉我这个好消息。

Thank you _______ _______ _______the good news.

9. 我喜欢跟我在许多方面都不同的人交朋友。

   I like to have friends ______ ______ _______ ________ ________ in many ways.

10. 他很风趣，经常使我们笑。

    He is _______. He often _______ _______ _______.

11. 汤姆与杰姆谁更聪明些？

    ______ is ______ ______, Tom ______ Jim?

12. 这对我很重要，但对她更重要。

    This is ______ ______me, but it's ______ ______ ______ ______.

13. 莉莉在班里是最外向的女孩。

    Lily is _______ _______ _______ girl in her class.

14. 我认为好朋友应使我感到快乐。

    I think a good friend _______ _______ _______ _______ happy.

阅读理解——根据要求完成下列内容

阅读下面的文章，并选择正确答案。

New rules and behavior standards for middle school students came out in March. Middle school is going to use a new way to decide who the top students are. The best students won't only have high marks. They will also be kids who don't dye their hair, smoke or drink. The following are some of the new rules.

Tell the truth. Have you ever copied someone else's work on an exam? Don't do it again! That's not something an honest students should do. If you have played computer games for two hours in your room, don't tell your parents you have done homework.

Do more at school. Good students love animals and care for other people. April is Bird-loving month in China. Is your school doing anything to celebrate? You should join! That way, you can learn more about animals and how to protect them. When more people work together, it makes it more fun for everyone.

Have you ever quarreled with your teammates when your basketball team lost? Only working together can make your team stronger. Be friendly to the people you are with. Try to think of others, not only yourself.

Be open to new ideas. Have you ever thought that people could live on the moon? Maybe you'll discover Earth II some day. Don't look down on new ideas. Everyone's ideas are important. You should welcome them, because new ideas make life better for everyone.

Protect yourself. Has someone ever taken money from one of your classmates? Don't let it happen to you. If you have to go home late, you should take care of yourself and let your parents know.

Use the Internet carefully. The Internet can be very useful for your studies. But some things on the Internet aren't for kids, so try to look at Web pages that are good for you. You can use the Web for fun or homework. Can't you find any good Web sites for children? Here are some: http://kids.Eastday.com, http: //www. chinakids.net.com.

1. The school new rules will help kids by telling them_________.

   A. how they can study well

   B. what they should do only at school

   C. what is right and what is wrong

   D. how they can protect themselves

2. According to the passage, which of the following is NOT true?

   A. Take care of yourself when you are out

   B. Tell the truth, even when you are wrong.

   C. Keep some animals to protect them.

   D. Use the Internet, but keep away from bad things.

3. The main idea of the fourth paragraph is about_________.

   A. making the team stronger

   B. working together with others

   C. learning from each other

   D. being strict with others

4. New ideas_________.

   A. should be looked down　　B. shouldn't be welcomed

   C. make people busy　　D. can make people live better

5. The best title of this article is_________.

   A. The school rules

   B. Being a top student

   C. New school rules and behavior standards

   D. A new way to be top students

情景写作——根据要求完成下列内容

根据中文意思和英文提示词语，并结合自己的想象，写出意思连贯、符合逻辑的英语短文。所给的英文提示词语必须全都用上，中文提示不必逐句翻译。

上星期五下午，王敏放学后乘公共汽车回家。在车上她发现司机在学英语。司机对王敏说了些什么？此事对你有何启示？你打算为2008年北京奥运会做些什么？

afternoon, go home, bus, in the bus, find, learn, surprised, weak, English, when, work hard, Beijing's Olympic Games, I think, modern

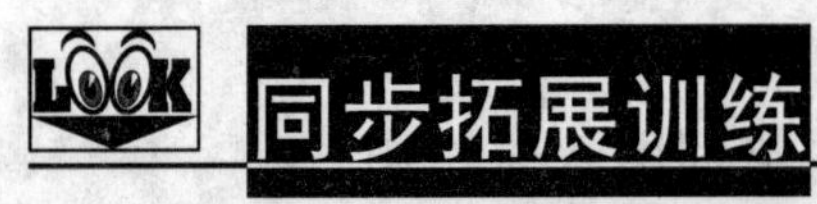

同步拓展训练 21

Lesson 61~63

听写检测——根据要求听写下列内容

Part A: 单词听写——听光盘录音，将听到的每个单词依次写在下面的横线上。

1.______ 2.______ 3.______
4.______ 5.______ 6.______
7.______ 8.______ 9.______
10.______ 11.______ 12.______
13.______ 14.______ 15.______
16.______ 17.______ 18.______
19.______ 20.______ 21.______
22.______ 23.______ 24.______
25.______ 26.______ 27.______
28.______ 29.______ 30.______
31.______ 32.______

Part B: 句子听写——听光盘录音，把课文内容听写在下面的横线上。

1.______
2.______
3.______
4.______
5.______
6.______
7.______
8.______
9.______
10.______

词汇游戏——根据汉语提示，将数字序号对应的单词填入表格中

横向提示		纵向提示	
横向提示	1. *adj.*周围的；6. *n.*大气层 8. *n.*宇航员；10. *adj.*亲密的 11. *adj.*有错误的；12. *n.*当局（常用复数） 15. *n.*种类；17. *n.*洪水，水灾 18. *n.*量；20. *n.*宇宙 21. *n.*根；22. *n.*控制 24. *n.*航天飞机 25. *adj.*遥远的 26. *n.*空间 27. *n.*婚礼	纵向提示	2. *n.*破坏，毁灭；3. *n.*星系 4. *n.*小片；5. *adj.*荒凉的 7. *n.*世纪；9. *n.*望远镜 13. *n.*招待会 14. *v.*变黑，发暗 15. *v.*喷撒 16. *n.*10 亿 19. *v.*威胁 22. *n.*圈子 23. *v.*发射

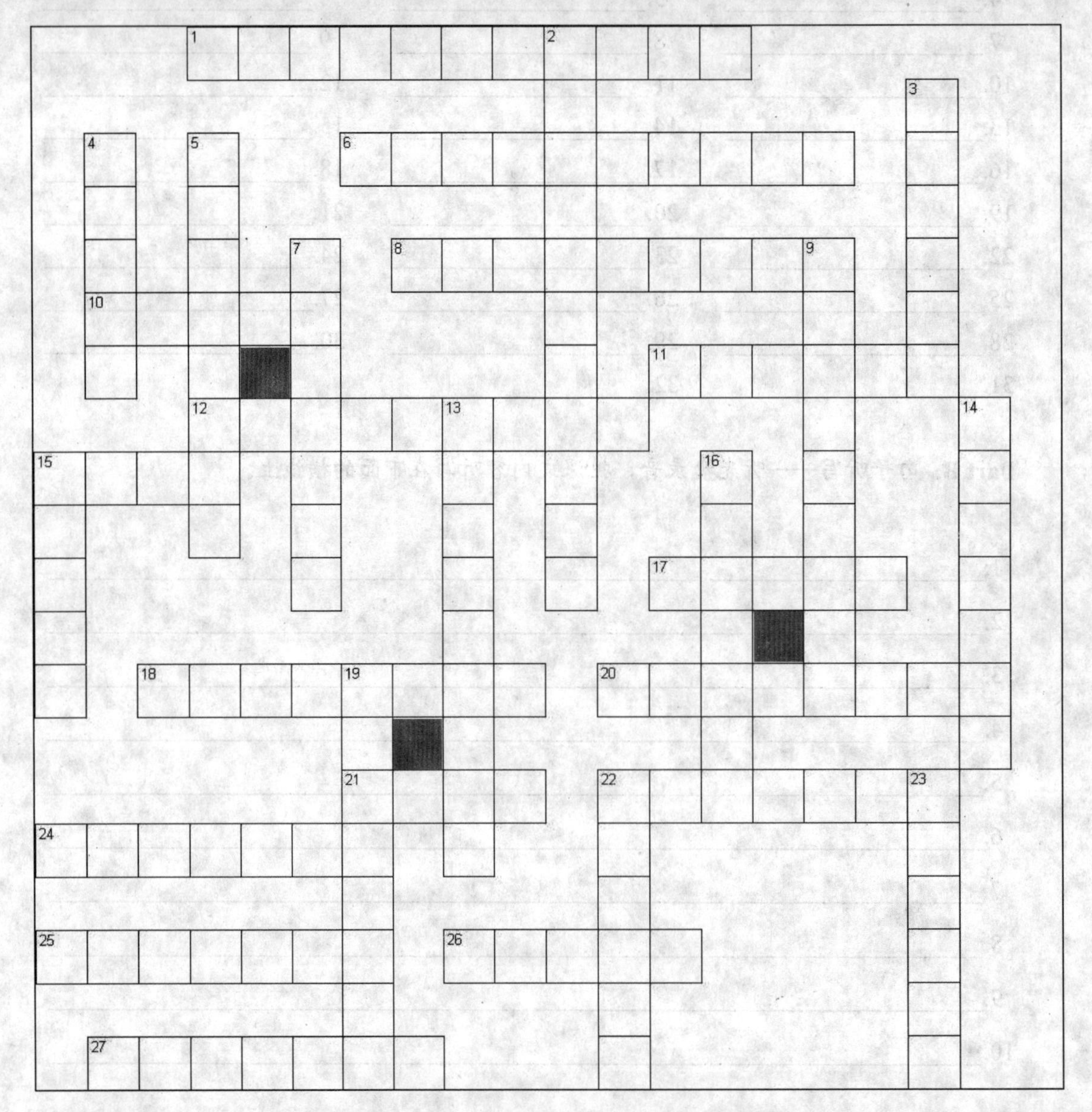

口语造句——根据要求完成下列内容

补全对话（每空一词）

A: Can I __1__ you, please ?

B: Yes, please.I'm __2__ for a sweater for myself.

A:OK. __3__ __4__ do you want, please?

B: Size L.

A: What about this one?

B: I don't like the colour. Have you got any blue ones __5__ that size?

A: Yes. Here you are.

B: I like it very much. How __6__ does it __7__, please ?

A: Fifty-five dollars.

B: That's much too __8__, I am afraid. Have you got anything cheaper?

A: How about this one? It's only twenty dollars.

B: OK. I'll take it. Here's the __9__.

A: Thank you. __10__ else?

B: No, thanks.

1. ________ 2.________ 3.________ 4.________ 5.________
6.________ 7.________ 8.________ 9.________ 10.________

语法精练——根据要求完成下列内容

根据句意，选用方框中所给词的适当形式填空。

serious, laugh, invite, help, smart, because, rain, show

1. Mr. Green won't go to the concert ______ he is really busy.
2. The radio says it will stop______.
3. He is very funny. He always makes his classmates______.
4. Last Saturday my best friend _______me with my math.
5. Lisa is very_______. She studies very well.
6. Thanks for _______me to your birthday party.
7. He doesn't like talking or laughing. He's_____ and quiet.

8. Could you _______us your family photos?

根据所给中文意思，完成句子。

9. 你去过长城吗？去过，去过两次。

   Have you _______ to the Great Wall? Yes. I have _______ there _______.

10. 我好长时间没有见到你了。你去哪儿了？

   I _____ _____you for a long time. Where ______ you ______?

11. 冲浪是我哥哥最喜爱的运动。

   _______ is my brother's ______sport.

12. 不管我说什么，他都不相信我。

   _____ _____what I say, he _____ _____me.

13. 高老师总是赞扬一班的学生。

   Miss Gao always _____ _____ _____the students of Class One.

14. 王先生已经戒烟了吗？

   ______Mr Wang _____ _____ _____ yet ?

阅读理解——根据要求完成下列内容

阅读下面的文章，并选择正确答案。

Each nation has many good people who help to take care of others. For example, some high school and college students in the United States often spend many hours as volunteers in hospitals, Orphanages or homes for the aged. They read books to the people in these places, or they just visit them and play games with them or listen to their problems.

Other young volunteers go and work in the homes of people who are sick or old. They paint, clean up, or repair their houses, do their shopping or mow their lawns. For boys who no longer have fathers there is an organization called Big Brothers. College students and other men take these boys to baseball games or on fishing trips and help them to get to know things that boys usually learn from their fathers.

Each city has a number of clubs where boys and girls can go to play games or learn crafts. Some of these clubs show movies or organize short trips to the mountains, the beaches, museums or other places of interest. Most of these clubs use a lot of high school and college students as volunteers because they are young enough to remember the problems of younger boys and girls.

Volunteers believe that some of the happiest people in the world are those who help to bring happiness to others.

1. Where can you often find volunteers in the United States?
   A. At a bus-stop. B. In a park. C. In a hospital. D. In a shop.
2. How do volunteers usually help those who are sick or old?
   A. They mow their lawns, do their shopping and clean up their houses.
   B. They cook, sew or wash their clothes.
   C. They tell them stories and sing and dance for them.
   D. They clean, wax and repair their cars.
3. What is Big Brothers?
   A. It's the name of a club.
   B. It's a home for children who have no brothers.
   C. It's the name of a film.
   D. It's an organization for boys who no longer have fathers.
4. Why do most of the boys' and girls' clubs use many high school and college students as volunteers?
   A. Because they have a lot of free time.
   B. Because they can still remember what they felt when they were younger.
   C. Because they know how to do the work.
   D. Because they like younger boys and girls.
5. What do volunteers believe?
   A. To make others happy, they have got to be unhappy.
   B. The happiest people in the world are those who make themselves happy.
   C. The happiest people in the world are those who are young and healthy.
   D. The happiest people in the world are those who help others and make others happy.

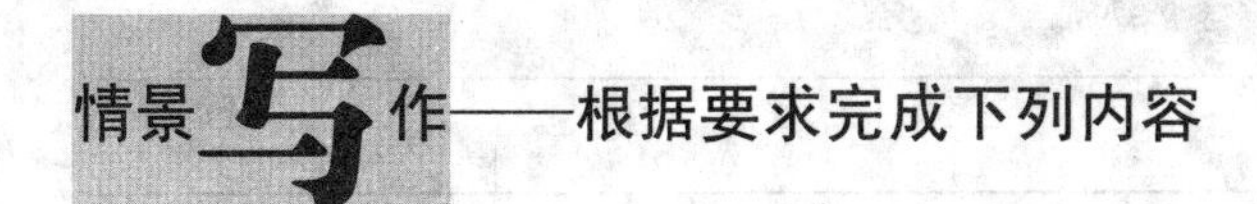

请以 My Experience in Examination 为题写一篇文章。

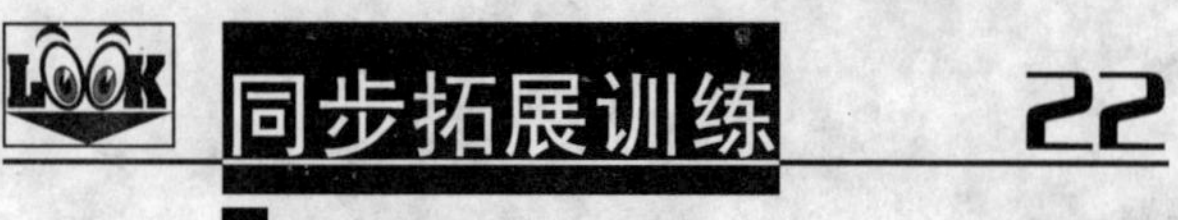

同步拓展训练 22

Lesson 64~66

听写检测——根据要求听写下列内容

Part A: 单词听写——听光盘录音，将听到的每个单词依次写在下面的横线上。

1.________	2.________	3.________
4.________	5.________	6.________
7.________	8.________	9.________
10.________	11.________	12.________
13.________	14.________	15.________
16.________	17.________	18.________
19.________	20.________	21.________
22.________	23.________	24.________
25.________	26.________	27.________
28.________	29.________	30.________
31.________	32.________	

Part B: 句子听写——听光盘录音，把课文内容听写在下面的横线上。

1.____

2.____

3.____

4.____

5.____

6.____

7.____

8.____

9.____

10.____

词汇游戏——根据汉语提示，将数字序号对应的单词填入表格中

横向提示	纵向提示
2. *n.*热心人；7. *v.*连接 10. *n.*大陆；11. *n.*港口 12. *v.*想像；13. *adv.*正式地 14. *n.*蜂蜡；16. *n.*调查 17. *n.*蜂房；20. *adj.*双的 21. *v.*走近 23. *n.*马戏团 24. *adj.*偏僻的 25. *v.*把……打包 26. *n.*入侵，侵略	1. *n.*通风；3. *n.*隧道 4. *adj.*幸运的；5. *v.*修复 6. *n.*兰开斯特；8. *v.*陪伴，随行 9. *v.*重新发现 14. *n.*轰炸机 15. *v.*重 18. *adj.*欧洲的 19. *n.*烟囱 22. *adj.*航空的 23. *n.*群

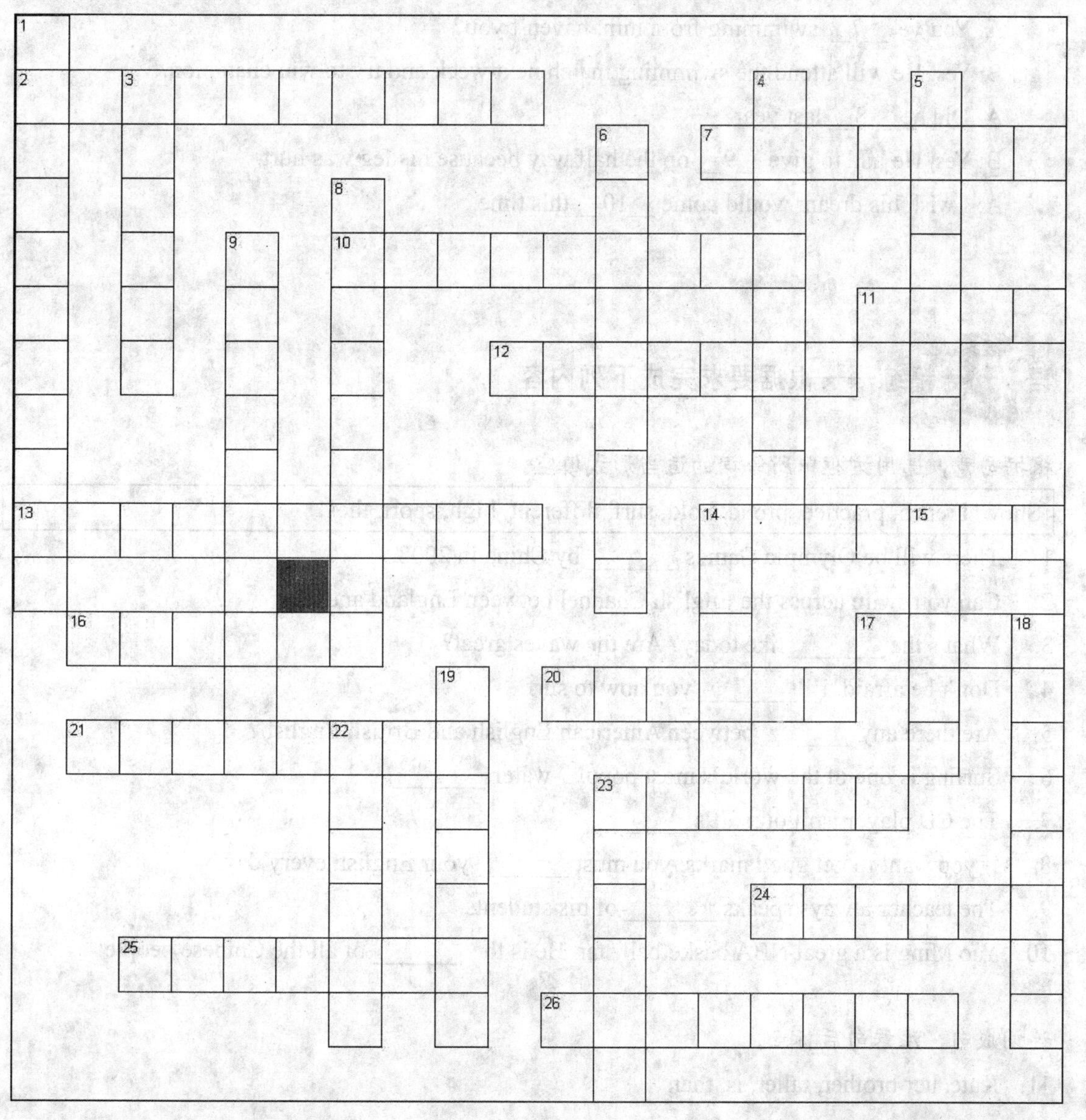

口语造句——根据要求完成下列内容

补全对话

A: Hi! What's the swimming __1__ today?

B: The water is warm. I do __2__ better than I did yesterday.

A: How __3__ have you __4__ here in Dalian?

B: __5__ last Monday.

A: Have you ever __6__ before?

B: No, I haven't. My brother is a good swimmer.

A: You've __7__ swimming from him, haven't you?

B: Yes. He will attend the swimming match next week and try to win champion.

A: Did he __8__ last year?

B: Yes. He had to give __9__ on the half way because his leg was hurt.

A: I wish his dream would come __10__ this time.

语法精练——根据要求完成下列内容

根据句意，选用方框中所给词的适当形式填空。

Show, French, practice, proud, hold, surf, different, high, sport, they

1. There will be Olympic Games _______ by China in 2008.
2. Can you swim across the English Channel between England and _______?
3. What's the _______ like today? Are the waves great?
4. Don't be afraid. I'll _______ you how to surf.
5. Are there any _______ between American English and British English?
6. Surfing is one of the world's most popular water _______.
7. The CD player isn't ours. It's _______.
8. If you want to get good marks, you must _______ your English every day.
9. The teacher always speaks _______ of his students.
10. Yao Ming is a great NBA basketball star. He is the _______ of all the Chinese people.

连词成句，注意句后标点。

11. Kate, her brother, taller, is, than

______________________________________.

12. than, me, he, more, outgoing, is

______________________________________.

13. who, calmer, Lily, is, Lucy, or

______________________________________?

14. Maria, do, like, what, you, about

______________________________________?

15. popular, me, friend, than, my best, is, more

______________________________________.

16. Sam, on, games, watching, TV, weekends, likes, on, soccer

______________________________________.

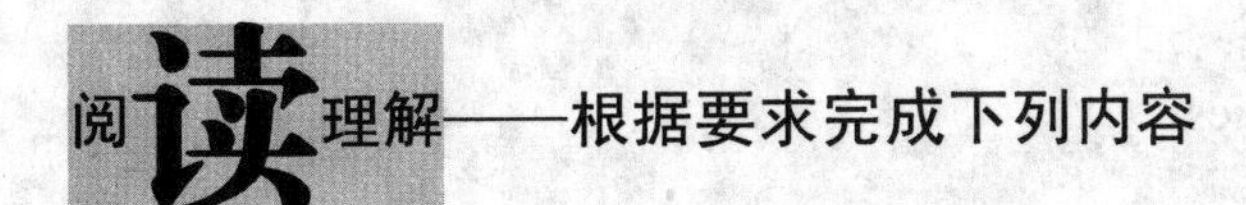

阅读下面的文章，并选择正确答案。

Students work very hard but many are unhappy. They feel heavy pressure from their parents. Most students are always being told by their parents to study harder so that they can have a wonderful life. Though this may be a good idea for those very clever students, it can have terrible results for many students because they have difficulties in their studies.

As it is reported, some students killed themselves. Some join the groups of troublemakers. Many of them have tried very hard at school but have failed in the exams and it makes their parents lose hope. Such students feel that they are hated by everyone else they meet and they don't want to go to school any longer, so they become dropouts.

It is surprising that though most parents are worried about their children, they do not help them in any way. Many parents feel that they are not able to help their children and that it is the teachers' work to help their children. To make matters worse, a lot of parents send their children to those schools opening in the evenings and on weekends. Those schools only help students to pass exams. It is a great surprise that almost three quarters of middle school students have been to such kind of schools.

Many schools usually have rules about everything, from the students' hair to their clothes and the things in their school bags. In fact, such strict rules may hurt the feelings of the students. Almost 40% of the students said that no one had taught them how to get on with others, how to tell right from wrong, how to show love to others, even to their parents.

1. Many students feel unhappy because________.
   A. their teachers don't like them
   B. they worry about their parents
   C. their parents put too much pressure on them
   D. they can't get on well with those clever students
2. Some of the students join the groups of trouble-makers because________.
   A. they want to kill themselves
   B. they can't do well in school
   C. they hate everyone else they meet
   D. they are afraid of making trouble
3. "Dropouts" are the students who________.
   A. make trouble in and out of school
   B. try hard but always fail in the exams
   C. lose hope and never do their homework
   D. leave school before finishing their studies
4. Which of the following is not true?
   A. Few students like heavy pressure.
   B. It's only the teachers' duty to help the students.
   C. Heavy pressure may be harmful to many children.
   D. Most parents only think of their children's exam results.
5. We should ________to help them feel less pressure.
   A. show more love to the students
   B. send the students to evening schools
   C. help the students choose school clothes
   D. make the students keep all the strict school rules

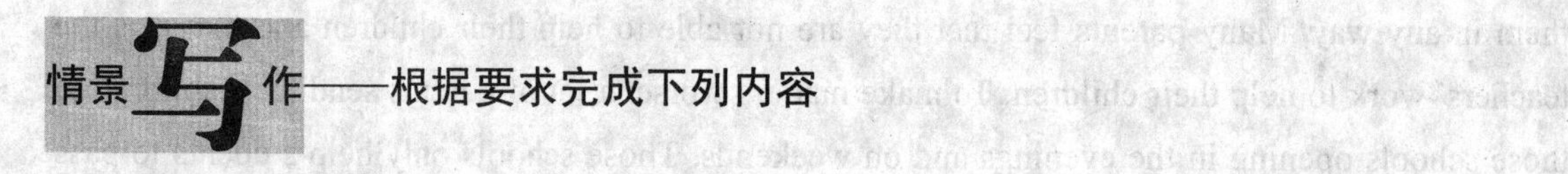

请以 An English Summer Camp 为题写一篇文章。

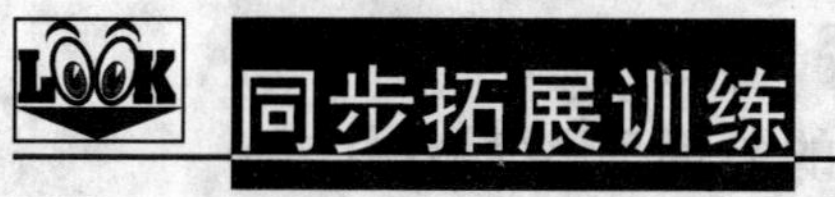

同步拓展训练 23

Lesson 67~69

听写检测——根据要求听写下列内容

Part A: 单词听写——听光盘录音，将听到的每个单词依次写在下面的横线上。

1.______ 2.______ 3.______
4.______ 5.______ 6.______
7.______ 8.______ 9.______
10.______ 11.______ 12.______
13.______ 14.______ 15.______
16.______ 17.______ 18.______
19.______ 20.______ 21.______
22.______ 23.______ 24.______
25.______ 26.______ 27.______
28.______ 29.______ 30.______
31.______ 32.______

Part B: 句子听写——听光盘录音，把课文内容听写在下面的横线上。

1.______
2.______
3.______
4.______
5.______
6.______
7.______
8.______
9.______
10.______

词汇游戏——根据汉语提示，将数字序号对应的单词填入表格中

横向提示	纵向提示
2. *n.*一生；5. *v.*取得，获得 8. *adj.*活动的；9. *v.*假设 12. *adj.*液态的；13. *n.*残骸 16. *adv.*猛烈地，剧烈地；17. *n.*谋杀 21. *n.*信心；23. *adj.*活着的 25. *v.*逃脱 26. *n.*刹车 28. *n.*踏板 29. *v.*营救 30. *adv.*应该	1. *v.*坚持做；3. *v.*命令，指示 4. *adj.*悲哀的；6. *n.*主考人 7. *n.*火山；10. *adj.*坚持的，固执的 11. *adj.*精彩的；14. *v.*害怕 15. *n.*执照，许可证；17. *v.*设法 18. *n.*礼物；19. *v.*反映 20. *v.*避开 22. *v.*毁坏 24. *n.*洞穴 27. *v.*（火山）喷发

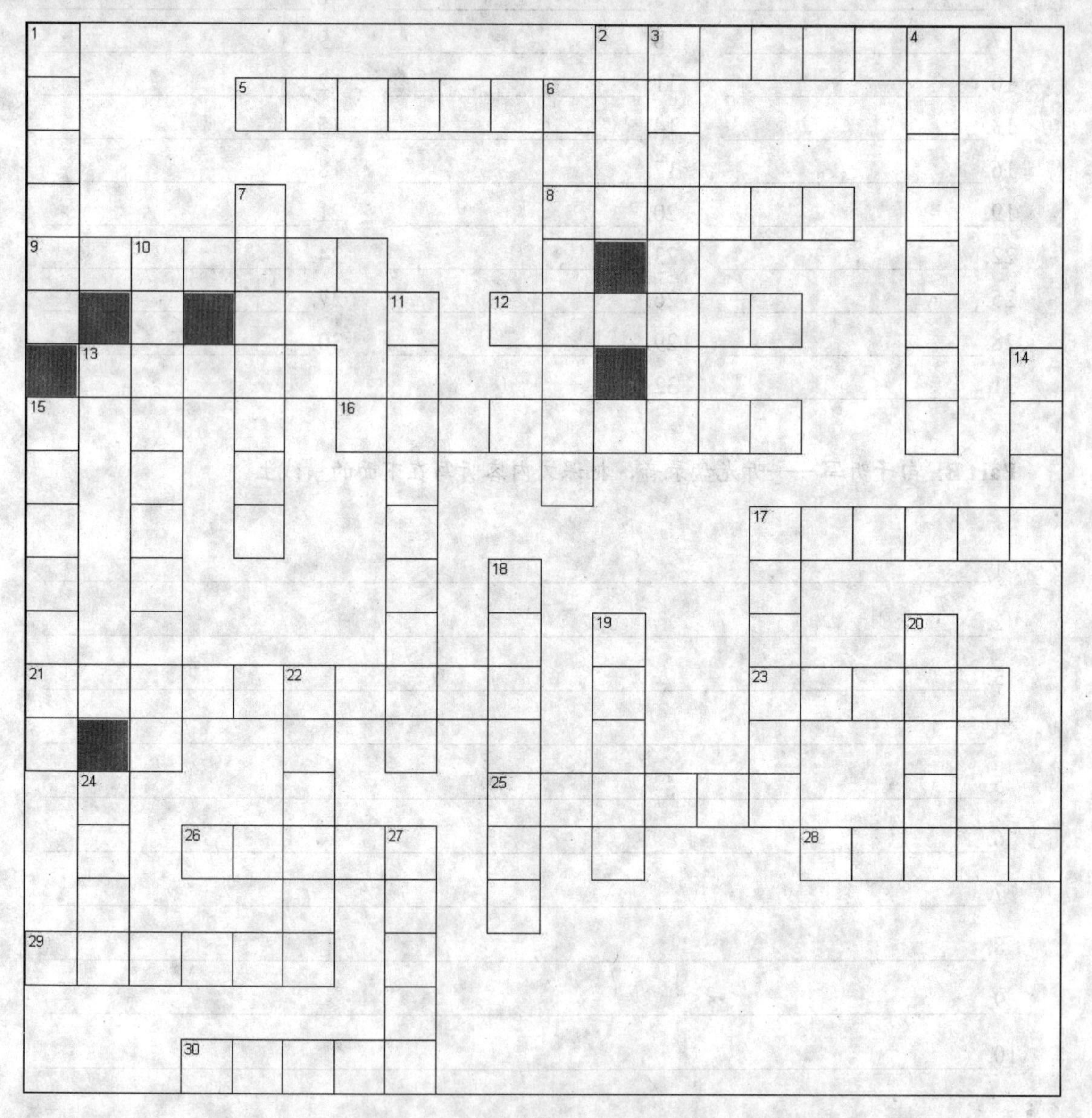

口语造句——根据要求完成下列内容

将下列句子排序成对话，把序号写在句子前面的横线上。

__ I am not sure. What does he look like?

__ No, he has black hair.

1 Do you know Tom in Class Nine?

__ Is he tall?

__ I think I know him. He always plays basketball after class.

__ He has a medium build.

__ Yes, he is.

__ Let me think. Does he have blonde hair?

__ Yes, that's him. He likes sports.

语法精练——根据要求完成下列内容

根据句意，选用方框中所给词的适当形式填空。

pick, throw, take care of, spit, for, since, do well in, used to

1. He has been a league member ________three years ago.
2. She has been like this ________several days.
3. Don't ________rubbish into the river.
4. ________our environment is very important.
5. Mr. Li ________smoke. He doesn't smoke now.
6. Have you ever ________flowers in a park?
7. Have you ever ________in a public place?
8. We are ________protecting the environment.

连词成句，注意句后标点。

9. you, can, party, my, come, birthday, to

____?

10. have, help, mom, I, to, my

____.

11. study, he, to, has, for, English, test.

____.

12. invitation, lot, a, thanks, for

____.

13. going, movie, with, I, my cousins, am, to, the

____.

阅读理解——根据要求完成下列内容

阅读下面的文章，并选择正确答案。

"Daddy, can I learn to play the violin?" young Sarah asked her father. She was asking for things and her father was not very pleased.

"You cost me a lot of money, Sarah," he said, "First you wanted to learn horse riding, then dancing, then swimming. Now it's the violin."

"I'll play every day, Daddy," Sarah said. "I'll try very hard."

"All right," her father said, "This is what I'll do. I'll pay for you to have lessons for six weeks. At the end of six weeks you must play something for me. If you play well, you can have more lessons. If you play badly, I will stop the lessons."

"OK. Daddy," Sarsh said, "That is fair."

He soon found a good violin teacher and Sarah began her lessons. The tuition was very expensive, but her father kept his promise.

The six weeks passed quickly. The time came for Sarah to play for her father. She went to the living room and said, "I'm ready to play for you, Daddy."

"Fine, Sarah," her father said. "Begin."

She began to play. She played very badly. She made a terrible noise.

Her father had one of his friends with him, and the friend put his hands over his ears.

When Sarah finished, her father said, "Well done, Sarch. You can have more lessons."

Sarah ran happily out of the room. Her father's friend turned to him. "You've spent a lot of money, but she still plays very badly," He said.

"Well, that's true," her father said. "But since she started learning the violin, I've been able to buy five apartments in this building very cheaply. In another six weeks I'll own the whole building!"

1. Sarsh's father was not pleased with her because________.
   A. she wanted to learn the violin
   B. she was rude
   C. she was always asking for things
   D. she was noisy
2. Sarah's father said he would pay for violin lessons for________.
   A. two weeks
   B. six weeks
   C. a month
   D. six months
3. Sarah played the violin________.
   A. well
   B. badly
   C. very well
   D. very badly
4. Her father gave her more lesson because________.
   A. she playes so well
   B. she was so interested in playing the violin
   C. he could buy more apartment cheaply because of Sarsh's noise
   D. he liked the violin
5. The best title of this story is________.
   A. Violin Lessons
   B. Sarah's Father
   C. Sarah's Violin Teacher
   D. Keep the Promise

In Canada you can find dogs, cats, horses, etc., in almost every family. These are their pets. People love these pets and regard them as their good friends. Before they keep them at their houses, they take them to animal hospitals to give them needles so that they won't carry disease. They have special animal food stores, though they can get animal food in almost every store. Some people spend around 200 Canadian dollars a month on animal food. When you visit people's homes, they would be very glad to show you their pets and they are very proud of them.

You will also find almost every family has a bird feeder in their garden. All kinds of birds are welcomed to come and have a good meal. They are free to come and go and nobody is allowed to kill any animals in Canada. They have a law against killing wild animals. If you killed an animal, you would be punished. If an animal happened to get run over by a car, people would be very sad about it.

People in Canada have many reasons to like animals. One of them might be: their family tie is not as close as ours. When children grow up, they leave their parents and start their own career. Then the seniors will feel lonely. But pets can solve this problem. They can be good friends and never leave them alone.

6. This passage shows that Canadians_____.
   A. love animals
   B. often kill animals
   C. hate animals
   D. don't keep their pets inside their houses

7. Children leave their parents when they grow up because_____.
   A. they don't love their parents any more
   B. they can only find jobs far from their parents
   C. their parents' houses are too small
   D. they want to start their career
8. They give their pets needles before keeping them at their houses because_____.
   A. the pets are sick
   B. the pets are wild
   C. they want to stop them from carrying disease
   D. they want them to sleep on the way home
9. Which is right according to the passage?
   A. People buy animal food for their pets only at the animal food stores.
   B. Pets eat better than people.
   C. Almost every family has a bird cage at his house.
   D. Any birds can come to the bird feeders to eat.
10. The passage mainly talks about_____.
   A. how to keep disease from pets　　B. pets in Canada
   C. how to take good care of pets　　D. life of the seniors in Canada

情景写作——根据要求完成下列内容

假如你是 Simon，请你写一封信给你的笔友，告诉他你的问题，并向他请求帮助。

1．经常上网，并花很多时间聊天。

2．经常晚回家，不能准时交作业。

3．父母和老师不喜欢我这样，让我放弃这个爱好，为此你很生气。

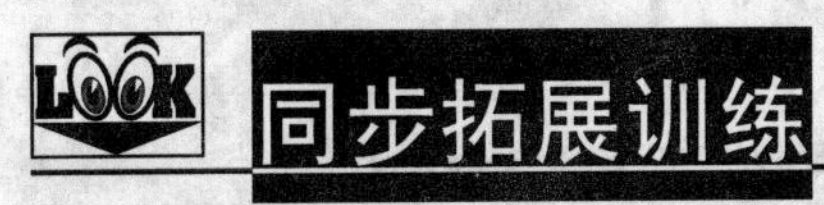

同步拓展训练 24

Lesson 70~72

听写检测——根据要求听写下列内容

Part A: 单词听写——听光盘录音，将听到的每个单词依次写在下面的横线上。

1.______ 2.______ 3.______
4.______ 5.______ 6.______
7.______ 8.______ 9.______
10.______ 11.______ 12.______
13.______ 14.______ 15.______
16.______ 17.______ 18.______
19.______ 20.______ 21.______
22.______ 23.______ 24.______
25.______ 26.______ 27.______
28.______ 29.______ 30.______
31.______ 32.______

Part B: 句子听写——听光盘录音，把课文内容听写在下面的横线上。

1.______
2.______
3.______
4.______
5.______
6.______
7.______
8.______
9.______
10.______

词汇游戏——根据汉语提示，将数字序号对应的单词填入表格中

横向提示	纵向提示
3. *n.*斗牛士；5. *adj.*著名的 6. *n.*批评；9. *n.*官员，行政人员 11. *n.*圆形竞技场地；14. *n.*扩音器，麦克风 15. *v.*鞠躬；17. *adj.*平均的 18. *adj.*极广大的；19. *n.*足迹 20. *v.*冲上去；23. *n.*公牛 24. *adv.*明显地 25. *v.*爆裂 26. *n.*塔 27. *adv.*同情地	1. *n.*斗牛；2. *n.*议会，国会 4. *adj.*准确的；7. *adj.*敏感地 8. *v.*检查 10. *n.*长度 12. *adj.*不知道的，未觉察的 13. *n.*马力 16. *n.*天文台 20. *adv.*笨拙地 21. *n.*竞赛 22. *v.*建起

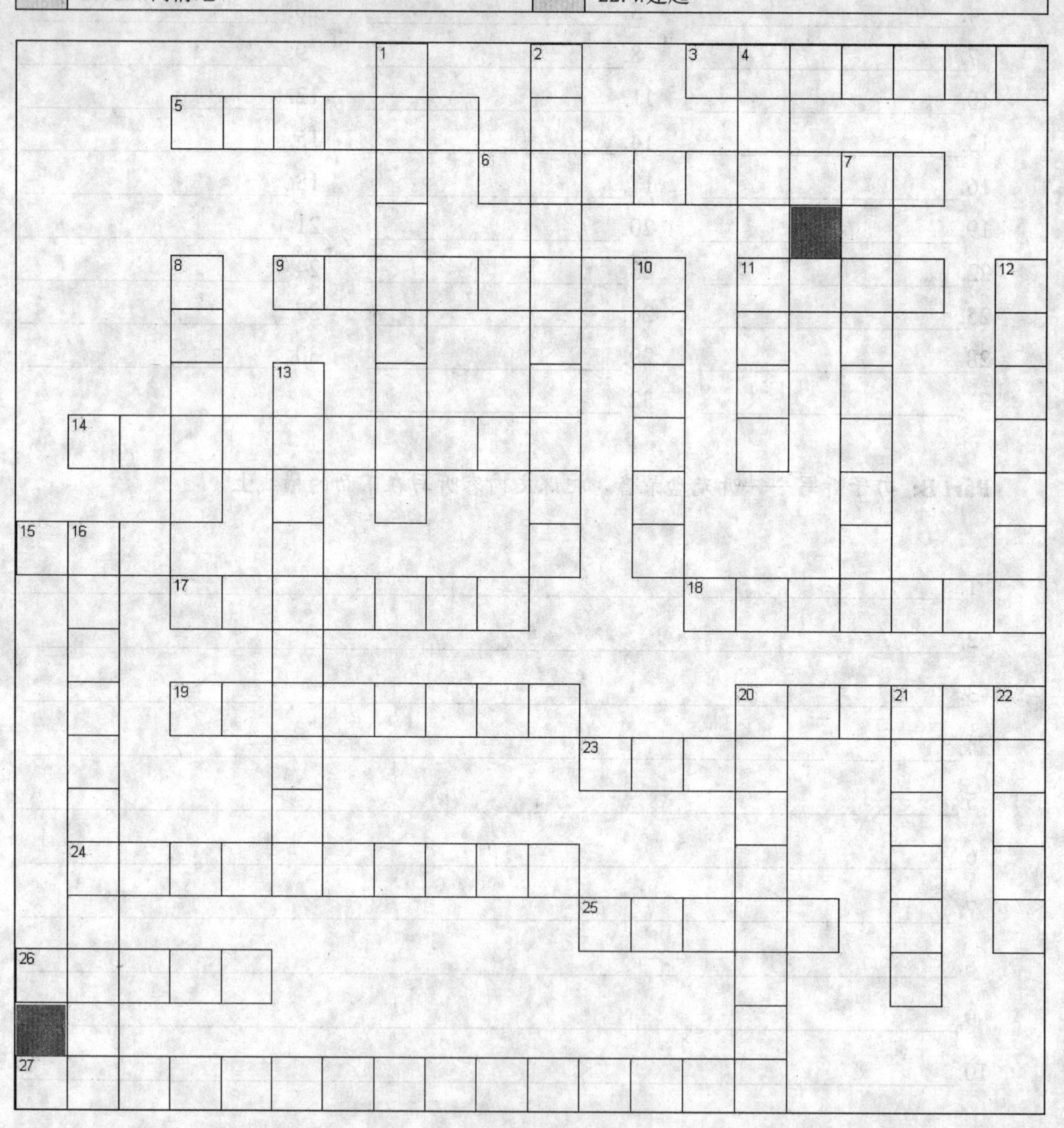

口语造句——根据要求完成下列内容

补全对话（一空一词）

A: Good morning, Doctor.

B: Good morning, young man. What's your __1__?

A: I don't __2__ well. I coughed terribly last night. And I __3__ a bad headache.

B: Have you taken your __4__?

A: Yes, I have. But I don't have a fever.

B: Emn. __5__ your mouth. Let me see. Well, you have just __6__ a cold. How __7__ have you been like this?

A: Ever since yesterday morning.

B: Have you had __8__ to eat this morning?

A: Yes, but I only had a glass of milk. I don't feel __9__ eating.

B: Don't worry. __10__ some medicine and drink more water. You will be all right very soon.

A: Thanks a lot.

B: You are welcome.

语法精练——根据要求完成下列内容

根据所给中文意思，完成句子。

1. 这周末他有太多的数学作业。

   He ________ ________ ________math homework this weekend.

2. 你能和我一起打网球吗？

   Can you ________ ________ ________ ________?

3. 他们下周有空。

   They ________ ________ ________next week.

4. 我一整天都要和叔叔去钓鱼。

   I'll ________ ________with my uncle the_____ _____.

5. 我们必须要为地理测验作准备。

   We _____ to _____ _____ the _____ _____.

根据句意，选用方框中所给词的适当形式填空。

play, little expensive, wake up, enjoy, slow, fall asleep, as soon as possible, because of

6. Most people were ill _______the cold weather.
7. He wants to see his doctor _______.
8. I think the market is the _____ place to buy clothes.
9. Tom _______very late this morning.
10. These songs are so _______to make me forget the sad thing.
11. Which is the _______way to travel, by train, by bus or by bike?
12. His parents encourage him to keep _______soccer.
13. I _______as soon as I went to bed yesterday evening.

阅读理解——根据要求完成下列内容

完形填空

What must you __1__ when you receive a present for your birthday? You have to sit down and write a thank-you letter. The words "Thank you" are very important. We have to use them often. We __2__ when someone gives us a drink, helps us to pick up things, hands us a letter, lends us a book, gives us a book or a present.

__3__ important word is "please". Many people forget __4__ it. It is not polite to ask someone to do something __5__ saying "please". We have to use it when we __6__ something, too. It may be a book or a pencil, more rice or more tea. It may be used in the classroom, at home, at the bus stop or in a shop. We have to use "please" to make people __7__.

We have to __8__ to say "sorry" too. When we have hurt someone, we go up and say we are __9__. When we have told a lie and felt sorry. We use __10__ word. When we have forgotten something or broken something. We use the word "sorry", too. "Sorry" is a word that can make people forget wrongs.

1. A. to do B. do C. say D. speak
2. A. say them B. say it C. talk them D. tell it
3. A. The other B. Other C. Another D. The others
4. A. using B. to use C. to using D. use
5. A. with B. and C. without D. or
6. A. ask B. ask for C. ask to D. ask about

7. A. happy B. happily C. happier D. happiest
8. A. forget B. learning C. studing D. learn
9. A. hungry B. angry C. sorry D. busy
10. A. same B. the same C. different D. one

阅读下面的文章，并选择正确答案。

As prices and building costs keep rising, the "do-it-yourself" (DIY) trend in the U. S. continues to grow.

"We needed furniture for our living room," says John Ross, "and we just didn't have enough money to buy it. So we decided to try making a few tables and chairs." John got married six months ago, and like many young people these days, they are struggling to make a home at a time when the cost of living is very high. The Rosses took a 2-week course for $ 280 at a night school. Now they build all their furniture and make repairs around the house.

Jim Hatfield has three boys and his wife died. He has a full-time job at home as well as in a shoe-making factory. Last month, he received a car repair bill for $ 420. "I was deeply upset about it. Now I've finished a car repair course. I should be able to fix the car by myself." He said.

John and Jim are not unusual people. Most families in the country are doing everything they can to save money so they can fight the high cost of living. If you want to become a do-it-yourselfer, you can go to DIY classes. And for those who don't have time to take a course, there are books that tell you how you can do things yourself.

11. We can learn from the text that many newly married people________.
A. find it hard to pay for what they need
B. have to learn to make their own furniture
C. take DIY courses run by the government
D. seldom go to a department store to buy things
12. John and his wife went to evening classes to learn how to________.
A. run a DIY shop B. make or repair things
C. save time and money D. improve the quality of life
13. When the writer says that Jim has a full-time job at home, he means Jim________.
A. makes shoes in his home B. does extra work at night
C. does his own car and home repairs D. keeps house and looks after his children
14. Jim Hatfield decided to become a do-it-yourselfer when________.
A. his car repairs cost too much B. the car repair class was not helpful
C. he could not possibly do two jobs D. he had to raise the children all by himself

15. What would be the best title for the text?

A. The Joy of DIY
B. You Can Do It Too!
C. Welcome to Our DIY Course!
D. Ross and Hatfield: Believers in DIY

情景写作——根据要求完成下列内容

母亲对每个人来说都是重要的，你可以介绍一下你的妈妈以及她对你的爱或者抒发你对母爱的感想。题目可以是 My Mother 或 Mother's Love。

同步拓展训练 25

Lesson 73~74

听写检测——根据要求听写下列内容

Part A: 单词听写——听光盘录音，将听到的每个单词依次写在下面的横线上。

1.______ 2.______ 3.______
4.______ 5.______ 6.______
7.______ 8.______ 9.______
10.______ 11.______ 12.______
13.______ 14.______ 15.______
16.______ 17.______ 18.______
19.______ 20.______ 21.______
22.______ 23.______ 24.______
25.______ 26.______ 27.______
28.______ 29.______ 30.______
31.______ 32.______

Part B: 句子听写——听光盘录音，把课文内容听写在下面的横线上。

1.______
2.______
3.______
4.______
5.______
6.______
7.______
8.______
9.______
10.______

词汇游戏——根据汉语提示，将数字序号对应的单词填入表格中

横向提示	纵向提示
1. *n.*权威，当局；8. *adj.*舒适的 10. *adj.*奇妙的，极好的；13. *n.*预防措施 14. *v.*发现 15. *n.*期间 19. *n.*舞台灯光 21. *v.*认出，发现 22. *n.*逃学的孩子 23. *n.*饼干，小点心 24. *adj.*完美的 26. *n.*冷笑	2. *adj.*缺乏想象力的；3. *n.*司法长官 4. *v.*旅行；5. *n.*边界 6. *n.*男演员；7. *v.*认出，承认 9. *adj.*远古的，旧的；11. *v.*出现 12. *v.*搭便车旅行；15. *n.*其间，同时 16. *v.*逃避，逃离 17. *v.*假装，伪装 18. *adj.*避阴的 20. *n.*告示 25. *n.*狂热者，迷

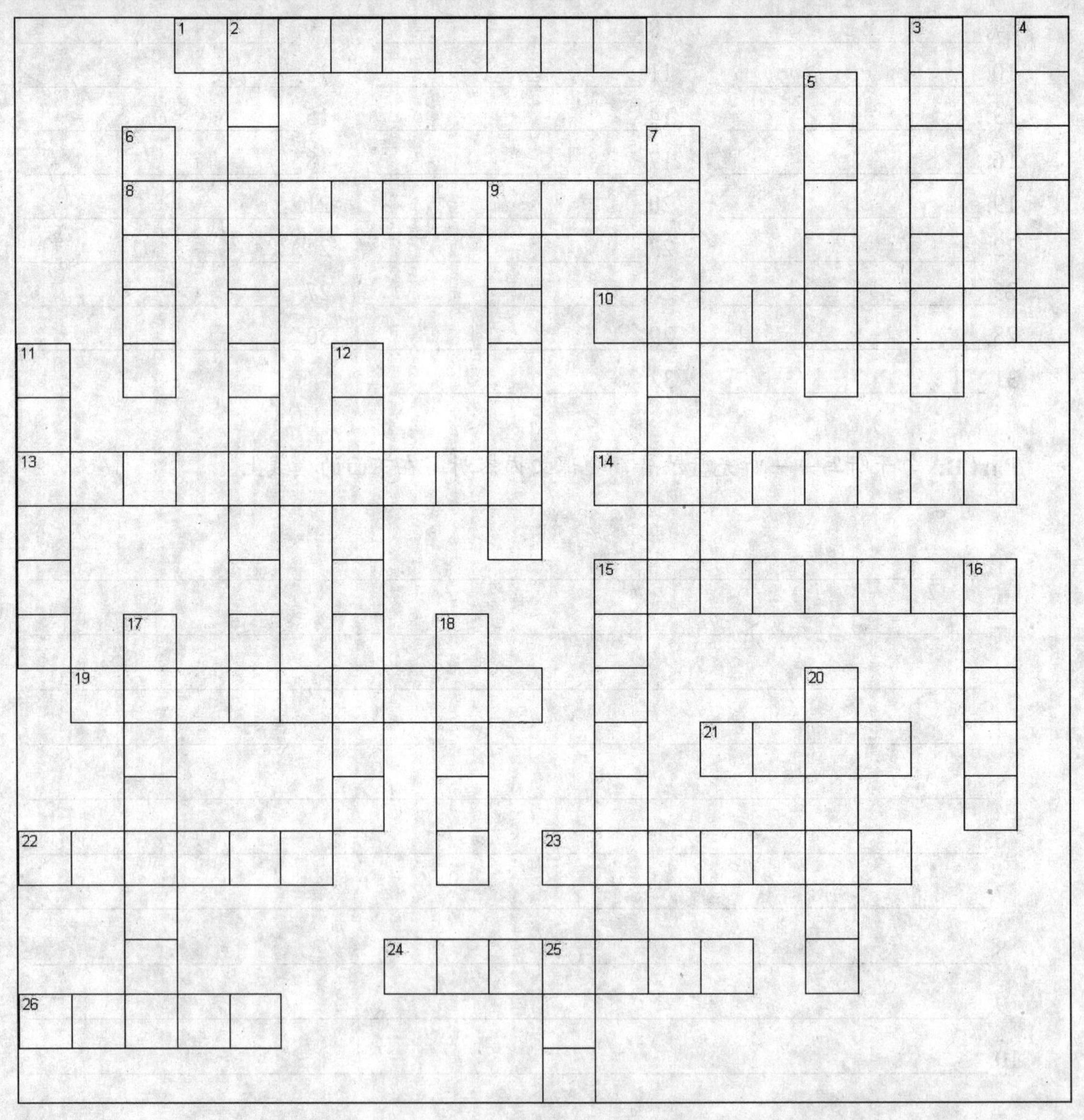

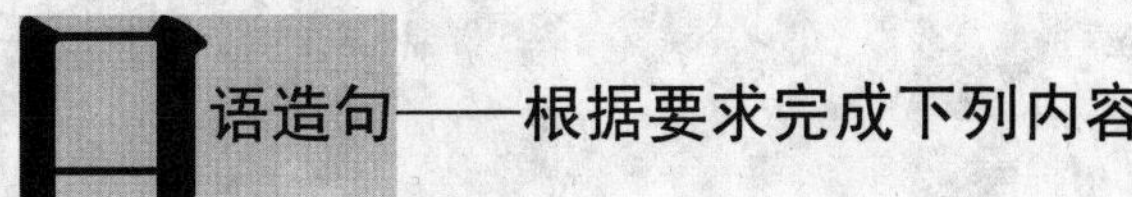

口语造句——根据要求完成下列内容

补全对话

Liu: Hello! Could I speak to Zhang Liu, please?

Zhang: Speaking. Is __1__ Liu Mei?

Liu: Yes. Are you free tomorrow?

Zhang: Why?

Liu: You know, my bag is broken. I want to buy a new __2__. Would you like to go __3__ with me ?

Zhang: Sure. But __4__ and __5__ shall we meet?

Liu: At ten o'clock, outside the gate of Hua Tai Market.

Zhang: I'm afraid I don't know the way to the market.

Liu: Well, listen to me carefully. Go down Suzhou Street and __6__ the second turning on the left. Then go __7__ until you reach Bei Tai Ping Qiao. The market is __8__ your right. By the way, you can catch a bus.

Zhang: __9__ __10__ do I need?.

Liu: Number 367.

Zhang: OK. See you then.

Liu: See you.

1.________ 2. ________ 3. ________ 4. ________ 5. ________

6. ________ 7. ________ 8. ________ 9. ________ 10. ________

语法精练——根据要求完成下列内容

下列各句中有一处是错的，请指出并改正。

1. I have much too homework to do today.
   A B C D
2. Thank you for call me.
   A B C D
3. They are talking in the phone now.
   A B C D

4. You can invite your classmates for your party.

A B C D

5. She can't goes to the mall this week.

A B C D

根据所给中文意思，完成句子。

6. 我们当中没有一个人去过欧洲。

______ ______ us ______ ______to Europe.

7. 快点！不然我们开会要迟到了。

Hurry up! ________we'll ________ ________ ________the meeting.

8. 我认为乘火车旅行比乘飞机旅行要便宜而且更乐享其中。

I think it is ________and ________ ________ to go on a trip by train than by plane.

9. 有时青年人觉得很难理解老年人。

Sometimes young people find ________ ________to ________old people.

10. 昨天下午直到雨停了，足球赛才开始。

The football game ________ ________ ________the rain ________yesterday afternoon.

11. 我从来也没有看过这么有趣的电影。

I have ______ ______ ______ ______interesting film.

12. 我妈妈不喜欢坐飞机匆忙旅行。

My mother doesn't like a ________ ________by ________.

阅读理解——根据要求完成下列内容

根据短文内容判断正误，正确写T，错误写F。

1970 was World Conservation Year. The United Nations wanted everyone to know that the world is in danger. They hoped that government would act quickly to conserve nature. Here is one example of the problem. At one time there were 1300 different plants, trees and flowers in Holland but now only 866 remain. The others have been destroyed by modern man and his technology. We are changing the earth, the air, water and everything that grows and lives. We can't live without these things. If things go like this, we shall destroy ourselves.

What will happen in the future? Perhaps it is more important to ask, "What must we do now?" The people who will be living in the world of tomorrow are the young of today. A lot of them know conservation is necessary. Many are helping to save our world. They plant trees, build bridges across rivers in forests, and so on. In a small town in the United States, a large number of girls cleaned the banks of 11 kilometres of their river. Young people may hear about conservation through a report called "No one's going to change our world", it was made by the beatles, Clift Richard and other singers. The money from it will help to conserve animals.

1. The United Nations wanted everybody to know that the world is dangerous.
2. There are fewer plants, trees and flowers in Holland because many kinds of plants, trees and flowers can't grow there any more.
3. We shall destroy ourselves if we are changing the earth, the air, water and everything that grows and lives.
4. The most important thing for us to do is to clean the banks of our rivers.
5. From this passage we know that we must conserve nature.

阅读下面的文章，并选择正确答案。

That day was like any other day in his life. After school Michael walked past the shop in the street corner. He stopped to look at the front row of shoes, and he felt sorry for himself. He really wanted to have a pair of shoes for his birthday.

He walked away sadly and thought of what to tell his mother. He knew she would give him anything if she could. But he also knew very well she had little money. He decided not to go home at once, as he looked worried and his mother would notice it. So he went to the park and sat on the grass. Then he saw a boy in a wheel chair. He noticed that the boy moved the wheels with his hands. Michael looked at him carefully and was surprised to see that the boy had no feet. He looked down at his own feet. "It's much better to be without shoes than without feet." he thought. There was no reason for him to feel so sorry and sad. He went away and smiled, thinking he was more lucky in life.

6. Michael left the shoe shop sadly because_________.

   A. the shoes in the shop were too big for him

   B. the shoes in the shop were too small for him

   C. he had no money to buy himself a pair of shoes

   D. he had too many shoes

7. Michael _______instead of going home.

   A. went to the park　　B. stayed in the shop

   C. played games at school　　D. played in the street

8. He knew that ________ if he got home at once.

A. his mother would be happy　　B. his mother would be worried

C. he would be very tired　　D. he would get anything he wanted

9. Michael saw a boy. The boy________.

A. was blind　　B. was deaf　　C. had no arms　　D. had no feet

10. Which of the following is true?

A. Mechael's mother was rich.

B. Good health is more important than anything else in the world.

C. The following day was Michael's birthday.

D. The boy in the wheel chair was Michael's friend.

情景写作——根据要求完成下列内容

请你参考所给信息，写一篇关于你的同学或朋友的小短文。

要求：

1. 短文中不得出现你的真实姓名和学校名
2. 可用所给信息，也可适当发挥
3. 词数：60～80

所给信息：Zhou Yi; 14; tall/short; thin/strong; kind; favorite sport; listen to music; read books

____

____

____

____

____

____

____

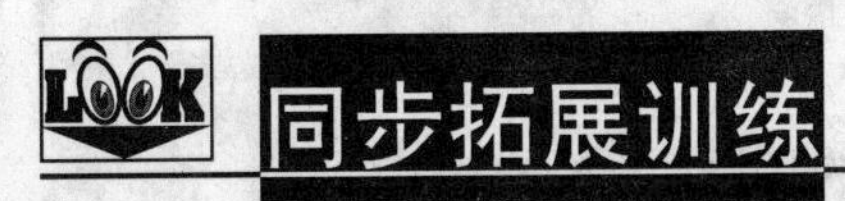

同步拓展训练 26

Lesson 75~76

听写检测——根据要求听写下列内容

Part A: 单词听写——听光盘录音，将听到的每个单词依次写在下面的横线上。

1.________	2.________	3.________
4.________	5.________	6.________
7.________	8.________	9.________
10.________	11.________	12.________
13.________	14.________	15.________
16.________	17.________	18.________
19.________	20.________	21.________
22.________	23.________	24.________
25.________	26.________	27.________
28.________	29.________	30.________
31.________	32.________	

Part B: 句子听写——听光盘录音，把课文内容听写在下面的横线上。

1.____

2.____

3.____

4.____

5.____

6.____

7.____

8.____

9.____

10.____

词汇游戏——根据汉语提示，将数字序号对应的单词填入表格中

横向提示		纵向提示	
横向提示	1. *n.*冠军；2. *n.*手提箱 7. *n.*旅客，乘客；8. *adj.*可怕的 11. *n.*通心面，空心面条；13. *adj.*在头上的 14. *n.*现场；15. *v.*打（庄稼） 17. *v.*期待，期望；18. *adj.*当地的 20. *n.*播音室；21. *adj.*厚的 22. *n.*播音员 23. *v.*加工 24. *n.*新闻简报 25. *n.*种植者	纵向提示	1. *n.*竞赛，竞争；2. *adj.*极好的 3. *n.*幸存者；4. *n.*一满车 5. *v.*收庄稼；6. *v.*收割，收获 9. *adj.*主要的 10. *n.*场面，场景 12. *adj.*目前的 14. *n.*梗 16. *n.*直升飞机 19. *v.*碰撞，坠毁 20. *v.*踩，跺

口语造句——根据要求完成下列内容

补全对话（每空一词）

A: __1__ me. Can you __2__ me the __3__ to the History Museum, please?

B: Let me see. Er, you go __4__ this street. __5__ the second turning on the __6__. Then walk on __7__ you reach Tian An Men Square. There you can __8__ it. It's on the __9__ side of the square.

A: __10__ a lot.

1. ________ 2. ________ 3. ________ 4. ________ 5. ________
6. ________ 7. ________ 8. ________ 9. ________ 10. ________

语法精练——根据要求完成下列内容

用 How many, how much 填空

1. ________mayonnaise do we need?
2. ________onions did you cut up?
3. ________cups of tea do you want?
4. ________cinnamon do they want?
5. ________yogurt do we need for the smoothie?
6. ________bottles of milk did he drink?
7. ________teaspoons of tomato sauce did you put on the sandwich?
8. ________water do you drink every day?

阅读理解——根据要求完成下列内容

完形填空

Thomas Edison was a famous American scientist. He was born __1__ 1847. When he was a child, he liked to find out __2__ things worked. He was in school for only three months. He asked his teacher a lot __3__ strange questions. Most of them __4__ not about his lessons. His teacher did not __5__ his new pupil. So he wanted to send Tom __6__ school. When he told this to

Edison's mother, she took her son __7__ school. She taught him __8__. The boy read a lot. Soon he became very __9__ in science. __10__ then Edison had already built a chemistry lab for himself.

1.	A. in	B. on	C. by	D. at
2.	any	B. some	C. what	D. how
3.	A. about	B. of	C. on	D. to
4.	are	B. is	C. were	D. was
5.	A. know	B. think	C. find	D. understand
6.	A. out from	B. away from	C. for	D. up
7.	A. to	B. into	C. out of	D. from
8.	A. himself	B. herself	C. themselves	D. itself
9.	A. happy	B. surprised	C. worried	D. interested
10.	A. At	B. After	C. Since	D. By

阅读下面的文章，并选择正确答案。

A computer company has a special person. He answers all the questions sent to him. The person is a 63-year-old man. He is known for always finding the right answers. On the Internet, more people are finding out about this clever man. He does not look like a computer expert. He has white hair and he is kind and polite. He feels that his age helps him with his work. People have asked questions about a lot of things and he remembers most of them.

He tries to return the answers within 24 hours on the Internet. The questions are very different each day. He loves his work. Other companies do not have such a person. Of course they don't have to pay any more money, either. But it's important for good computer companies to have a person to answer the questions. It keeps the computer buyers happy. Happy buyers will keep coming back.

11. How does the special person answer the questions?
    A. He answers the questions in the letters, then he sends them off in the post office.
    B. He asks the people to come to the company and get the answers.
    C. He answers the questions on the Internet.
    D. He asked others to answer the questions instead.
12. People know him because________.
    A. he is head of the company
    B. he has white hair and he is kind and polite
    C. he does not look like a computer expert

D. he can always find the right answers to their questions

13. Which of the following sentences has NOT been mentioned?

A. He remembers almost all the things that people ask about.

B. He's old and he doesn't have to work at all.

C. He thinks that his age is helpful.

D. He is 63 years old.

14. In the sentence, he tries to return the answers within 24 hours, "within" means________.

A. before　　B. after　　C. in　　D. at

15. What will happy computer buyers do?

A. They'll stop asking questions.

B. They'll stop buying because they have what they want.

C. They'll go to other computer companies for cheaper computers.

D. They'll come back for more business.

情景写作——根据要求完成下列内容

假如你明天要进行一次植树活动，老师讲解了有关注意事项，你的同学 Mike 还不太清楚。现在请你把老师讲的要点用英语对 Mike 讲一遍，并把要讲的话写下来。

1. 挖坑，不要太深
2. 在坑中插根直竹竿
3. 在坑中放入树苗，靠近直竿
4. 盖土，用脚踩实
5. 把树苗固定在竹竿上
6. 浇水

注意：1. 可以增加适当的细节，使所写的语言连贯

2. 词数：80 左右

____

____

____

____

____

LOOK
同步拓展训练 27
Lesson 77~78

听写检测——根据要求听写下列内容

Part A: 单词听写——听光盘录音，将听到的每个单词依次写在下面的横线上。

1.________	2.________	3.________
4.________	5.________	6.________
7.________	8.________	9.________
10.________	11.________	12.________
13.________	14.________	15.________
16.________	17.________	18.________
19.________	20.________	21.________
22.________	23.________	24.________
25.________	26.________	27.________
28.________	29.________	30.________
31.________	32.________	

Part B: 句子听写——听光盘录音，把课文内容听写在下面的横线上。

1.____

2.____

3.____

4.____

5.____

6.____

7.____

8.____

9.____

10.____

词汇游戏——根据汉语提示，将数字序号对应的单词填入表格中

横向提示		纵向提示	
横向提示	1. *n.*满意，满足；5. *v.*以……为名 8. *adj.*成功的；10. *n.*香烟 11. *n.*歌手；12. *n.*庙 15. *adj.*欣喜的；17. *v.*使镇定 19. *n.*手术 24. *n.*（照相）底片 25. *adj.*巨大的，庞大的 27. *n.*疾病 28. *n.*神经 29. *n.*愉快，快乐	纵向提示	1. *n.*皮，皮肤；2. *n.*集中，专心 3. *n.*切片；4. *n.*脾气 6. *v.*受苦，受害；7. *v.*幸免于 9. *n.*体形，人像；13. *n.*木乃伊 14. *v.*持续；16. *adv.*通常地 18. *n.*症状；20. *n.*胃口，食欲 21. *v.*显示出 22. *n.*树脂 23. *adj.*罕见的，杰出的 26. *n.*斑点

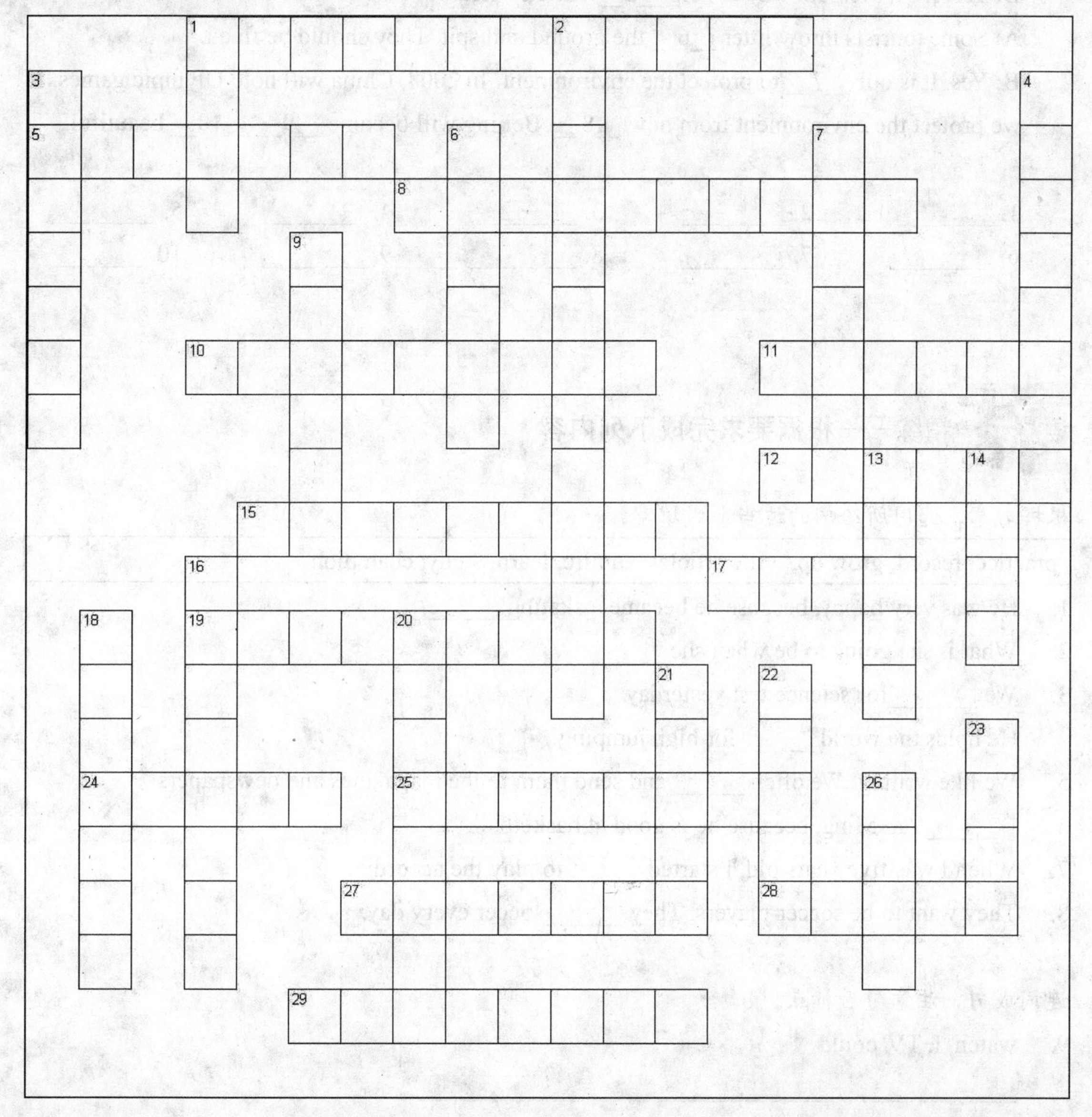

口语造句——根据要求完成下列内容

补全对话

A: Where have you __1__?

B: I've been to the Great Wall.

A: What did you do there?

B: I picked __2__ some rubbish and __3__ into dustbins with my classmates in the mountains.

A: It's really nice. __4__ the environment is very important.

B: Yes. It's a pleasant way to help __5__ our city clean.

A: Some tourists throw litter __6__ the ground and spit. They should be fined.

B: Yes. It is our __7__ to protect the environment. In 2008, China will hold Olympic games. If we protect the environment from now __8__, Beijing will become __9__ __10__ beautiful.

1.________ 2. ________ 3. ________ 4. ________ 5. ________
6. ________ 7. ________ 8. ________ 9. ________ 10. ________

语法精练——根据要求完成下列内容

根据句意，选用所给词的适当形式填空。

practice, record, grow up, write articles, admire, learn, study, champion

1. He was very happy, because he became a skating______.
2. What is she going to be when she_______.
3. We _______for science test yesterday.
4. He holds the world ______for high jumping.
5. We like writing. We often ______and send them to the magazines and newspapers.
6. I ______Yao Ming, because he is good at basketball.
7. When I was five years old, I started ______to play the accordion.
8. They want to be soccer players. They ______soccer every day.

连词成句，注意句后标点。

9. watch, I, TV, could

____?

10. out, I, stay, could,late

____?

11. could, bike, use, I, your

____?

12. taking, dog, thanks, my, for, care, of

____.

13. take, please, the, trash, out

____.

14. forget, room, clean, your, don't, to

____.

阅读理解——根据要求完成下列内容

阅读下面的文章，并选择正确答案。

Last week Fred had to go to New York. It was his first time there, and he didn't know his way around the city. He had a meeting at 10 o'clock, and he wanted to be on time. The meeting was in the Peterson Building on 34th Street, but Fred didn't know where that was. Seeing two men standing on a corner, he asked them.

"Excuse me," he said, "but can you tell me how to get to the Peterson Building on 34th Street?"

"Sure," answered one of them. "You can get there in five minutes. Go to the next corner and turn left. Walk three blocks and there you are."

But the other man said, "There's a better way. Go on the bus here at the comer. It stops right near the Peters Building."

"Not Peters," Fred told him, "Peterson."

Then the first man said, "On, that's on East 34th Street, not West 34th. It's quite a distance from here. You will have to take the subway."

But the second man told Fred, "No, don't go by subway. Take the crosstown bus. It goes to the Peterkin Building."

"Peterson. Not Peterkin," Fred looked at his watch. It was almost ten o'clock. "Thanks a lot," he said. "I think I'll take a taxi."

When he got into the taxi, he saw the two men arguing and pointing in different directions. Next time he wanted to know how to get to a place, he'd better ask a policeman!

1. Fred had to go to New York because________.

A. he had a meeting there

B. he lived there

C. he went to see his friend

D. he didn't go there before

2. He wanted to go to________.

A. the Peters Building

B. New York

C. the Peterson Building

D. the Peterkin Building

3. The Peters Building is on_______

A. South 34th Street

B. North 34th Street

C. East 34th Street

D. West 34th Street

4. How did Fred go there? He went there________.

A. on foot

B. by taxi

C. by subway

D. by bus

5. The story tells us that if you don't know how to get to a place, you'd better ask________.

A. a policeman B. a woman C. a man D. a boy

If you go into the forest with friends, stay with them. If you don't, you may get lost. If you get lost, this is what you should do.

Sit down and stay where you are. Don't try to find your friends-let them find you. You can help them to find you by staying in one place.

There is another way to help your friends or other people to find you. You can shout or whistle three times. Stop. Then shout or whistle three times again. Any signal given three times is a call for help. Keep up the shouting or whistling, always three times together. When people hear you, they will know that you are not just making noise for fun. They will let you know that they have heard your signal is given twice. It is an answer to a call for help.

If you don't think that you will get help before night comes, try to make a little house-cover up the hole with branches with lots of leaves. Make yourself a bed with leaves and grass.

When you need some water, you have to leave your little branch house to look for a stream. Don't just walk away. Pick off small branches and drop them as you walk in order to find the way back.

When you are lost, the most important thing to do is to stay in one place.

6. If you get lost in the forest, you should ______.

A. just cry and shout

B. walk around the forest and shout

C. stay in one place to give signals

D. build a house

7. How to let people believe that you are not just making noise for fun? You should ________.

A. shout that you are lost

B. keep up either shouting or whistling always three times together

C. shout or whistle only once

D. deep silent

8. When you heard two shouts or two whistles you know that ______.

A. the birds are singing　　B. something will happen

C. something terrible will happen　　D. people will come to help you

9. When you are lost in the forest but you want to leave your place to get some water, what should you do?

A. Pick up small branches.

B. Look for a bottle.

C. Leave marks as you go to a stream in order to find your way back.

D. Make a hole in the ground.

10. This article tells you ______.

A. what you should do if you are lost in the forest

B. what you should do if you want to get some water from a stream

C. how to spend the night in the forest

D. how to find food and clothes in the forest

情景写作——根据要求完成下列内容

根据提示，请以凯特的名义给韩梅写封信，要求格式正确、内容全面、表述准确、词数 70 个左右（不包括已给出的内容）。凯特的地址是：美国康涅狄克州（Connecticut）西巷市（Westport）花园大街（Gardener Street）173 号。写信日期是 2007 年 4 月 8 日。

信的内容如下：

1．老师说中国是一个大国，人口最多。

2．虽然中国距离美国很远，但我已经看到了好多有关中国的电视节目。

3．我对中国很感兴趣，我希望了解更多关于你们生活的情况。

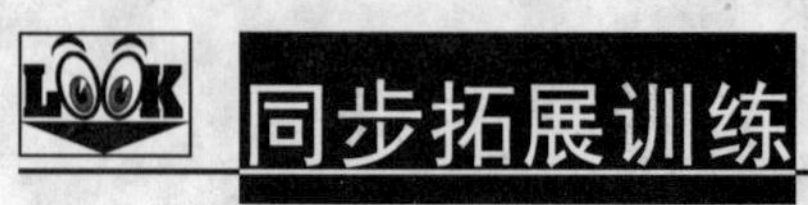

同步拓展训练 28

Lesson 79~80

听写检测——根据要求听写下列内容

Part A: 单词听写——听光盘录音，将听到的每个单词依次写在下面的横线上。

1.______ 2.______ 3.______
4.______ 5.______ 6.______
7.______ 8.______ 9.______
10.______ 11.______ 12.______
13.______ 14.______ 15.______
16.______ 17.______ 18.______
19.______ 20.______ 21.______
22.______ 23.______ 24.______
25.______ 26.______ 27.______
28.______ 29.______ 30.______
31.______ 32.______

Part B: 句子听写——听光盘录音，把课文内容听写在下面的横线上。

1.______
2.______
3.______
4.______
5.______
6.______
7.______
8.______
9.______
10.______

词汇游戏——根据汉语提示，将数字序号对应的单词填入表格中

横向提示	纵向提示
2. *adv.*幸运地；4. *v.*安放 5. *n.*展览；7. *n.*机会，场合 8. *adj.*各种各样的；9. *n.*经验，体验 10. *n.*学院；13. *v.*害怕，担惊 14. *n.*展览；16. *adv.*十分地，彻底地 17. *v.*保持 21. *adj.*急于了解，好奇的 23. *n.*利润 24. num.百万 25. *n.*蒸汽	1. *n.*宫殿；3. *adj.*不平常的 6. *adj.*奇妙的，极好的 10. *adj.*好奇的，求知的 11. *adj.*不高兴的 12. *n.*高度 15. *n.*父（母）亲 18. *n.*博物馆 19. *n.*铁 20. *n.*假期 22. *n.*炸弹

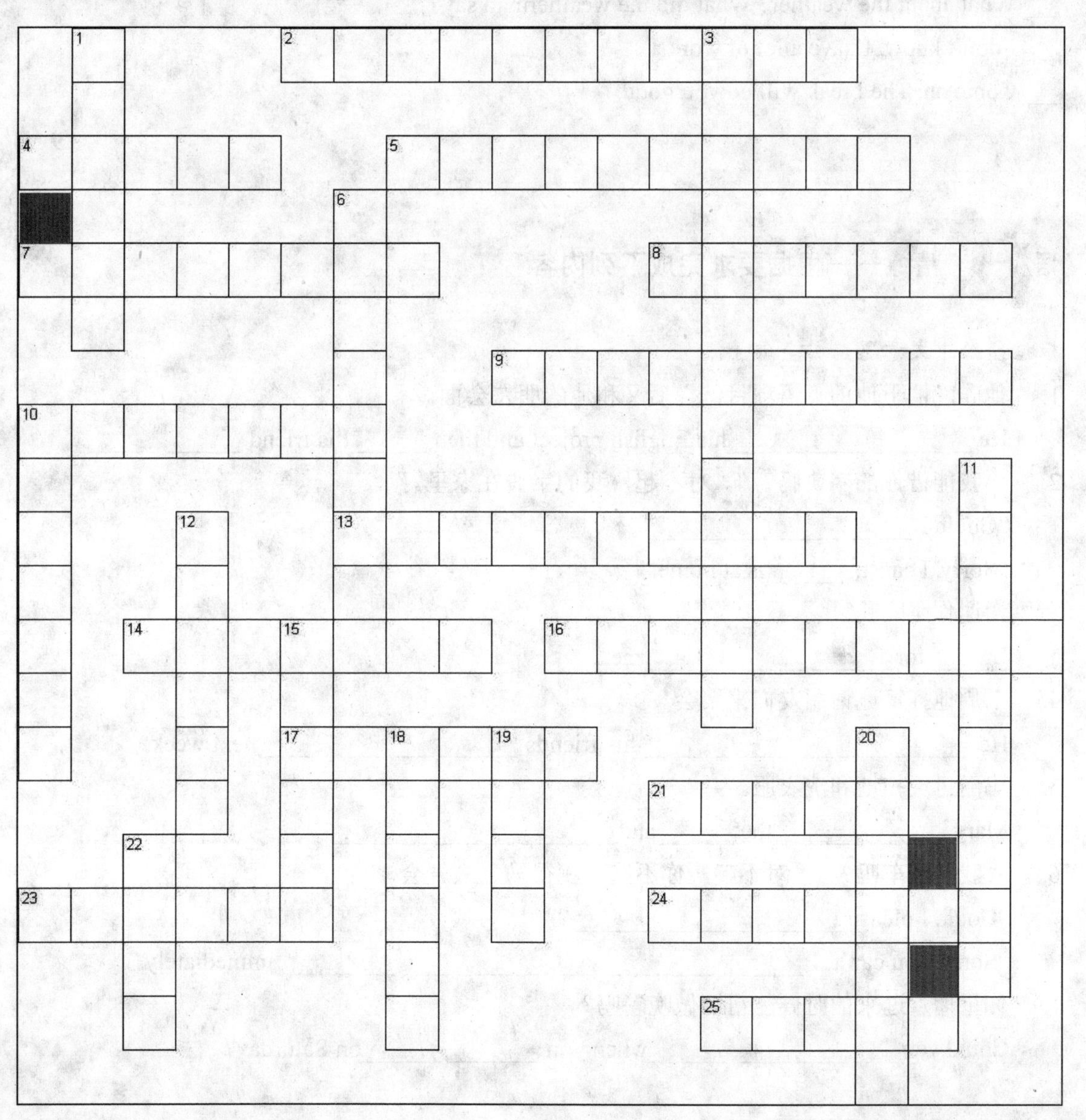

口语造句——根据要求完成下列内容

将下列句子排序成对话，把序号写在句子前面的横线上。

___ Yes. Do you want to go?

___ Let's go to the coast this weekend, Tom.

___ Yes. I'm sure it's would Okay. I'll go.

___ He's predicting clear skies.

___ Is that right?

___ What about the weather? What did the weatherman say?

___ I don't know. I have a lot of work.

___ Come on. The break will do you good.

语法精练——根据要求完成下列内容

根据所给中文意思，补全句子。

1. 他昨晚忙于他的英语项目，之后又和他的朋友会面。

   He ______ ______ ______his English project and then ______his friend ______ ______.

2. "我能借你的字典吗？""对不起，我的字典在家里。"

   "Could I ______ ______ ______?"

   "Sorry, I can't. ______ is at home."

3. 谢谢你照顾我。

   ______ for ______ ______ ______me.

4. 下周他打算邀请朋友们来聚会。

   He ______ ______ ______ ______ his friends ______ ______ ______next week.

5. 玛丽讨厌扫地和洗衣服。

   Mary ______ ______the ______and ______ ______ ______.

6. "我能搭车吗？""对不起，你不能。我得马上去开会。"

   "Could I please ______ ______ ______?"

   "Sorry, you can't. I ______ ______ ______ ______ ______ ______immediately."

7. 你星期六过来的时候能帮忙做晚餐吗？

   Could you ______ ______ ______when you ______ ______on Saturday?

阅读理解——根据要求完成下列内容

阅读下面的文章，并选择正确答案。

The police received a report that six men had stopped a truck. It was carrying some dry goods and two bags full of something important. The six men attacked the driver. After searching for three hours, the police found the truck near the river. The driver was sitting on a bag in the truck and his hands were tied behind his back. The thieves had tied a handkerchief round his mouth so that he wouldn't shout. The police climbed into the back of the truck and freed the driver. They asked him what had happened.

"I was stopped soon after I left the bank," the driver explained. "Six men stopped me and made me drive to the river, 'If you shout,' one of them said, 'we'll kill you!' When I got to the river, they tied me up. Then they threw me into the back of the truck. There were two bags in it and they took one of them."

"How much money did the bag contain?" a police officer asked.

"It didn't contain any money at all," the driver laughed.

"It was full of letters. This one contains all the money. I have been sitting on it for three hours."

1. Where did the truck start its journey?

   A. From the bank　　B. Near the river

   C. In the street　　D. From a post office

2. The driver could not report it to the police immediately because ________.

   A. he was thrown into the back of the truck

   B. he was sitting on a bag

   C. he was tied up and a handkerchief was tied round his mouth

   D. the truck broke down

3. The six men got away with________.

   A. a lot of money　　B. many letters

   C. plenty of dry goods　　D. money and letters

4. The six men did not take away the other bag. That was probably because________.

   A. they didn't notice the bag under the driver

   B. they thought that there was nothing important in the bag

   C. they didn't like that bag

   D. the bag is too small to be seen

5. The thieves tied up the driver________.

A. when they stopped the truck

B. when they got on the truck

C. when the truck got to the river

D. after they threw the driver into the back of the truck

Robert had just moved into the street and he felt strange and that he was not wanted. He knew that perhaps the other boys were trying to get an idea of what kind of a boy he was. This did not help to make him less lonely. He was new and he had to be tested. Still, proving himself would not be all that easy. He did not want to run with bad boys or get into something against the law to prove that he was strong. No! He must show what he was made of in a more helpful way. That would be better when he got the idea.

The next day was Saturday. He knew that most of the boys would be down on the playground and choose up sides for the Saturday game. Robert knew he could play well and that just might be enough to prove he was strong-and to make friends with them. He arrived early and did his step exercises. He shot the ball several times and did some other exercises-the most difficult and most wonderful in basketball. Then the boys came.

Robert went through what he had done before the game and showed what he could do. No one said a word. The boys just looked at each other and thought about it. In the end, when it was all over, the biggest of the group just smiled and shook his head. Robert knew he had made it.

6. What does "This did not help to make him less lonely" mean?

A. Robert felt more lonely because the other boys wanted to test him.

B. Robert did not want himself to be less lonely.

C. Robert felt as lonely as before when the other boys tried to find out what kind of a boy he was.

D. The other boys did not want to make Robert feel less lonely.

7. Why would it not be easy for Robert to prove himself?

A. Because he was not sure if he was really strong.

B. Because he was new and was not wanted in the street.

C. Because the other boys had found out what kind of a boy he was.

D. Because he must choose the best one among different ways.

8. When did Robert decide to prove himself by playing basketball?

A. After he had thought about the two wrong ways.

B. Long before he moved into the street.

C. When the other boys came down to the playground.

D. As soon as he showed what he was made of in front of the other boys.

9. What did the biggest of the group mean by shaking his head?

A. He did not want to say anything about what Robert had done.

B. He had not thought Robert could play so wonderfully.

C. He did not want to make friends with Robert.

D. He did not think Robert played basketball well.

10. The name of the story should be _______.

A. Three Ways to Prove Oneself　　B. Robert Is Lonely

C. Just One of the Boys　　D. A Saturday Basketball Game

情景写作——根据要求完成下列内容

根据汉语提示，写一篇 80 个词左右的文章。题目是 The Importance of Learning English。

在现代社会中，英语变得越来越重要。在许多国家英语作为一门外语被广泛使用。世界上大部分的商业信件都是用英语写成的；世界上 3/4 的书和报纸都是用英语印刷的；互联网上的许多信息也是英文的。此外，中国与外国的交流也越来越多，中国的对外开放政策和加入 WTO 都激励着更多的人学习英语。英语已经成为连接不同国家人们的一座桥梁。年轻人如果想拥有一个更美好的未来，必须学好英语。

____

____

____

____

____

同步拓展训练 29

Lesson 81~82

听写检测——根据要求听写下列内容

Part A: 单词听写——听光盘录音，将听到的每个单词依次写在下面的横线上。

1.________	2.________	3.________
4.________	5.________	6.________
7.________	8.________	9.________
10.________	11.________	12.________
13.________	14.________	15.________
16.________	17.________	18.________
19.________	20.________	21.________
22.________	23.________	24.________
25.________	26.________	27.________
28.________	29.________	30.________
31.________	32.________	

Part B: 句子听写——听光盘录音，把课文内容听写在下面的横线上。

1.________________________________

2.________________________________

3.________________________________

4.________________________________

5.________________________________

6.________________________________

7.________________________________

8.________________________________

9.________________________________

10.________________________________

汇游戏——根据汉语提示，将数字序号对应的单词填入表格中

横向提示		纵向提示	
横向提示	1. *v.*逃跑；4. *n.*动物，生物 9. *adj.*上了年纪的；11. *n.*黑暗 12. *v.*行礼；15. *n.*来复枪，步枪 16. *adj.*闪闪发光的；18. *adv.*有时候，偶尔 19. *v.*拖 23. *adv.*大胆地 25. *n.*囚犯 26. *adv.*迅速地 27. *n.*海员，水手 28. *n.*怪物	纵向提示	2. *adj.*猛烈的；3. *adj.*强大的，有力的 5. *adv.*最后，终于；6. *v.*闪耀 7. *n.*渔民，渔夫；8. *adv.*明显地 10. *v.*认识到，实现；13. *n.*制服 14. *v.*发现；16. *n.*海员 17. *adj.*奇怪的，不寻常的 20. *adj.*灰白的 21. *n.*打击 22. *n.*肩 24. *n.*桨鱼

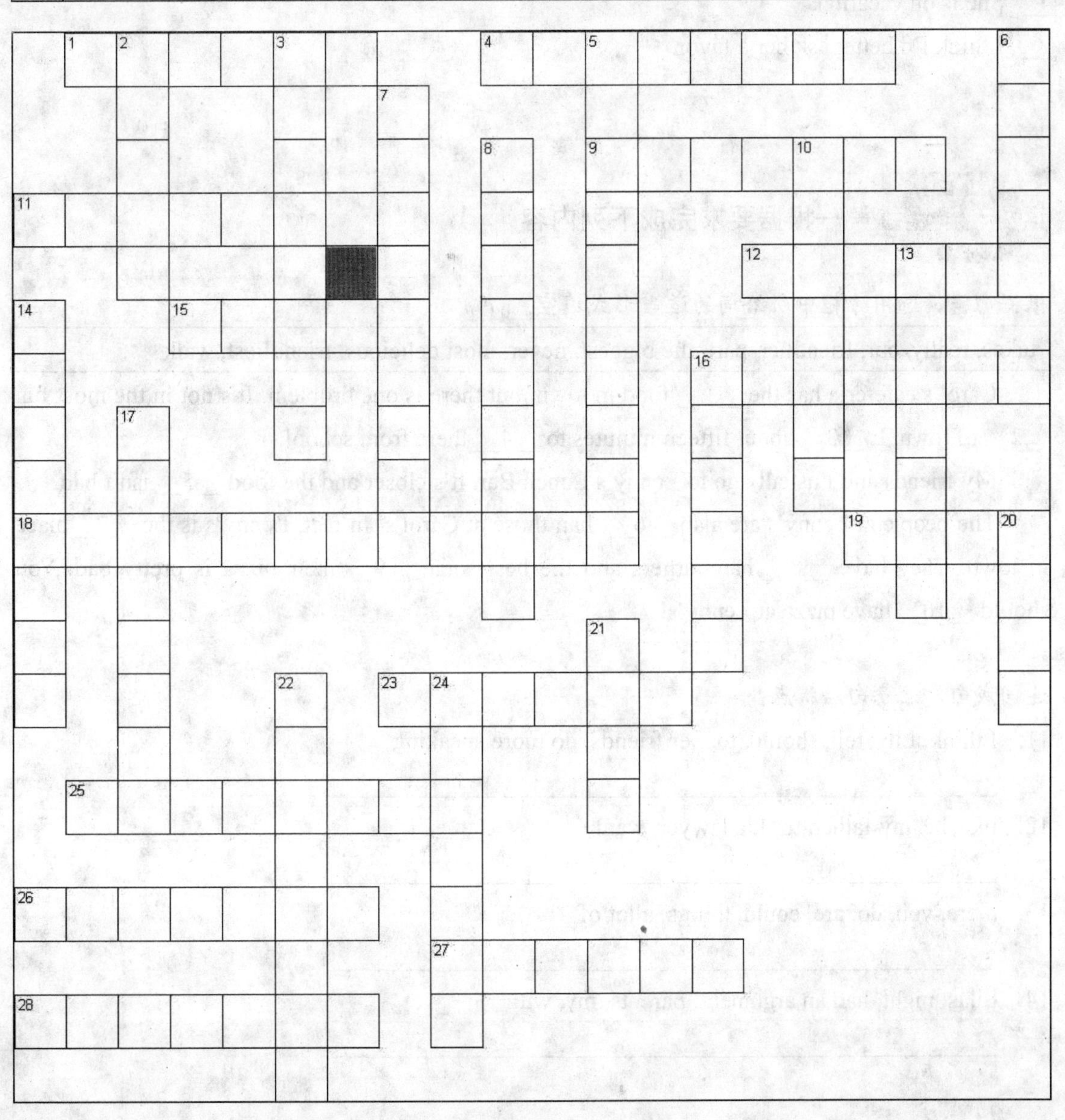

口语造句——根据要求完成下列内容

将下列句子排序成对话，把序号写在句子前面的横线上。

__ Why don't you ask Sophie?

__ Mary, will you and your husband be able to go to the dance with us this Saturday?

__ Then how about your mother-in-law?

__ Oh, we'd love to go, if we can get a baby-sitter.

__ Let's keep our fingers crossed.

__ She is on vacation.

__ I think I'd better ask her a favor.

语法精练——根据要求完成下列内容

根据句意，选用方框中所给词的适当形式填空。

takes, really, but, friendlier, part, the biggest, never, most delicious, friendliest, walk

Carol's cafeteria has the __1__ food in town, but there is one problem. It's not in the most fun __2__ of town. It __3__ about fifteen minutes to __4__ there from school.

My friends and I usually go to Lenny's Lunch Bar. It's closer and the food __5__ isn't bad.

The people at Lenny's are also __6__ than those at Carol's. In fact, Lenny's is the __7__place in town. They have __8__ hamburgers and the best soda, __9__ their pizza is pretty bad. You should __10__ have pizza at Lenny's!

连词成句，注意句后标点。

11. I think, Lily, tell, should, to, her friends, do more speaking

____.

12. like, be, my father, to, I, a lawyer, want

____.

13. there, you, do, are, could, things, a lot of

____.

14. I, last night, had an argument, parents, my, with

____.

15. that, goes, it, everything, well, seems

____.

16. he, as, same, haircut, the, do, I, has

____.

17. me, popular, best friend, than, is, my, more

____.

阅读理解——根据要求完成下列内容

阅读下面的文章，并选择正确答案。

Man has been to the moon. It has been the first step to the future travels in space. The moon is much nearer to the earth than all the planets. Venus, the nearest planet to the earth is millions of kilometers away! Travelling to the planets will be man's next step. It will be more difficult than traveling to the moon and certainly more exciting.

In 1997, an American spaceship reached Mars, the second nearest planet to the earth. A wonderful robot slowly walked on the planet and worked hard. It sent a lot of information back to the earth. The most exciting piece was that there used to be a lot of water on Mars. The American scientists wanted to find the answer to the question, "Is there any life in Mars?" Unluckily, no life was found there, but American scientists do not lose heart. Russian spaceships have found that it is so hot on Venus that there must be no life there.

Spaceship of the future will be bigger and faster. They will be able to carry people for travels to the moon or the planets.

Man may in the future find planets like the earth and make them his home. But there is still a long, long way to go. Man should learn to know that the earth will be his only home for a long time and begin to love and take good care of it.

1. The first step to the future travels in space is the ________.

A. travelling to Mars　　B. travelling to the moon

C. travelling to Venus　　D. travelling to the sun

2. The nearest planet to the earth is ________.

A. Mars　　B. Venus　　C. the moon　　D. the sun

3. The American scientists ________ that they can find living things on Mars.

A. believe　　B. are sure　　C. are not sure　　D. think

4. There must be no life on Venus because ________.

A. there is little are there B. it is too cold there

C. there is no water there D. it is too hot there

5. It will be possible for people to travel to the moon or the planets in the future because spaceships________.

A. will be bigger B. will be faster

C. will be comfortable D. will be bigger and faster

If you visit London nowadays, you will see a lot of buses and cars on the road, you will also see a lot of bikes because nowadays more and more people travel by bike.

There are a lot of reasons for this. First, it's very cheap to use a bike, and it's quick too. You often wait for a bus for half an hour. When the bus comes, there are so many other buses and cars on the roads that the bus moves very slowly. The underground train is quick but very expensive and often crowded.

I traveled to work by bus for about four years. I often arrived at work late, and tired. Then one day, about two years ago, a colleague said, "I go to work by bike, why don't we travel together?"

"Because my bike's old," I answered, "and there are so many buses and cars on the road. I will feel frightened..."

"You needn't feel frightened !" said my friend, "If you follow me and we ride slowly, you will be fine."

Although we went slowly, we arrived at work quickly. The bus ride took forty minutes and the bike ride took half an hour!

The next day I bought myself a new bike. Now I don't feel afraid. I love cycling to work. I take a different road every day. I arrive at work very quickly. I've got a little more money now, and very important, I feel fit and well.

Many people think in the same way as I do. That's why you see a lot of bikes on the road. Who knows, perhaps in the future we'll have roads for bicycles only. I hope so!

6. In London nowadays there are________.

A. not many bikes on the road but a lot of buses and cars

B. lots of bikes, buses and cars on the road

C. a lot of bikes but not many cars and buses

D. a lot of people walking on the roads

7. Buses move slowly________.

A. because there are a lot of other buses and cars on the road too

B. although there are a lot of other buses on the roads

C. as there aren't many other buses on the roads

D. for there are many bikes on the roads

8. The writer_________ .

A. traveled to work by bus four years ago

B. always arrived at work late

C. stopped going to work by bus two years ago

D. stopped going to work by bike two years ago

9. A lot of people_________ .

A. agree with the writer about cycling in London

B. are now rich and important

C. don't agree with the writer about cycling in London

D. are making roads for bicycle only

10. After cycling to work, the writer wasn't always late for work, was he? _________.

A. No, he was　　　　B. Yes, he was

C. No, he wasn't　　　　D. Yes. he wasn't

情景写作——根据要求完成下列内容

根据以下要点，写出有关北京举办 2008 年奥运会的短文。

1. 北京 2008 年将举办奥运会，全国人民都为之骄傲。
2. 此次奥运会将进一步加深世界各国人民之间的相互了解，促进中国经济的快速发展。
3. 北京人也正全力以赴为奥运会做准备，他们正忙于学英语和建造更多的建筑物。

英文提示：

Olympic Games, proud, develop, fast, economy, try one's best, get ready for, be busy doing, build.

____

____

____

____

____

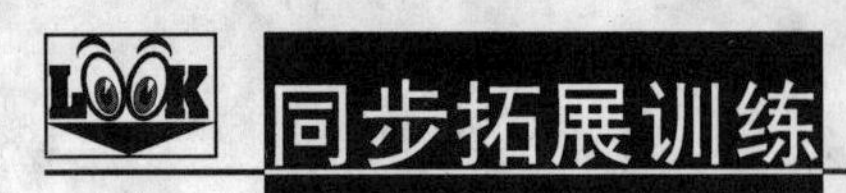

同步拓展训练 30

Lesson 83~84

听写检测——根据要求听写下列内容

Part A: 单词听写——听光盘录音，将听到的每个单词依次写在下面的横线上。

1.______	2.______	3.______
4.______	5.______	6.______
7.______	8.______	9.______
10.______	11.______	12.______
13.______	14.______	15.______
16.______	17.______	18.______
19.______	20.______	21.______
22.______	23.______	24.______
25.______	26.______	27.______
28.______	29.______	30.______
31.______	32.______	

Part B: 句子听写——听光盘录音，把课文内容听写在下面的横线上。

1.______

2.______

3.______

4.______

5.______

6.______

7.______

8.______

9.______

10.______

词汇游戏——根据汉语提示，将数字序号对应的单词填入表格中

横向提示	纵向提示
4. *v.*不赞成，反对；5. *adj.*激进的 9. *v.*减轻 12. *n.*压力，麻烦 14. *n.*程度 18. *n.*感激 22. *adj.*进步的 23. *n.*反对者，对手 25. *n.*脾气，情绪 26. *adv.*正确地，严密地 27. *n.*公共汽车司机	1. *adj.*从前的；2. *v.*正式提出，宣布 3. *adj.*私人的，私有的；6. *adj.*普通的，全面的 7. *adj.*政治的；8. *v.*自动提出，自愿 10. *v.*继续；11. *n.*选举 13. *adj.*怀疑的；15. *n.*条件，环境 16. *n.*大学；17. *n.*协议 19. *n.*入口，门口 20. *v.*打败 21. *v.*退休，隐退 24. *n.*新闻界

1 2 3 4 5 6 7 8 9 10 11 12 13 14 15 16 17 18 19 20 21 22 23 24 25 26 27

口语造句——根据要求完成下列内容

将下列句子排序成对话，把序号写在句子前面的横线上。

__ Is four o'clock all right with you?

__ I'd love to. What time shall I come?

__ Please come and join us for Sunday dinner.

__ Sure, I can come anytime.

__ By the way, when's the big event? I mean your wedding.

__ Why don't you bring your girl friend? Daniel is coming, too. We haven't gotten for ages.

__ We haven't set a date, but we're thinking about an autumn wedding.

语法精练——根据要求完成下列内容

根据句意，用方框中所给词的适当形式填空。

on computers, be, an astronaut, win, suffer, gentleman, make time, except, invite, large

1. My best friend wants to be _______ in the future.
2. They decided to clear up bowling and make it a _______ game again.
3. Kids will study at home_______. They won't go to school.
4. They are very busy with their work, but try to ______ for fun.
5. Will people live ______ 200 years old?
6. We all pass the math exam _______ Li Ping.
7. I think most of the students are _______ from exhaustion and stress.
8. Which movies _______ Oscars at Academy Awards last year?
9. The hole is _______ enough for a young tree.
10. They _______ us to the party last Sunday.

按要求改写下列各句，每空一词，缩写算一词。

11. They built the house two years ago.（改为被动语态）

    The house _______ _______ two years ago.

12. We should plant trees every year.（改为被动语态）

    Trees should _______ _______ every year.

13. They sell pork in the shop.（改为被动语态）

    Pork ________ ________ in the shop.

14. Both she and I are teachers.（改为否定句）

    ______ she ________ I am a teacher.

15. They speak English in class.（改为被动语态）

    English ________ ________ by ________ in class.

16. We often use keys for locking doors.（改为被动语态）

    Keys ________ often ________ ________ locking doors.

17. This jacket is made of wool.（对划线部分提问）

    ________ ________ this jacket made of?

18. A stamp is used for sending letters.（对划线部分提问）

    ________ is a stamp ________ ________?

阅读理解——根据要求完成下列内容

阅读下面的文章，并选择正确答案。

Last Friday, after doing all the family shopping in town, I wanted to have a rest before catching the train. So I bought a newspaper and some chocolate and went into the station coffee shop with a long table to sit at. I put my heavy bag down on the floor, put the newspaper and chocolate on the table to keep a place, and went to get a cup of coffee.

When I came back with the coffee, there was someone sitting next to me. It was one of those strange-looking young men, with dark glasses, torn clothes and long hair. But I wasn't surprised at such a young man. What surprised me most was that he had started to eat my chocolate!

I was quite uneasy about him, but I didn't want to get into trouble. I just looked down at the front page of the newspaper and took a bit of chocolate. The boy looked at me. Then he took a second piece of chocolate. Still I didn't say anything. When he took a third piece, I felt more angry than uneasy. I thought, "Well, I shall have the last piece." and I got it.

The boy gave me a strange look, then stood up. As he left, he shouted out, "This woman is crazy!" Everyone looked at me. That was embarrassing enough. But it was worse when I finished my coffee and got ready to leave. My face went red when I found I had made a mistake.

It wasn't my chocolate. Mine was just under my newspaper.

1. The woman went to town_______.

   A. to do some shopping for her family

   B. to have a rest

   C. to buy some chocolate and coffee

2. When she came back with the coffee, the woman was surprised because_____.

   A. a strange-looking young man was sitting next to her

   B. the young man had dark glassed and torn clothes on

   C. he was eating the chocolate

3. The woman was not happy because_______.

   A. she thought the chocolate was hers

   B. she was afraid of such a young man

   C. it was not polite to eat chocolate

4. The woman found her mistake_______.

   A. after she left the coffee shop

   B. after she finished reading the newspaper

   C. just before she left the coffee shop

Venice is the "Queen" of the Adriatic Sea. Every year thousands of people from all over the world travel to Italy to visit the city. Do you know why they like to go there for a visit?

Venice is a very beautiful city. It is quite different from other cities in the world. There aren't any roads and streets in the city, so there aren't any cars and buses. There are many canals in the city. There is one big canal and one hundred and seventy-seven small canals. People move up and down the canals in boats to go to work, go shopping or visit their friends.

But Venice is sinking. It is going down and the water is going up. In 2040 Venice will be under water. The Adriatic Sea will cover the city. The Venetians love their city and want to stay there. So they want to save Venice from the sea. They do not want to leave. How can they save Venice? They can build some strong huge walls and gates in the sea. The gates will close to keep too much water out. Thus Venice will not sink.

5. From this short article we know Venice is _______.

   A. a very beautiful woman of the Adriatic Sea

   B. the most important woman in Italy

   C. a very important and beautiful place of the Adriatic Sea

   D. the most important city in Italy

6. People from all parts of the world go to visit Venice because _______.

A. there are 177 canals in the city

B. it is sinking into the Adriatic Sea

C. there are a lot of kinds of boats on the canals

D. it is not only beautiful but also quite different from other cities

7. The Venetians usually go to work or visit their friends _______.

A. by bus　　B. by bike　　C. in cars　　D. in boats

8. Year by year the Adriatic Sea _______ and Venice _______.

A. is rising…is sinking　　B. is going down…is going up

C. has risen…has sunk　　D. will go up…will go down

9. Because the Adriatic Sea will cover it, the Venetians _______.

A. have to leave Venice in 2040

B. will try to do something to save their city

C. want to stay there until the water covers the city

D. do not love the city any longer

情景写作——根据要求完成下列内容

根据中文大意，写出意思连贯、符合逻辑、不少于 50 词的短文。所给英文提示词供选用。

假设你叫王明，昨天收到了笔友 David 的 E-mail，得知他不久要到北京来学习中文。他想了解如何学好中文。请你用英文给他回复一封 E-mail，介绍学习中文的体会和方法，提出你的建议，并表达你想帮助他学好中文的愿望。

提示词语：Chinese, be, useful, many foreigners, learn, now, difficult, different from, it is important…, listen, talk, read, write

____

____

____

____

____

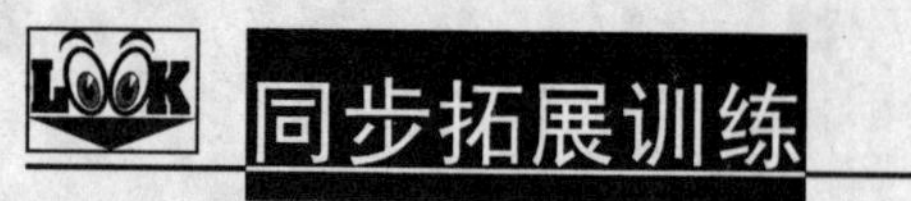

同步拓展训练 31

Lesson 85~86

听写检测——根据要求听写下列内容

Part A: 单词听写——听光盘录音，将听到的每个单词依次写在下面的横线上。

1.________ 2.________ 3.________
4.________ 5.________ 6.________
7.________ 8.________ 9.________
10.________ 11.________ 12.________
13.________ 14.________ 15.________
16.________ 17.________ 18.________
19.________ 20.________ 21.________
22.________ 23.________ 24.________
25.________ 26.________ 27.________
28.________ 29.________ 30.________
31.________ 32.________

Part B: 句子听写——听光盘录音，把课文内容听写在下面的横线上。

1.________________________________
2.________________________________
3.________________________________
4.________________________________
5.________________________________
6.________________________________
7.________________________________
8.________________________________
9.________________________________
10.________________________________

词汇游戏——根据汉语提示，将数字序号对应的单词填入表格中

横向提示		纵向提示	
横向提示	1. *v.*转向；7. *v.*捐助，援助 9. *n.*签名本，相册；12. *n.*沮丧 14. *n.*同伙，伙伴；15. *v.*驾驶 18. *n.*礼物，赠品 19. *adj.*好奇的 20. *n.*园艺 22. *adv.*绝望地 23. *n.*浮标 25. *n.*鼓励 26. *n.*告别	纵向提示	2. *v.*告诉，通知；3. *adv.*缓慢地，轻轻地 4. *v.*漂动，漂流；5. *n.*校长 6. *n.*爱好，嗜好；8. *adv.*不情愿地 10. *v.*评论，谈及；11. *n.*敬意 13. *v.*标记；14. *n.*巧合 15. *n.*快艇 16. *adv.*完全地，一概地 17. *adj.*巨大的 21. *v.*致力于 24. *n.*总数

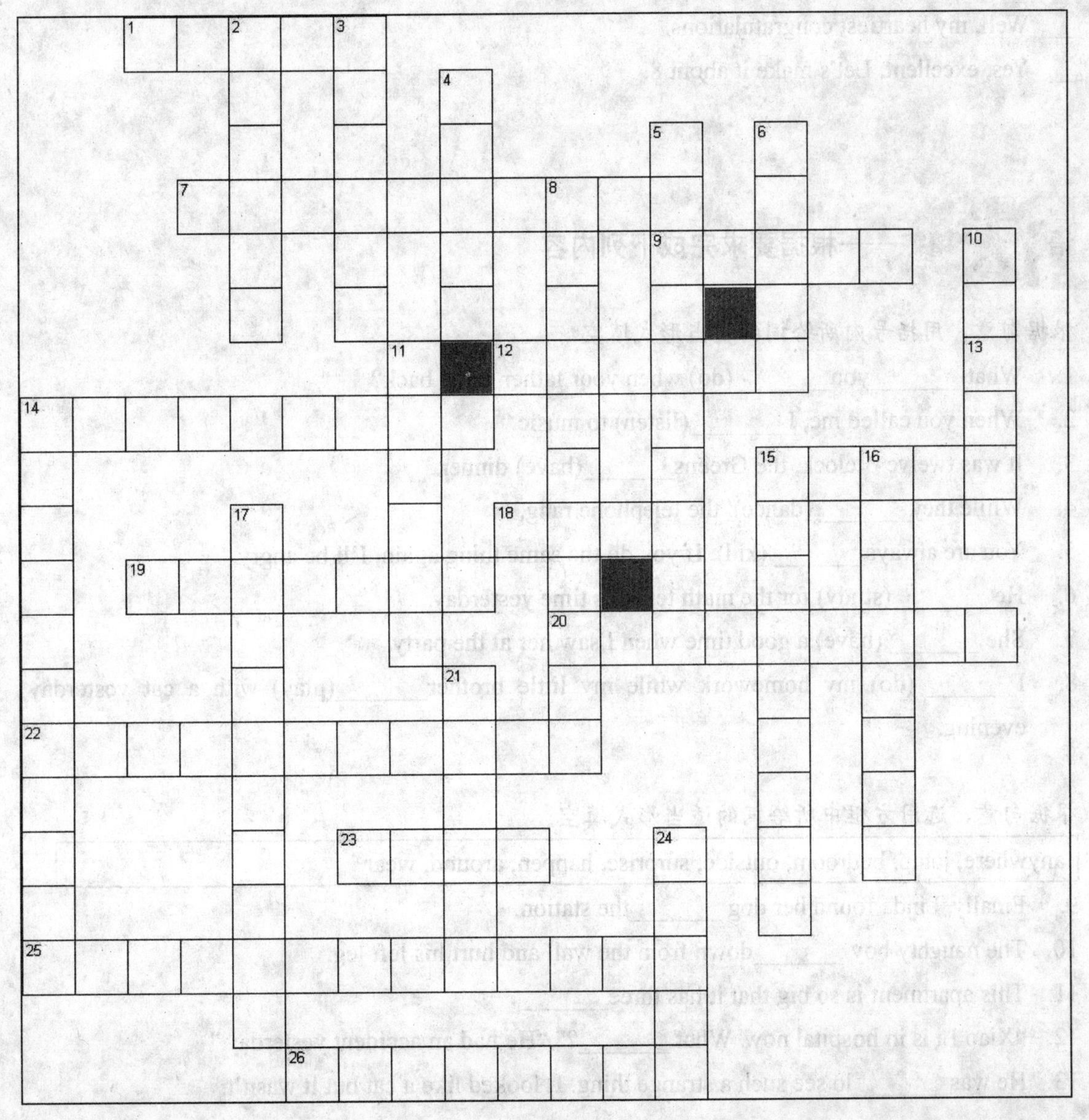

口语造句——根据要求完成下列内容。

将下列句子排序成对话，把序号写在句子前面的横线上。

__ I'd love to, but today happens to be my wedding anniversary and we're going out tonight to celebrate.

__ What about coming with me to my club? You'd get to know quite a lot of interesting people there.

__ Thank you very much., I would manage to come along tomorrow night, if that would suit you.

__ Very well. Thanks.

__ Well, my heartiest congratulations.

__ Yes, excellent. Let's make it about 8.

语法精练——根据要求完成下列内容

根据句意，用括号内所给词的适当形式填空

1. What _______ you_______ (do) when your father came back?
2. When you called me, I_______ (listen) to music.
3. It was twelve o'clock, the Greens_______(have) dinner.
4. While they_______ (dance), the telephone rang.
5. You are always_______ (kid). If you do the same thing again, I'll be angry.
6. He _______ (study) for the math test this time yesterday.
7. She _______ (have) a good time when I saw her at the party.
8. I_______ (do) my homework while my little brother_______(play) with a cat yesterday evening.

根据句意，选用方框中所给词的适当形式填空。

anywhere, jump, bedroom, outside, surprise, happen, around, wear

9. Finally, Linda found her dog _______the station.
10. The naughty boy _______down from the wall and hurt his left leg.
11. This apartment is so big that it has three_______.
12. "Xiao Li is in hospital now. What _______?" "He had an accident yesterday."
13. He was _______lo see such a strange thing. It looked like a cat but it wasn't.

14. Where is my CD? I can't find it_______.
15. Look! Jack _______a T-shirt and jeans.
16. I was doing some washing at _______five in the afternoon.

阅读理解——根据要求完成下列内容

阅读下面的文章，并选择正确答案。

There was once a bad king. All his people hated him very much. One day in a summer he was swimming by himself in a river.

The king was a good swimmer, but while he was in the middle of the river, he was ill. He cried out "Help! Help!" At that time two farmers were working in the field near the river.

They ran over, jumped into the water and saved the king. They didn't know that he was the king until they pulled him out of the water.

The king was very happy, so he said to the farmers, "You have saved my life. Now you may ask for anything, and I'll give it to you."

One of the farmers said, "My son broke his leg last week, and he can't walk. Please send him a good doctor." The king agreed. Then he said to the other farmer. "And what can I do for, old man?"

The old man was very clever. He thought for a few minutes and then he answered, "You can do a very important thing for me." "What's that?" asked the king. He thought that the old man would ask for some money or something else.

"Don't tell anybody that we have saved you," the old farmer answered.

1. Where was the king swimming one day in a summer?

   A. In a river. B. In a lake. C. In the sea.

2. Who came to save him?

   A. His son. B. Two fanners. C. A farmer.

3. When did the farmers know that he was the king?

   A. Before they jumped into the water.

   B. When they were in the water.

   C. After they pulled him out of the water.

4. What did the king do after he was saved?

   A. He promised to be a good king.

B. He promised to give the farmers anything they wanted.

C. He promised not to swim again.

5. Why did the king need help in the water?

A. Because he wasn't good at swimming.

B. Because somebody pulled him into the water.

C. Because he was ill.

The other day I heard an American say to a Chinese student of English "You speak good English." But the students answered, "No, no. My English is very poor." The foreigner was quite surprised at the answer. Thinking he had not made himself understood or the student had not heard him clearly, he said, "Yes, indeed, you speak very well." But the Chinese student still kept saying "No." In the end the foreigner gave up and didn't know what to say.

What is wrong with the student's answer? It is because he didn't accept a compliment as the English people do. He should have said "Thank you!" instead of "No". He actually understood what the American had said. But he thought he was too proud. According to the Western culture, if someone says the dishes you have cooked are very delicious, you should say "Thank you". If someone says to a woman "You look so beautiful with the new clothes on." she should be very happy and answer "Thank you!" In our country we think being modest is a good thing, but in the west, if you are modest and say: "No, I am afraid I can't do it well," then the others will take it for granted that you really can not do it. If you often say "No, you will certainly be looked down upon by others". If asking for a job, one says something like "Yes, I can certainly do it" instead of "Let me have a try on the job.", he or she will expect to get it. So in the west, one should always be confident. Without self-confidence, he can not go anywhere. Confidence is one of great importance to one in a country where competition is quite keen.

6. Why was the American surprised at the Chinese students' answer?

A. Because he wondered whether the student could really speak good English.

B. Because he would not like others to say "No".

C. Because he could hardly hear what the student had said.

D. Because the way to accept a compliment in China is not the same as that in the Western countries.

7. As the student kept saying "No", the American ______.

A. became disappointed

B. got angry

C. lost interest

D. could not continue the talk because he really didn't know what else he could say

8. According to the Western culture, if one is given a compliment, he or she should say ________.

A. Pardon B. Excuse me C. Yes, thanks a lot D. Thank you

9. Why does a man in the West who asks for a job say something like "Yes, I can certainly do it"? ________.

A. Because he is not modest

B. Because he should give an impression that he's just fit for the job in order to get the job

C. Because he could do nothing but speak that way

D. Because he just wanted to have a try.

10. What does the passage tell us? ________

A. The Chinese people are modest while the Westerners are confident.

B. Confidence is more important than modesty.

C. How to accept compliments given by Westerners.

D. About the Western culture.

情景写作——根据要求完成下列内容

假如你叫李明，去年在因特网上结识了一位笔友 Jack。他正在学习中文，常从网上了解中国。他将于下周参观你的学校。请你根据下表所提供的信息，用英语向你的同学介绍 Jack。

Name: Jack	Age: 16
City: London, England	Family: father, mother, a sister
School: Park School	Favourite subject: maths
Interests: music, football	Free Time Activities: surfing the Internet, learning Chinese

参考词汇：activity 活动；surf the Internet 上网

____

____

____

____

____

____

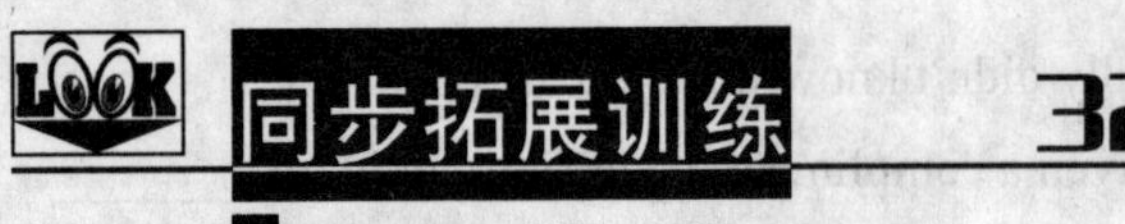

同步拓展训练 32

Lesson 87~88

听写检测——根据要求听写下列内容

Part A: 单词听写——听光盘录音，将听到的每个单词依次写在下面的横线上。

1.______	2.______	3.______
4.______	5.______	6.______
7.______	8.______	9.______
10.______	11.______	12.______
13.______	14.______	15.______
16.______	17.______	18.______
19.______	20.______	21.______
22.______	23.______	24.______
25.______	26.______	27.______
28.______	29.______	30.______
31.______	32.______	

Part B: 句子听写——听光盘录音，把课文内容听写在下面的横线上。

1.______

2.______

3.______

4.______

5.______

6.______

7.______

8.______

9.______

10.______

词汇游戏——根据汉语提示，将数字序号对应的单词填入表格中

横向提示		纵向提示	
横向提示	1. *n.*雇主；6. *v.*坍塌 12. *n.*炸药；13. *n.*容器 16. *adv.*因此，所以；18. *v.*进展，进行 21. *prep.*在……之下 22. *n.*谋杀 25. *v.*陷入，使陷入困境 26. *v.*引起，促成 27. *v.*犯（罪） 28. *v.*救援，营救 29. *n.*层	纵向提示	2. *n.*麦克风；3. *v.*推想，假设 4. *n.*探长；5. *v.*提醒 7. *n.*震动；8. *v.*放下，降低 9. *n.*矿井；10. *n.*其间，其时 11. *v.*确认，证实；14. *adj.*更迟的 15. *adv.*顺利地；17. *n.*不在犯罪现场 19. *n.*地面，表面 20. *adj.*不平常的 23. *v.*钻孔 24. *v.*证明，证实

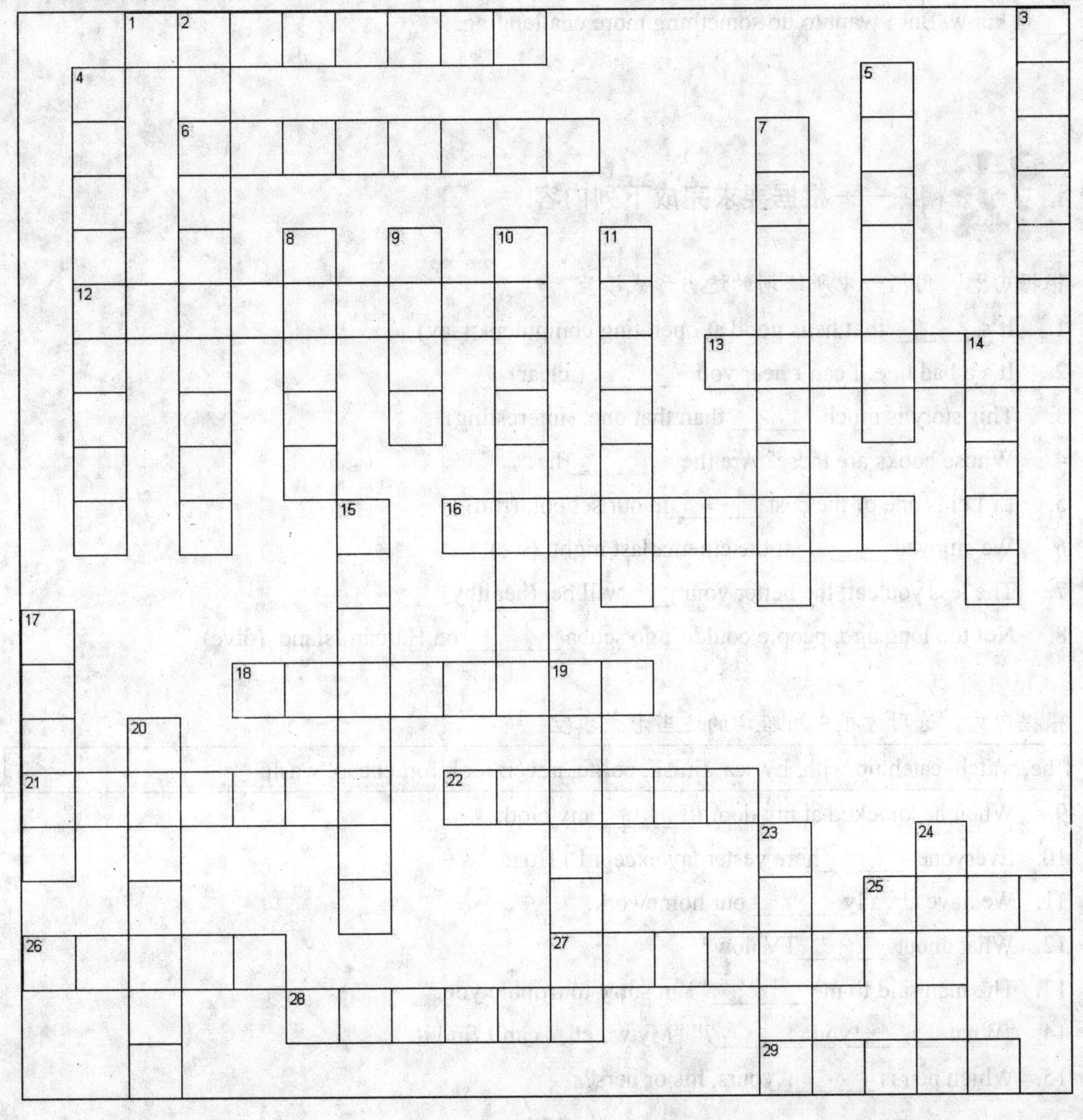

口语造句——根据要求完成下列内容

将下列句子排序成对话，把序号写在句子前面的横线上。

__ Ok. But I'd like to ask you to consider about it carefully.

__ Hello, David. Long time no see.

__ I'm going to resign.

__ Hi, Tom. How nice to see you.

__ Really? But what a good job you now have!

__ What are you doing all these days?

__ I know. But I want to do something more challenging.

语法精练——根据要求完成下列内容

根据句意，用括号中所给词的适当形式填空。

1. It's _______ that he is good at operating computers. (say)
2. It's a bad line. I can't hear you _______. (clear)
3. This story is much _______ than that one. (interesting)
4. Whose books are these? Are they _______ (he)?
5. Li Lei is one of the best _______ in our school, (run)
6. We enjoyed _______ at the cinema last night, (we)
7. The less you eat, the better your ____ will be. (healthy)
8. Not too long ago, people couldn't go scuba _______ on Hainan Island, (dive)

根据句意，选用方框中所给词的适当形式填空。

be, watch, catch up with, by sea, finish, polite, never, look for, cheap, wash

9. When he knocked at my door, I _______ my clothes.
10. Everyone _______ here yesterday except Li Hua.
11. We have already _______ our homework.
12. What about _______ TV now?
13. The man said to me _______ "I'm sorry to trouble you."
14. "What _______ you _______?" "My watch, I can't find it."
15. Which pen is _______,yours, his or hers?

16. If you work hard, you can ________your classmates soon.
17. Last year I went to Da Lian ________.
18. She is always careful. She has________ lost her things.

阅读理解——根据要求完成下列内容

阅读下面的文章，并选择正确答案。

Jess really felt very happy. When he arrived at his seat in the classroom that morning, he found an invitation on his desk. It was from several of his classmates asking him to join them on a camping trip. This was the first time he was asked to join in an out-of-school activity. Why were they asking him now? Noboby seemed to like him. In fact, he had been so lonely that <u>he drowned his feeling with food</u>. As a result, he had put on a lot of weight, and this gave the kids something more to make fun of him.

Cindy, who was standing near Jess when he read the invitation, went out quickly to tell the others that the trick had worked. Everyone was pleased that Jess thought that was true. But there was no camping trip. The whole thing was made up.

At first, Cindy thought it was fun. But later, when Jess told her that he was going to buy a sleeping bag with his savings, Cindy had second thoughts. She knew that Jess's family had little money, and she hated to see him spend his savings on something he would never use. Cindy also hated to tell Jess the truth. Her close friends would be angry with her. What could she do now?

1. Choose the best title for this story.
   A. Jess And His School
   B. Jess And His Friends
   C. An Invitation For Jess
   D. Jess And His Camping Trip
2. The sentence "he drowned his feeling with food" means________ .
   A. he ate a lot to make himself feel less lonely
   B. he asked for a lot of food from his classmates
   C. he brought his food to his classmates
   D. he had a lot of food to put on weight
3. What would happen if Cindy told Jess the truth?
   A. Jess would go on the camping trip himself
   B. Everyone would be angry with Cindy.
   C. Cindy might have trouble with her close friends.

D. Jess would be thankful to his classmates.

4. If Jess really bought a sleeping bag, _______?

A. everyone else would also buy one　　B. it would be the best in the class

C. Cindy would pay for it　　D. he would have it for no use

阅读下面的表格，选择正确答案。

WHERE TO STAY IN BOSWELL YOUR GUIDE TO OUR BEST HOTELS

Name/Address	Room Number	Single Room	Double Room	Special Attractions
FIRST HOTEL 222 Edward Road Tel. 4146433	120	$ 25	$ 35	Air-conditioned rooms French restaurant Night club Swimming pool Shops Coffee shop and bar Telephone, radio and TV set in each room Close to the city center
FAIRVIEW HOTEL 129 North Road Tel. 5915620	450	$ 12	$ 18	Close to the airport Telephone in each room Bar, Restaurant, Garage Swimming pool
ORCHARD HOTEL 233 Edward Road Tel. 6416446	470	$ 15	$ 20	Facing First Hotel European restaurant TV set Coffee shop Nightclub Laundry and dry-cleaning shops
OSAKA HOTEL 12364 Venning Road Tel. 6438200	180	$ 30	$ 50	Air-conditioned rooms Japanese and Chinese Restaurants Swimming pool Large garden Shops

5. If you want to eat Chinese food, you will go to the restaurant in _______.

A. the Fairview Hotel B. the First Hotel

C. the Orchard Hotel D. the Osaka Hotel

6. The cheapest price for a single bed is _______ in _______in Boswell.

A. $ 12, the First Hotel B. $ 15, the Osaka Hotel

C. $ 12, the Fairview Hotel D. $ 25, the Orchard Hotel

7. The number of the rooms in the hotel with the best special attractions is _______.

A. 120 B. 470 C. 450 D. 180

8. If a Japanese traveler likes to eat in a French restaurant, _______is the right place for him to go to.

A. 233 Edward Road B. 12364 Venning Road

C. 222 Edward Road D. 129 North Road

9. Which hotel faces the Orchard Hotel?

A. The First Hotel B. The Osaka Hotel

C. The Fairview Hotel D. No Hotel

情景写作——根据要求完成下列内容

班委会决定将于 6 月 18 日上午举行初三离校前的最后一次班级活动。假如你是班长，请你根据表格中的活动内容，用英语写一篇短文，向你们班外籍老师汇报这次活动的安排。

时间	内容
8:00-9:00	1.谈谈“长大后你想做什么?”；2.谈谈如何过暑假
9:00-10:10	1.唱歌、跳舞；2.表演短剧；3.其他
10:10-11:00	1.打扫教室；2.修理桌椅；3.其他
11:00-11:30	1.拍照；2.互留电话号码、地址；3.其他

Our class is going to have a farewell party on the morning of June 18.______________________

____

____

____

____ At 11:30, the party will be over.

同步拓展训练 33

Lesson 89~90

听写检测——根据要求听写下列内容

Part A: 单词听写——听光盘录音，将听到的每个单词依次写在下面的横线上。

1.________ 2.________ 3.________
4.________ 5.________ 6.________
7.________ 8.________ 9.________
10.________ 11.________ 12.________
13.________ 14.________ 15.________
16.________ 17.________ 18.________
19.________ 20.________ 21.________
22.________ 23.________ 24.________
25.________ 26.________ 27.________
28.________ 29.________ 30.________
31.________ 32.________

Part B: 句子听写——听光盘录音，把课文内容听写在下面的横线上。

1.____
2.____
3.____
4.____
5.____
6.____
7.____
8.____
9.____
10.____

词汇游戏——根据汉语提示，将数字序号对应的单词填入表格中

横向提示		纵向提示	
横向提示	2. *adj.*特别喜爱的；6. *n.*因素 7. *n.*理智，头脑；10. *n.*潜水员 11. *n.*报幕员；13. *v.*吓，使恐怖 16. *adv.*明显地；17. *n.*品种 18. *n.*节目，程序；19. *n.*油煎土豆片 20. *adv.*常常，频繁；24. *n.*鲸 25. *n.*鳐 27. *n.*笼 28. *v.*失败，不及格 29. *adj.*失望的	纵向提示	1. *n.*喜剧；3. *adv.*笨拙地 4. *adv.*不幸地；5. *adj.*巨大的 8. *v.*演出；9. *n.*艺人 12. *n.*鲨鱼；14. *v.*使惊吓 15. *adj.*枯燥，无味；16. *v.*过度捕捞 21. *v.*排队 22. *adj.*地方的，当地的 23. *n.*小错误 26. *n.*鳕鱼 27. *n.*全体工作人员

口语造句——根据要求完成下列内容

将下列句子排序成对话，把序号写在句子前面的横线上。

__ We're in the same boat. With both boys in college, it's been tough. We simply can't afford a vacation this year.

__ Are you taking a vacation this summer?

__ Maybe next year things will be better.

__ What do you mean?

__ Yes, but we're not going anywhere.

__ Everything is sky high. We don't have enough money for a vacation. How about you?

语法精练——根据要求完成下列内容

根据句意，选用方框中所给词的适当形式填空。

burn, travel, not smoke, give, go, be, leave, not hear, good, have

1. The doctor told my father _______any more.
2. We saw a fire _______in the place when we came into the house.
3. They _______to New York for many times.
4. Where is the teacher? She _______to her office.
5. Do you know what time the ship _______?
6. Mrs. Brown _______from her son for nearly one year.
7. Please _______each child one cake.
8. They said they _______a very good summer holiday.
9. We like _______by air very much.
10. Who is the _______teacher in your school?

根据所给中文意思，完成句子。

11. 没有消息就是好消息。

    _______news _______good news.

12. 给予（别人东西）要比收到（别人东西）好。

    It's better to _______ _______ to _______.

13. 鱼儿离不开水。

Fish can't live _______ _______.

14. 你能告诉我校长住在哪里吗？

Could you tell me _______ the headmaster ________?

15. 我不知道一班有多少共青团员。

I don't know _______ _______ League members _______ _______ in Class One.

阅读理解——根据要求完成下列内容

根据短文内容判断正误，正确写 T，错误写 F。

Christmas is the biggest festival of the year, but people in the West enjoy many other festivals too. Here are a few of them:

Saint Valentine's Day: 14 February

Saint Valentine's Day is the day for lovers. On this day, people send a card to the person they love. You do not write your name in the card: the person you love must guess who sent them the card. Some people receive more than one card! Presents husbands and wives often give each other may be roses or chocolates. All these cards and presents give the same message: I love you.

Easter Day: a Sunday in March or April

Easter is a three-day religious holiday. It starts on a Friday called "Good Friday". On this day, people eat a kind of bread called hot cross buns. These buns have a cross drawn on them in sugar. They taste good either hot or cold. Easter Day is the following Sunday. On this day, people eat chocolates in the shape of large eggs. There are usually some sweets inside the eggs. The day after Easter Day is a holiday in many countries. People often travel during Easter to see friends or have a holiday. Easter marks the beginning of spring.

Halloween: 31 October

People believe that ghosts and witches come out at night on Halloween. Young people like to dress up in scary clothes and wear masks on their faces. Children go from house to house playing "trick or treat". They want to receive some sweets; otherwise they will play a trick on the house owner. Some people cut out the inside of a pumpkin, make a scary face on it and put a candle inside it. Then they put the pumpkin in the window of their house to frighten people.

1. Lovers send Valentine cards.
2. The message of the cards and presents given on Saint Valentine's Day is "Happy Valentine's Day."

3. The day after Easter is a holiday.
4. "Trick or treat" is a game where children ask for sweets, or else they will play a trick on someone.
5. They put a pumpkin in their window because they want other people to eat it.

情景写作——根据要求完成下列内容

假定你叫李华，在因特网上看到第九届宁波国际服装节（the 9th Ningbo International Fashion Fair）组委会招聘2008"宁波国际服装节"志愿者（volunteer）的广告。请你用英语写一封简短的邮件，介绍自己的情况（见下表），表示愿意为服装节做一些工作，请组委会考虑并尽早予以答复。

姓名	李华	性别	男	出生年月	1989年5月
就读学校	宁波14中	兴趣爱好	英语口语，电脑，旅游		
电话号码	87856789	E-mail 地址	lihua@163.com		

注意：词数80左右；要求语句连贯

参考词汇：be born, be interested in, do something for, as soon as possible, send somebody an e-mail

____

____

____

____

____

____

同步拓展训练 34

Lesson 91~92

听写检测——根据要求听写下列内容

Part A: 单词听写——听光盘录音，将听到的每个单词依次写在下面的横线上。

1.______ 2.______ 3.______
4.______ 5.______ 6.______
7.______ 8.______ 9.______
10.______ 11.______ 12.______
13.______ 14.______ 15.______
16.______ 17.______ 18.______
19.______ 20.______ 21.______
22.______ 23.______ 24.______
25.______ 26.______ 27.______
28.______ 29.______ 30.______
31.______ 32.______

Part B: 句子听写——听光盘录音，把课文内容听写在下面的横线上。

1.______
2.______
3.______
4.______
5.______
6.______
7.______
8.______
9.______
10.______

词汇游戏——根据汉语提示，将数字序号对应的单词填入表格中

横向提示		纵向提示	
	1. *n.*棚子；5. *v.*按铃 6. *n.*飞行器；9. *n.*卧室 10. *v.*包含；12. *adv.*立刻，马上 14. *n.*门铃；18. *n.*神秘 20. *v.*解释 22. *prep.*向，朝 23. *n.*飞行员 25. *n.*语气，腔调 26. *n.*梯子 27. *n.*照片		1. *adj.*讽刺的，讥笑的；2. *adv.*后来 3. *n.*望远镜；4. *n.*气球 7. *v.*支配，控制；8. *v.*打断，妨碍 11. *adj.*睡着的，睡熟的；13. *v.*下来，下降 15. *adj.*皇家的；16. *v.*侦察 17. *v.*通知，告诉 19. *n.*轨迹，踪迹 21. *v.*忘记 23. *v.*更喜欢，宁愿 24. *adv.*熟（睡）

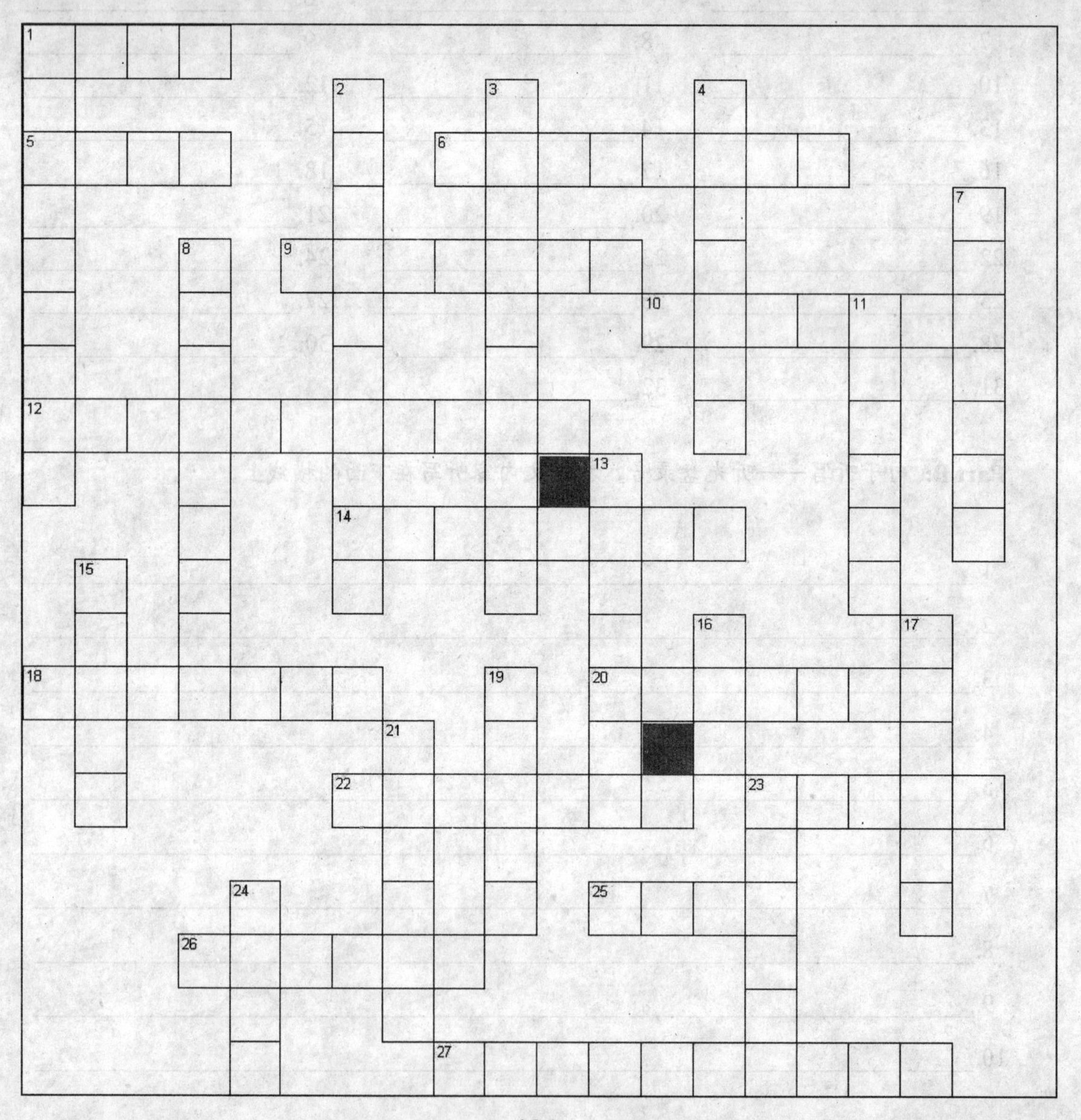

口语造句——根据要求完成下列内容

将下列句子排序成对话，把序号写在句子前面的横线上。

__ Yes, but isn't it your dinner time?

__ I'd like to have you come my house tomorrow evening if you are free.

__ Yes, it surely is. I'm inviting you to dinner.

__ All right. I'll be expecting you around six tomorrow evening.

__ Well, I've nothing in particular to do. But what time shall I come?

__ Is six o'clock convenient for you?

__ Oh, thank you. I'm sure I will come.

语法精练——根据要求完成下列内容

根据句意，用括号中所给词的适当形式填空。

1. They are not Chinese but________. (French)
2. Where is salt________? (produce)
3. Knives are used of________things. (cut)
4. There is a ________door in front of us. (lock)
5. English is the most widely ________in the world. (speak)
6. How ________the strange thing is! (interest)
7. She was ________if it was a real king's hat. (surprise)
8. When was the Palace Museum ________? (build)
9. The big bottle is used for________. You mustn't throw it. (drink)
10. He's waiting for you at the front______ to the building, (enter)

根据句意，选用方框中所给词的适当形式填空。

try one's best, far, dive, delicious, sight-seeing, whether, in a month,on the Internet

11. The food I cook is very ______.
12. Could you tell me _____ that's a fast train or not?
13. London is a little ______ from here, isn't it?
14. Let's go scuba _______.
15. We'll _______to help people who are in trouble.

16. The Greens will be back to New York ______.
17. My uncle is looking for information about Paris ________.
18. Some people go to a place of interest for ______.

阅读理解——根据要求完成下列内容

阅读下面的文章，并选择正确答案。

An old friend from California was going to spend a few days with me. He called me from the station to tell me that he had arrived. I wasn't able to leave the office, but I had got ready for his visit. I told him where my new house was and that I had left the key under the doormat（门垫）. Because I knew it would be very late before I could get home, I asked him to make himself at home and help himself to anything in the fridge.

Two hours later, my friend phoned me from the house. At the moment he said he was listening to some music after a nice meal. He had found two fried eggs, and had helped himself to some cold chicken in the fridge. Now he said he was drinking a glass of orange and he wished me to go back soon. When I asked him if he had any trouble in finding the house, he answered he didn't find the key under the doormat. But the window by the apple tree was open and he climbed in through the window. I listened to this in surprise. There was no apple tree outside my window at all. But there is one by the window of my next door neighbor's house!

1. The writer left the key under the doormat for______.
   A. his uncle B. himself C. his friend D. his children
2. The writer told his friend to look after himself before he got home because____.
   A. he would get home very late
   B. his friend would stay with him for a few days
   C. his friend would not mind that
   D. he would not be able to return home that day
3. His friend told him on the phone that________.
   A. he found the house without any trouble
   B. he enjoyed himself very much in the house
   C. he found the key very easily
   D. he liked his new house

4. How did the writer's friend come into the house?

A. He used the key to open the door.

B. He got in easily because the door was open.

C. He got in through the window.

D. He knocked at the door.

5. Which of the followings is right?

A. The writer's friend went into the wrong house.

B. The writer's friend liked the neighbor's house.

C. The writer's house was easy to find.

D. The window of the writer's room was open.

The weather was very cold. Snow was falling. The roads were covered with ice and a strong wind was blowing. It was not a goodnight to be outside.

Thomas, however, had to walk home from work. He had to walk along a country road.

As he walked the cold wind beat against his chest.

"I will be warmer," he thought, "I wear my coat backwards."

He stopped walking for a moment, took off his coat, and put it back on backwards.

"That's much better," he thought, and walked on through the thickly falling snow.

A few minutes later a car hit him. The driver of the car had not seen him soon enough. When he tried to stop, the car skidded on the ice.

The driver got out of his car and ran to help Thomas.

Soon a police car arrived. The policeman ran to look at Thomas who was lying on the ground.

"I'm afraid he's dead," he told the driver.

The driver could not believe this.

"He can't be dead," he cried, "I hardly touched him. Look at my car. There's not a mark on it."

"He's dead," the policeman said. "There is no doubt."

"Yes," the driver of the car said, "but only to turn his head around the right way."

6. Why was Thomas walking in such bad weather?

A. He had to get home from work. B. His car had broken down.

C. He had missed his bus. D. He was lost.

7. How did Thomas make himself warmer?

A. He walked quickly. B. He wore a lot of clothes.

C. He put his coat on backwards. D. He drank some hot tea.

8. What happened to Thomas?

A. His car skidded on the ice.　　B. He was slipped on the ice.

C. He died of the cold.　　D. He was hit by a car.

9. Who killed Thomas?

A. The story doesn't tell us　　B. The driver of the car

C. The policeman　　D. He killed himself

10. The best title of the story would be _______.

A. A Traffic Accident　　B. A Cold Winter Night

C. Right Way or Wrong Way　　D. Don't Help Others

情景写作——根据要求完成下列内容

英语是中学的一门重要课程，然而，有的同学因学习方法不当而学习效果不佳，有的同学因畏惧困难而放弃了英语学习。针对这些现象，《学生英文报》展开了“怎样学好英语”的大讨论，请你以 Talking about English learning 为题，用英语给该报投一篇稿子，谈谈你对英语学习的看法以及你学习英语的成功经验，并给学习有困难的同学提几条你对学好英语的建议。要点如下：

1. Why do you learn English?
2. How do you learn English?
3. Your suggestions

____

____

____

____

____

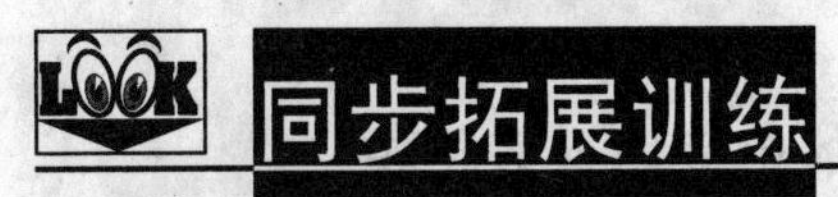

同步拓展训练 35

Lesson 93~94

听写检测——根据要求听写下列内容

Part A: 单词听写——听光盘录音，将听到的每个单词依次写在下面的横线上。

1.________ 2.________ 3.________
4.________ 5.________ 6.________
7.________ 8.________ 9.________
10.________ 11.________ 12.________
13.________ 14.________ 15.________
16.________ 17.________ 18.________
19.________ 20.________ 21.________
22.________ 23.________ 24.________
25.________ 26.________ 27.________
28.________ 29.________ 30.________
31.________ 32.________

Part B: 句子听写——听光盘录音，把课文内容听写在下面的横线上。

1.________
2.________
3.________
4.________
5.________
6.________
7.________
8.________
9.________
10.________

词汇游戏——根据汉语提示，将数字序号对应的单词填入表格中

横向提示		纵向提示	
	1. *v.*使竖立；2. *v.*建造，构造 6. *n.*构架，框架；9. *adj.*实际的，真实的 12. *adv.*特别，尤其；13. *v.*指导，传授 14. *v.*运送 19. *n.*三轮车 21. *n.*港口 23. *n.*金属 25. *n.*铜 26. *n.*自由 27. *v.*支持，支撑		1. *n.*试验；3. *adv.*正式 4. *n.*雕像；5. *n.*纪念碑 7. *adj.*勉强的，不愿意的；8. *adj.*水下的 10. *n.*外形，轮廓；11. *n.*入口，门口 15. *n.*底座；16. *n.*场地 17. *adj.*高尚的，壮丽的 18. *v.*赠送 20. *v.*比赛，对抗 22. *v.*设计，计划 24. *v.*喘气

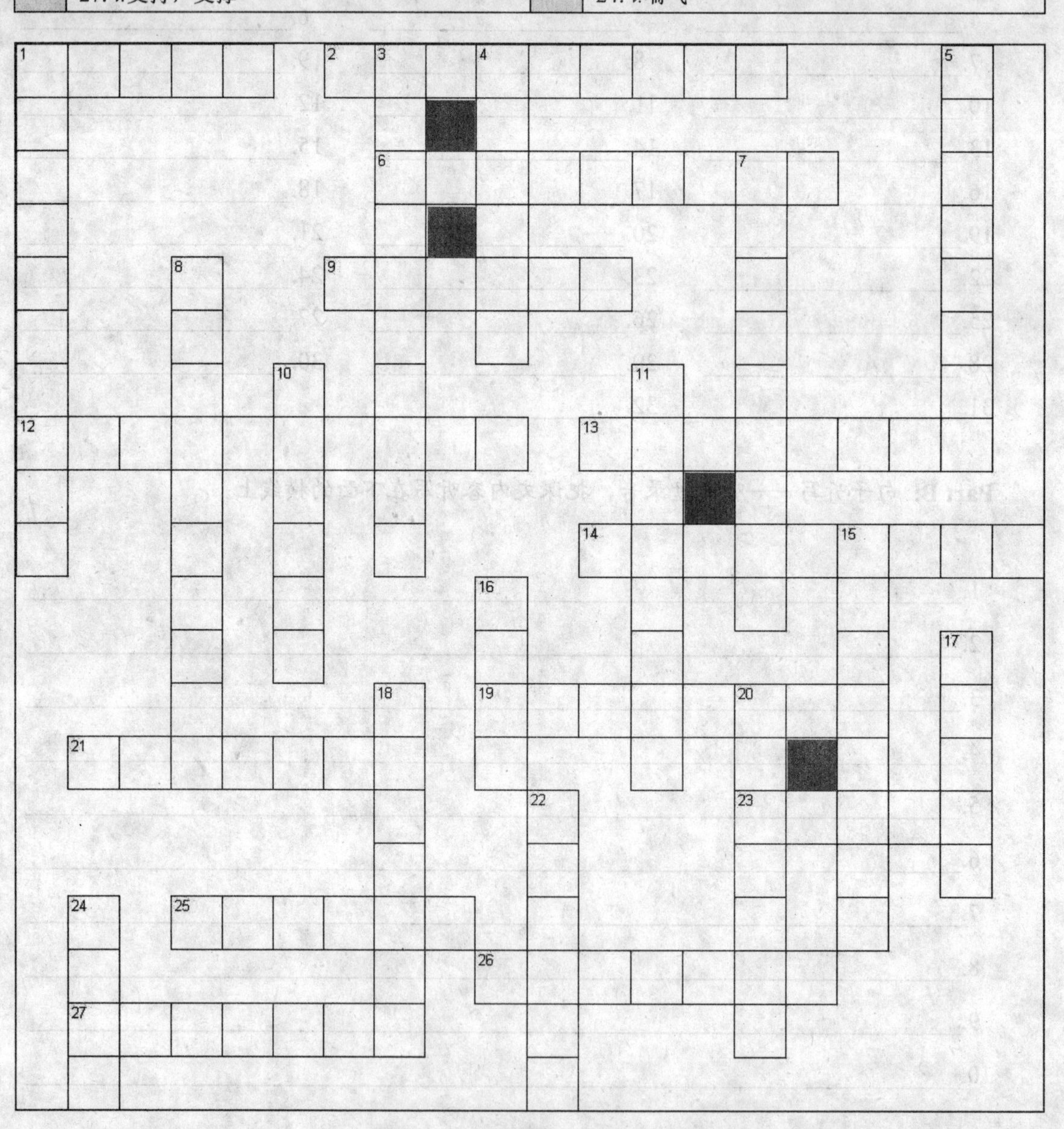

口语造句——根据要求完成下列内容

将下列句子排序成对话，把序号写在句子前面的横线上。

__ Yes, I am.

__ Are you by any chance going to the airport?

__ My car is here. I can give you a ride.

__ No, not at all. I'm going there anyway.

__ How are you going to get there?

__ Thank you very much. It's very kind of you.

__ By taxi.

__ Don't let me trouble you.

语法精练——根据要求完成下列内容

根据句意，用括号中所给词的适当形式填空。

1. Our classroom is 4 metres _______. (widely)
2. She has been to America several _______. (time)
3. Today is Tree _______Day. (plant)
4. We've already planted _______of trees since last year. (million)
5. The _______you study, the more you will learn. (hard)
6. The _______month of the year is March. (three)
7. Our room is the_______of the three. (big)
8. You must see your uncle as _______as possible. (often)
9. My sister is_______than I. (careful)
10. I will go to the cinema this evening. Would you like to come with_______? (I)

按要求改写下列各句，每空一词。

11. Both my father and I went to the cinema yesterday evening.（改为否定句）

    _______ my father _______ I went to the cinema yesterday evening.

12. You must hand in your homework now.（改为被动语态）

    Your homework _______ _______ _______in now.

13. The key is used for locking our classroom door.（就划线部分提问）

________ ________ the key ________ for ?

14. I bought the car last year.（改为被动语态）

    The car ________ ________ last year.

15. She has had the bike for 5 years.（就划线部分提问）

    ________ ________ has she had the car ?

16. Must I water the flowers every day?（给出否定回答）

    ________, you ________.

17. "Don't be late for school." Tom's father said to him.（改为一个简单句）

    Tom's father ________ Tom ________ ________ ________ late for school.

18. "Would you like to go to the party?" Meimei asked me.（改为一个主从复合句）

    Meimei asked me ________ I ________ ________ to go to the party.

19. She's got some books about art, ________ she?（改成反意疑问句）

20. There are some apples in the basket.（改为否定句）

    There ________ ________ apples in the basket.

阅读理解——根据要求完成下列内容

阅读下面的文章，并选择正确答案。

Mabel is a cashier in a big shop in New York. People can buy medicine, watches, sweets, and many other things. They pay Mabel for the things they buy.

At the shop people can also buy lottery tickets. They pay one dollar for a lottery ticket. There are pictures on the ticket. Some pictures are winning pictures. Some pictures are losing pictures. Most people win nothing. Some people win two dollars. A few lucky people win thousands of dollars.

One day Mabel was working at the shop. She sold three lottery tickets to a woman. The woman looked at the pictures on the tickets. Then she threw the tickets on the counter and walked away. "These are losing pictures", she thought.

Mabel picked up the tickets and looked at them. She was surprised. Then she was excited. One ticket was a winning ticket.

"Excuse me!" Mabel called to the woman. "You won $ 50000!"

The woman came back to the counter. She took the winning ticket and looked at it. "You are right." she said. "I won $ 50000." The woman walked away slowly, looking at the ticket again and again. Then she turned around. "Thank you! Thank you very much!" she said to Mabel.

Why did Mabel give the woman the ticket? Why didn't she keep the ticket? Didn't she want to get $ 50000?

"Of course I want the money," Mabel said. "But it was her ticket. It wasn't my ticket."

"Well, I am sorry that you are not rich," her mother said. "But I am happy that you are honest."

1. Mabel ______at the big shop .

A. receives and pays out money　　B. puts things on the shelves

C. helps people choose things　　D. carries things for old people

2. One lottery ticket costs________.

A. nothing　　B. three dollars　　C. two dollars　　D. one dollar

3. The woman was lucky because ______ .

A. all her three tickets were winning tickets

B. all her three tickets were losing tickets

C. Mabel found the winning ticket and gave it back to her

D. she found the winning ticket by herself

4. Mabel didn't keep the winning ticket because_______.

A. she won $ 50000, too

B. her mother told her not to do so

C. she didn't want to have anything that was not hers

D. her mother was very rich

5. When Mabel's mother learned about her story, she was very_______.

A. angry　　B. surprised　　C. disappointed　　D. happy

Babies love chocolate and sometimes they also eat the paper around it. My cat enjoys a meal of good, thick paper, old letters, for example. She doesn't like newspapers very much.

Of course, the best paper comes from wood. Wood comes from trees, and trees are plants. Vegetables and fruit are plants too, and we eat a lot of them. So can we also eat wood and paper.

Scientists say: "All food comes in some way from plants." Well, is that true? Animals eat grass and grow fat. Then we eat their meat. Little fish eat little sea-plants; then bigger fish swim along and eat the…Chickens eat bits of grass and give us…Think for a minute. What food not come from plants in some way?

Scientists can do wonderful things with plants. They can make food just like meat and cheese. And they can make it without the help of animals. It is very good food too. Now they have begun to say: "We make our paper from wood. We can also make food from wood. The next thing is not very difficult." What is the next thing? Perhaps it is food from paper. Scientists say: "We can turn paper into food. It will be good, cheap food too; cheaper than meat or fish or eggs."

So please keep your old books and letters. (Don't feed them to your cat) One day, soon, they will be on your plate. There is nothing like a good story for breakfast.

6. What does the best paper come from?

A. Vegetables B. Food C. Plant D. Wood

7. From the passage, we can infer that_________ do not come from plants in some way.

A. few kinds of food B. meat and fish

C. cheese and chickens D. wood and paper

8. What's the main idea of this passage?

A. All food comes from plants in some way.

B. It will not be long before food can be made from paper.

C. Scientists can do wonderful things with plants.

D. Scientists can make food without the help of animals.

9. The writer asks us to keep our old books and letters because_________.

A. they are useful for reading

B. they may be used to feed cats

C. we can make food from them soon

D. we can read them before meals

10. The best title for the passage is_________.

A. Food from Plants

B. Plants, Animals and Food

C. Keep Your Books and Letters

D. What Can We Make with Old Paper?

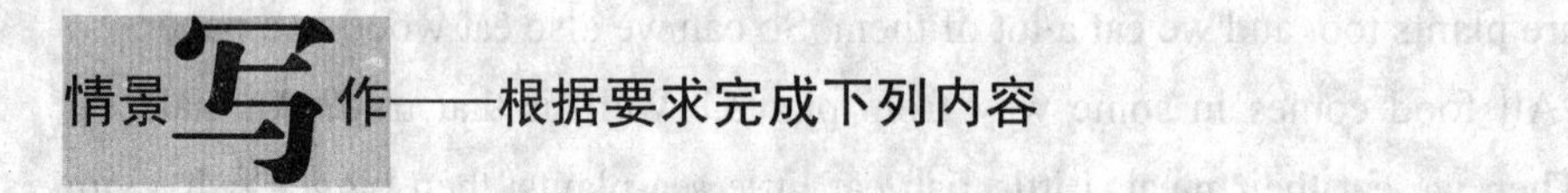

请以 How People Spend Their Holiday 为题写一篇文章。

同步拓展训练 36

Lesson 95~96

听写检测——根据要求听写下列内容

Part A: 单词听写——听光盘录音，将听到的每个单词依次写在下面的横线上。

1.________ 2.________ 3.________
4.________ 5.________ 6.________
7.________ 8.________ 9.________
10.________ 11.________ 12.________
13.________ 14.________ 15.________
16.________ 17.________ 18.________
19.________ 20.________ 21.________
22.________ 23.________ 24.________
25.________ 26.________ 27.________
28.________ 29.________ 30.________
31.________ 32.________

Part B: 句子听写——听光盘录音，把课文内容听写在下面的横线上。

1.________________________________
2.________________________________
3.________________________________
4.________________________________
5.________________________________
6.________________________________
7.________________________________
8.________________________________
9.________________________________
10.________________________________

词汇游戏——根据汉语提示，将数字序号对应的单词填入表格中

横向提示		纵向提示	
	1. *adj.*感人的；2. *adj.*苍白的，无力的 5. *v.*呼喊，惊叫；6. *n.*大使馆 7. *n.*幻想故事；8. *v.*投，掷 13. *n.*大使；15. *v.*考虑，照顾 16. *adj.*可怕的，令人吃惊的；21. *n.*灯笼 23. *n.*景象，壮观，场面 25. *n.*洞，孔 26. *v.*欢迎 27. *v.*漂流 28. *n.*子弹		1. *n.*混乱，脏乱；3. *n.*机会，场合 4. *n.*节日；9. *v.*指导，带领 10. *n.*旅行，旅程 11. *adv.*冷淡地，枯燥无味地 12. *adj.*正确的，精确的；14. *adv.*肯定地 17. *n.*天，天堂；18. *adj.*不幸的 19. *n.*地下室 20. *adj.*愉快的，高兴的 22. *v.*派任 24. *n.*人群

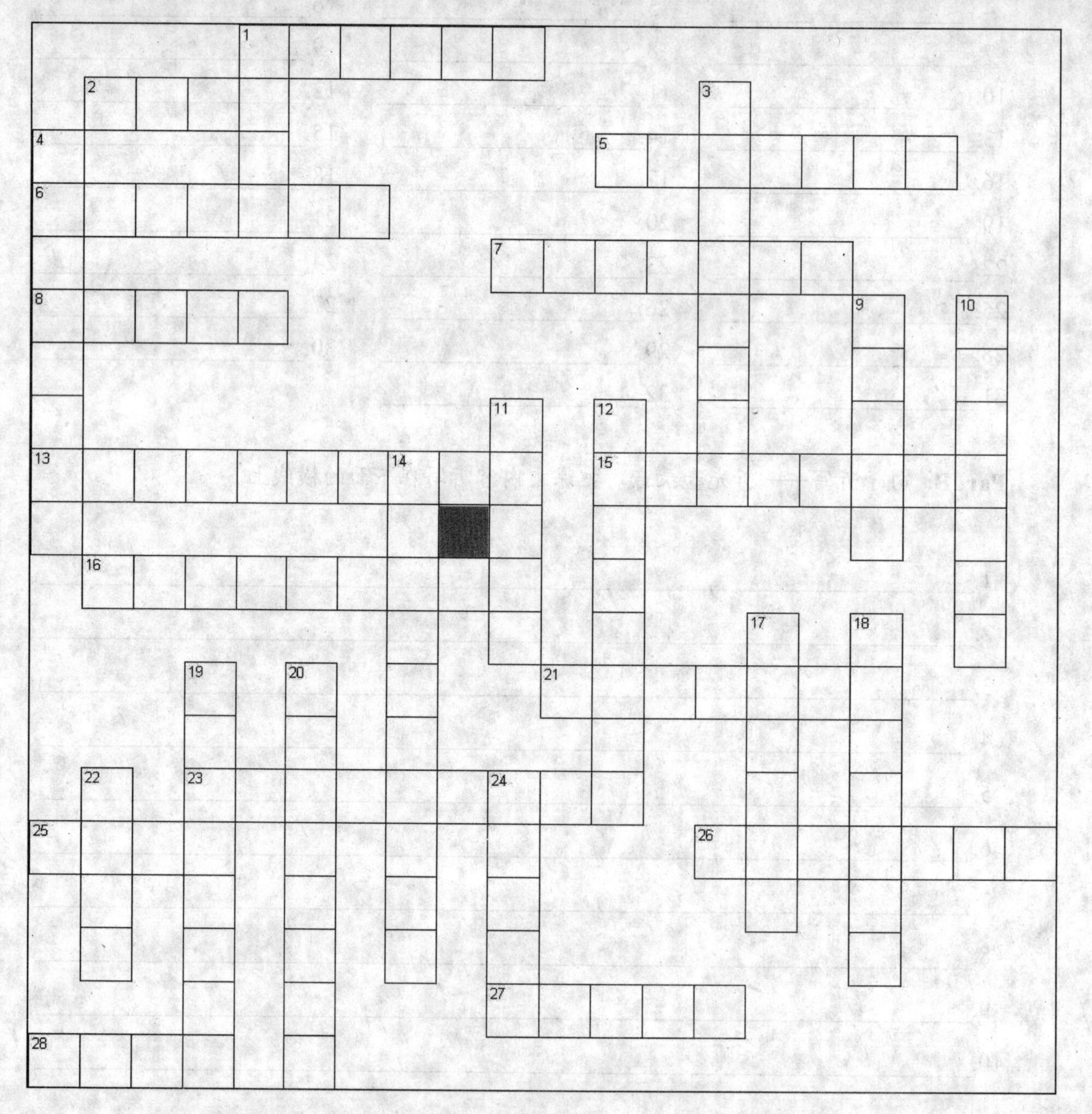

口语造句——根据要求完成下列内容

将下列句子排序成对话，把序号写在句子前面的横线上。

__ That does look easy. I think I'll make some tonight.

__ Would you like some cookies? I just made them.

__ No, they're really quite easy, Wait a minute, I've got the recipe right here. See these are the ingredients, and then you just follow the directions.

__ Thank you. Yes, I would.

__ I guess I'll try a chocolate one first. Mmm… this is delicious. Are they hard to make?

__ These are chocolate, and those are almond-flavored.

语法精练——根据要求完成下列内容

连词成句，注意句后标点。

1. college, think, go, should, you, to, I

______________________________.

2. going, he, travel, world, the, is, around, to

______________________________.

3. Mr., Li, by, three, a, teaching, years, made, living, ago

______________________________.

4. you, bus, party, if, take, to, the, the, you, be, will, late

______________________________.

5. don't, people, who, in, trouble, laugh, at, the, are

______________________________.

6. since, have, I, the , piano, been, practising, 10:30

______________________________.

7. running, Maria, been, minutes, 15, has , for

______________________________.

8. Mary, he, has, last, since, known, year.

______________________________.

9. Peter, he, years, was, Chinese, been, old, studying, since, six , has

____.

10. we, our, savings, have, run , out of

____.

根据句意，选用方框中所给词的适当形式填空。

sing, join, work, repair, knock at, teach, buy, write, like, leave

11. When I was doing my homework, I heard someone _____ the door.
12. Your radio can ________in two days.
13. Listen! Who ________in the next room?
14. She ________in the middle school for fourteen years.
15. These books ________by our English teachers.
16. ________you ________ Chinese food ?
17. Jane______this hat last week.
18. The train _______when he got to the station.
19. She ________the League last year.
20. Uncle Wang_________ in the workshop at nine this morning.

阅读理解——根据要求完成下列内容

根据短文所提供的信息填写下面的表格

Paul McCartney is one of the greatest stars of the twentieth century. Paul comes from an ordinary family, but he is now the third richest man in Europe. He has worked at music for nearly forty years and today he is one of the world's most famous musicians.

He was born in Liverpool, England, on 18th June, 1942. He started to play the guitar seriously when he was fourteen. When he was fifteen he met and formed a band with another boy from Liverpool, John Lennon. This was perhaps the most important point in his life.

In 1961, Paul and John helped to form the Beatles, which became the most successful band ever in the history of rock music. Their second song, Please please me, went straight to the top of the British chart in 1963. During the 1960s the Beatles continued to make successful songs. But in 1970, after they had been playing together for ten years, the band broke up.

In 1972, Paul formed a new band, Wings, but it was never as successful as the Beatles. And it broke up after seven years. Since the 1980s Paul has written pop music and has worked on films. He has also opened a school in Liverpool.

In 1969, Paul got married. He loved his wife Linda very much. They had children and a happy life for many years. But Linda died in April 1998. Paul was very sad. Paul McCartney is one of the best songwriters and musicians that no rock fan will ever forget.

Date	What happened to Paul
1942	1.
1956(14 years old)	started to play the guitar seriously
1957	2.
1961	3.
1963	Their second song went to the top of the British chart.
1969	4.
1970	5.
1998	His wife died.

情景写作——根据要求完成下列内容

假如你叫 Li Ying，请依据下表所列内容给你想结识的英国笔友 Linda 发一封电子邮件介绍你的情况，邮件的开头和结尾已给出。

Name	Li Ying	Sex	Girl	Age	16
Hometown	Zigong	School	No. 15 Middle School		
Likes	travel, dance, computer games, songs, shopping				
Dislikes	stay at home, basketball, football				

May, 8

Dear Linda,

____

____

____

____

____

Yours,

Li Ying

同步拓展训练

参考答案

同步拓展训练 1

听写检测①

1.private *adj.*私人的
2.conversation *n.*谈话
3.theatre *n.*剧场，戏院
4.seat *n.*座位
5.play *n.*戏
6.loudly *adv.*大声地
7.angry *adj.*生气的
8.angrily *adv.*生气地
9.attention *n.*注意
10.bear *v.*容忍
11.business *n.*事
12.rudely *adv.*无礼地，粗鲁地
13.until *prep.*直到
14.outside *adv.*外面
15.ring *v.*（铃或电话等）响
16.aunt *n.*姑，姨，婶，舅母
17.repeat *v.*重复
18.send *v.*寄，送
19.postcard *n.*明信片
20.spoil *v.*使索然无味，损坏
21.museum *n.*博物馆
22.public *adj.*公共的
23.friendly *adj.*友好的
24.waiter *n.*服务员，招待员
25.lend *v.*借给
26.decision *n.*决定
27.whole *adj.*整个的
28.single *adj.*唯一的，单个的
29.actor *n.*演员
30.lunchtime *n.*午餐时间
31.arrive *v.*到达
32.teach *v.*教授

口语造句

1.learning; 2.problem; 3.pronunciation; 4.don't; 5.difficult
6.about; 7.forget; 8.write; 9.way; 10.help

语法精练

1.can; 2.do; 3.club; 4.join; 5.can't; 6.like; 7.swimming; 8.want; 9.sings; 10.Are
11.used to, chat; 12.in, past few; 13.weren't, No; 14.seems, have, lot; 15.how to; 16.worry about, stressed out; 17.used, hate, doesn't, about; 18.used to, more interested, sending messages

阅读理解

1.B; 2.A; 3.C; 4.D; 5.A; 6.D; 7.B; 8.A; 9.D; 10.A
11.A；12.B；13.D；14.C；15.C

同步拓展训练 2

听写检测

1.exciting *adj.*令人兴奋的
2.receive *v.*接受，收到
3.firm *n.*商行，公司
4.different *adj.*不同的
5.centre *n.*中心
6.abroad *adv.*在国外
7.pigeon *n.*鸽子
8.message *n.*信息
9.cover *v.*越过
10.distance *n.*距离
11.request *n.*要求，请求
12.spare part 备件
13.service *n.*业务，服务
14.beggar *n.*乞丐
15.food *n.*食物
16.pocket *n.*衣服口袋
17.call *v.*拜访，光顾
18.brother *n.*兄弟
19.Australia *n.*澳大利亚
20.month *n.*月
21.visit *v.*参观，访问
22.place *n.*地方，地点
23.garage *n.*修车厂
24.telephone *n.*电话
25.carry *v.*携带，运送
26.minute *n.*分钟
27.move *v.*搬家
28.knock *v.*敲
29.return *n.*回报
30.sing *v.*唱歌
31.meal *n.*一餐，一顿饭
32.neighbour *n.*邻居

① 句子听写部分答案详见相应课文，以增强读者语境学习的效果，并加深记忆。

口语造句

1.are you doing； 2.am studying； 3.am cleaning；4.go；5.sounds；6.is swimming；7.swimming；8.go

语法精练

1.Are you a musician?

2.Please call Liz at 790-4230.

3.Maybe you can be in our school concert.

4.Are you good with children?

5.I can play the guitar but I can't play it well.

6.We want two good singers for our rock band.

7.Jane can't play volleyball well.

8.What club do you want to join?

9.Can you help kids with swimming

10.Come and join us.

11.must belong

12.Whose, can't be, for

13.could, likes

14.dropped, on

15.running, could

16.swimming, an ocean

17.wake, is pretending, asleep

18.must be, only, who's

阅读理解

1.B；2.C；3.C；4.A；5.A；6.C；7.B；8.A；9.A；10.B；11.C；12.B；13.A；14.C；15.C；16.C；17.D；18.C；19.D

同步拓展训练3

听写检测

1.detective *n.*侦探
2.airport *n.*机场
3.expect *v.*期待，等待
4.valuable *adj.*贵重的
5.parcel *n.*包裹
6.diamond *n.*钻石
7.steal *v.*偷
8.main *adj.*主要的
9.airfield *n.*飞机起落的场地
10.guard *n.*警戒，守卫
11.precious *adj.*珍贵的
12.stone *n.*石子
13.sand *n.*沙子
14.competition *n.*比赛，竞赛
15.neat *adj.*整齐的，整洁的
16.path *n.*小路，小径
17.wooden *adj.*木头的
18.pool *n.*水池
19.welcome *n.& v.*欢迎
20.crowd *n.*人群
21.gather *v.*聚集
22.hand *n.*指针
23.shout *v.*喊叫
24.refuse *v.*拒绝
25.laugh *v.*笑
26.plane *n.*飞机
27.thief *n.*贼，小偷
28.building *n.*建筑物
29.beautiful *adj.*美丽的
30.vegetable *n.*蔬菜
31.interesting *adj.*有趣的
32.prize *n.*奖赏，奖品

口语造句

2；4；1；6；3；5

语法精练

1.Monday；2.Tuesday；3.February；4.fifth；5.week
6.twelve；7.hours；8.December；9.Saturday；10.Wednesday
11. see；12. Why；13. Because；14.Where；15.Africa；16.What；17.grass；18.them

阅读理解

1.C；2.B；3.B；4.A；5.A

同步拓展训练 4

听写检测

1.jazz *n.*爵士乐
2.musical *adj.*音乐的
3.instrument *n.*乐器
4.clavichord *n.*古钢琴
5.recently *adv.*最近
6.damage *v.*损坏
7.key *n.*琴键
8.string *n.*（乐器的）弦
9.shock *v.*使不悦或生气，震惊
10.allow *v.*允许，让
11.touch *v.*触摸
12.turn *n.*行为，举止
13.deserve *v.*应得到，值得
14.lawyer *n.*律师
15.bank *n.*银行
16.salary *n.*工资
17.immediately *adv.*立刻
18.luck *n.*运气，幸运
19.captain *n.*船长
20.sail *v.*航行
21.harbour *n.*港口
22.proud *adj.*自豪
23.important *adj.*重要的
24.keep *v.*保持，保留
25.living room 客厅，起居室
26.belong to 属于
27.grandfather *n.*祖父
28.restaurant *n.*饭店
29.borrow *v.*借，借入
30.pay back 偿还，报答，报复
31.surprise *n.*惊奇，惊喜
32.famous *adj.*著名的，出名的

口语造句

1.C；2.D；3.A；4.E；5.B

语法精练

1.wants to be；2.The thieves are afraid of；3.awful, counts, his；4.helps, patients；5.establish a international school；6.has some danger；7.people go out；8.an exciting；9.as soon as possible；10.doesn't want to work

阅读理解

1.B；2.C；3.A；4.D；5.C；6.B；7.A；8.C；9.B；10.B
11.D；12. C；13.C；14.D

同步拓展训练 5

听写检测

1.group *n.*小组，团体
2.pop singer 流行歌手
3.club *n.*俱乐部
4.performance *n.*演出
5.occasion *n.*场合
6.amusing *adj.*有趣的，好笑的
7.experience *n.*经历
8.wave *v.*招手
9.lift *n.*搭便车
10.reply *v.*回答
11.language *n.*语言
12.journey *n.*旅行
13.secretary *n.*秘书
14.nervous *adj.*精神紧张的
15.afford *v.*负担得起
16.weak *adj.*弱的
17.interrupt *v.*插话，打断
18.at present 现在，目前
19.arrive *v.*到达
20.station *n.*车站
21.stay *n.*停留，暂住
22.difficult *adj.*困难的
23.village *n.*乡村，村庄
24.south *n.*南部，南
25.apart *adv.*分离，分别地
26.neither *adj.*两者都不
27.during *prep.*在……期间
28.feel *v.*感觉，觉得
29.enter *v.*进入
30.business *n.*商业，生意
31.firm *n.*公司
32.salary *n.*薪水，工资

口语造句

1；8；3；2；5；9；6；4；10；7；11

语法精练

1.dangerous；2.clerk；3.waiter；4.hospital；5.reporter；6.fun；7.store；8.difficult；9.thieves；10.count

11. best loved, on display

12. reminds me of

13.who can't sing, clearly

14. who is, playing different kinds of

15. Whatever, do, forget, safety

16.Though, he, went on working

17.As, know, whoever, break, laws

18. has been on, about ten minutes

阅读理解

1.C；2.D；3.B；4.C；5.A；6.D；7.D；8.C；9.B；10.A

11.D；12.B；13.D；14.C；15.A

同步拓展训练6

听写检测

1.park *v.*停放（汽车）
2.traffic *n.*交通
3.ticket *n.*交通违章罚款单
4.note *n.*便条
5.area *n.*地段
6.sign *n.*指示牌
7.reminder *n.*提示
8.fail *v.*无视，忘记
9.obey *v.*服从
10.appear *v.*登场，扮演
11.stage *n.*舞台
12.bright *adj.*鲜艳的
13.stocking *n.*长筒袜
14.sock *n.*短袜
15.pub *n.*小酒店
16.landlord *n.*店主
17.bill *n.*账单
18.wrong *adj.*错误的
19.lucky *adj.*幸运的
20.without *prep.*没有，不
21.enjoy *v.*享受，欣赏
22.attention *n.*注意，注意力
23.actress *n.*女演员
24.in spite of 尽管
25.take part in 参加
26.terrible *adj.*极坏的，可怕的
27.beside *prep.*在……旁边
28.look for 寻找
29.answer *v.*回答
30.immediately *adv.*立刻，马上
31.return *v.*返回
32.garden *n.*花园

口语造句

1.C；2.A；3.E；4.H；5.G；6.B；7.F；8.I；9.J；10.D

语法精练

1. Is Kate doing her homework?；Yes, she is.；No, she isn't.

2. Are his parents talking with the teachers?；Yes, they are.；No, they aren't.

3. Is Jim cleaning his room?；Yes, he is.；No, he isn't.

4. Are your friends eating breakfast?；Yes, they are.；No, they aren't.

5. Is your aunt cooking dinner?；Yes, she is.；No, she isn't.

6.photographers；7.hiking；8.collecting；9.miss；10.gentle；11.reminds；12.change；13.suggestion；14.potatoes；15.Italian

阅读理解

1.T；2.F；3.F；4.F；5.T；6.T；7.D；8.C；9.A；10.A；11.B；12.C；13.D；14.B；15.C；16.D

同步拓展训练 7

听写检测

1.hurry v.匆忙
2.ticket office 售票处
3.pity n.令人遗憾的事
4.exclaim v.大声说
5.return v.退回
6.sadly adv.悲哀地，丧气地
7.catch v.抓到
8.fisherman n.钓鱼人，渔民
9.boot n.靴子
10.waste n.浪费
11.realize v.意识到
12.mad adj.发疯
13.reason n.原因
14.sum n.量
15.determined adj.坚定的
16.at any moment 随时
17.hurry v.赶紧，匆忙
18.certainly adv.的确，当然
19.at once 马上，立刻
20.performance n.表演
21.Wednesday n.星期三
22.favourite adj.特别喜爱的
23.worry v.担心，烦恼
24.unlucky adj.不幸的
25.rubbish n.垃圾，废物
26.spend v.花费，消耗
27.give up 放弃
28.important adj.重要的，重大的
29.interested adj.感兴趣的
30.aeroplane n.飞机
31.probably adv.大概，或许
32.offer v.提供，出价

口语造句

1.stayed；2.had；3.cleaned；4.did；5.It；6.went；7.about；8.did；9.played；10.and；11.went；12.had；13.But；14.wasn't

语法精练

1. Do you like cold weather?
2. What an interesting place it is!
3. How was the weather there?
4. How is it going with you?
5. We are taking photos of the pyramids.
6. I'm looking at five thousand years of history.
7. Everyone is having a good time.
8. How cold the weather is!
9.Is it cool in Paris now?
10. The weather is windy and cold.
11. to hand out；12. worked out；13. has run out of；14. put off
15. has given away；16.clean, up；17. call, up；18. to fix up；19. homeless；20. project

阅读理解

1. Winter；2.She enjoys skating；3. Autumn；4. It's not too hot, and not too cold；5. Winter is over
6.A；7.C；8.D；9.D；10.B；11.B；12.A；13.C；14.B；15.B

同步拓展训练 8

听写检测

1.dream v.做梦，梦想
2.age n.年龄
3.channel n.海峡

4.throw v.扔，抛
5.complete v.完成
6.modern adj.新式的，与以往不同的
7.strange adj.奇怪的
8.district n.地区
9.manager n.经理
10.upset adj.不安
11.sympathetic adj.表示同情的
12.complain v.抱怨
13.wicked adj.很坏的，邪恶的
14.contain v.包含，内装
15.honesty n.诚实
16.envelope n.信封
17.receive v.收到
18.travel v.旅行
19.address n.地址
20.regularly adv.有规律地
21.decide v.决定
22.cost v.花费
23.surprise n.惊奇
24.beautiful adj.美丽的
25.stay v.暂住
26.lovely adj.可爱的
27.strange adj.陌生的，奇怪的
28.enter v.进入
29.start v.出发，开始，着手
30.interrupt v.打断，打扰
31.knock v.敲
32.outside adj.外面的，外界的

口语造句

1.C；2.A；3.E；4.D；5.B

语法精练

1. Could you tell me the way to the post office?
2. My cousin doesn't like milk at all.
3. What would you like on your pizza?
4. Where can I find the classical CDs?
5. He went to the library and did some reading.
6. have been, twice；7. do, want, for；8. place where, weather
9. plan on driving, Singapore；10. is saving money
11. provide, with, spots；12.surfing, be away
13. take a trip, in the south of China；14. am considering visiting
15. this time of year；better pack

阅读理解

1.B；2.C；3.D；4.A；5.B；6.B；7.D；8.C；9.C；10.A
11.T；12.F；13.F；14.T；15.F

同步拓展训练9

听写检测

1.railway n.铁路
2.porter n.搬运工
3.several pron.几个
4.foreigner n.外国人
5.wonder v.感到奇怪
6.critic n.评论家
7.paint v.画
8.pretend v.假装
9.pattern n.图案
10.curtain n.窗帘，幕布
11.material n.材料
12.appreciate v.鉴赏
13.notice v.注意到
14.whether conj.是否
15.hang v.悬挂
16.critically adv.批评地
17.upside down 上下颠倒地
18.tent n.帐篷
19.field n.田地，田野
20.smell v.闻起来，闻到

21.wonderful *adj.*极好的
22.campfire *n.*营火，篝火
23.creep *v.*爬行
24.sleeping bag 睡袋
25.comfortable *adj.*舒适的，安逸的
26.soundly *adv.*香甜地，深入地
27.leap *v.*跳跃，跳起
28.heavily *adv.*大量地
29.stream *n.*小溪
30.form *v.*形成
31.wind *v.*蜿蜒
32.right *adv.*正好

口语造句

2, 7, 11, 10, 4, 6, 3, 1, 5, 8, 9

语法精练

1. What time does he eat breakfast?
2. My brother usually goes to bed at nine.
3. We make a shower schedule.
4. When does he usually get up?
5. I practice the guitar at around seven.
6. What time do you leave home in the morning?
7. long have, doing
8. have been to, twice
9. should, get(buy), for
10. has worked, for
11. mind(my)sitting, not at all
12. doesn't swimming, does, Yes, does
13. has, been, neither have I

阅读理解

1.F；2.T；3.F；4.F；5.F
6.D；7.B；8.C；9.D；10.A

同步拓展训练 10

听写检测

1.rare *adj.*罕见的
2.ancient *adj.*古代的，古老的
3.myth *n.*神话故事
4.trouble *n.*麻烦
5.effect *n.*结果，效果
6.taxi *n.*出租汽车
7.land *v.*着陆
8.plough *v.*耕地
9.lonely *adj.*偏僻的，人迹罕至的
10.roof *n.*楼顶
11.block *n.*一座大楼
12.flat *n.*公寓房
13.desert *v.*废弃
14.polo *n.*水球
15.cut *v.*穿过
16.row *v.*划（船）
17.kick *v.*踢
18.towards *prep.*朝，向
19.nearly *adv.*几乎
20.sight *n.*眼界，视域
21.owner *n.*主人，所有者
22.park *v.*停放汽车（等）
23.because of 因为，由于
24.garage *n.*车库
25.ugly *adj.*丑陋的，难看的
26.stone *n.*石头
27.unusual *adj.*不平常的
28.service *n.*服务
29.passenger *n.*乘客，旅客
30.occasion *n.*场合，机会
31.businessman *n.*商人
32.lonely *adj.*孤独的，寂寞的

口语造句

1.F；2.E；3.B；4.A；5.C

语法精练

1. What's Tom's cousin's favorite subject?
2. Why do you like math?
3. His favorite color is red.
4. Who is your science teacher?
5. When does he usually get up?
6. can exchange
7. how, can get to
8. fact, many differences between, and
9. saw him, was lying on, reading
10. if, turns around
11. interest, cartoons more than
12. makes big plans
13. to hang out

阅读理解

1.C；2.C；3.B；4.D；5.A；6.A；7.C；8.A；9.C

同步拓展训练 11

听写检测

1.retire *v.*退休
2.company *n.*公司
3.bicycle *n.*自行车
4.save *v.*积蓄
5.workshop *n.*车间
6.helper *n.*帮手，助手
7.employ *v.*雇佣
8.grandson *n.*孙子
9.once *adv.*曾经，以前
10.temptation *n.*诱惑
11.article *n.*物品，东西
12.wrap *v.*包裹
13.simply *adv.*仅仅
14.arrest *v.*逮捕
15.darkness *n.*黑暗
16.explain *v.*解释，叙述
17.coast *n.*海岸
18.storm *n.*暴风雨
19.towards *prep.*向，朝；接近
20.rock *n.*岩石，礁石
21.shore *n.*海岸
22.light *n.*灯光
23.ahead *adv.*在前面
24.cliff *n.*峭壁
25.struggle *v.*
26.hospital *n.*
27.expensive
28.used to 过
29.spare part
30.factory *n.*工
31.success *n.*
32.honest *adj.*
直的

口语造句

1.F；2.B；3.A；4.C；5.D

语法精练

1. What do you usually do on weekends?
2. He often goes to the movies on Sunday.
3. They shop twice a month.
4. How often does Mr. Li watch TV?
5. How often do you exercise?
6. We should drink milk every day.
7. Teenagers should sleep at least eight hours for every night.
8. important, interested in
9. used to be
10.an appointment, arrive, on tim
11.need to know, dinner table
12. should try different methods
13. not visit, without calling
14. gradually, living
15. go out of, to make, feel

阅读理解

1.A；2.C；3.A；4.D；5.D；6.
9.A；10.C；11.A；12.B；13.D

同步拓展训练 12

听写检测

1.station *n.*（警察）局
2.most *adv.*相当，非常
3.while *n.*一段时间
4.regret *v.*后悔
5.far *adv.*非常
6.rush *v.*冲
7.act *v.*行动
8.straight *adv.*径直
9.fright *n.*害怕
10.battered *adj.*撞坏的
11.shortly *adv.*很快，不久
12.afterwards *adv.*以后
13.record *n.*
14.strong *adj*
15.swimmer
16.succeed
17.train *v.*训
18.anxiously

9.intend v.打算
0.solid adj.固体的，硬的
1.receive v.收到，接到
2.local adj.地方的，当地的
3.smiling adj.微笑的
24.pick up 获得，找到
25.amused adj.愉快的，开心的
26.expect v.期待，期望
27.steal v.偷，偷窃
28.exciting adj.令人兴奋的
29.thief n.小偷，贼
30.damage v.损害，伤害
31.recognize v.认可，认出
32.arrest v.逮捕

语造句

；3；1；8；6；4；2；9；5；7

法精练

B（去掉 an）；2. C（改为 want）；3. C（改为 nurses）

A（改为 a reporter）；5. B（改为 has）

misled；7. spending；8. moves；9. becoming；10. to set up

. shows；12. write down；13. thankful；14.makes；15. hurry up

读理解

C；2.A；3.D；4.D；5.D

C；7.D；8.D；9.B；10.B；11.C；12.A；13.A；14.C；15.C；16.B；17.A；18.D；19.C

同步拓展训练 13

写检测

Olympic adj.奥林匹克的
hold v.召开
government n.政府
mmense adj.巨大的
stadium v.露天体育场
standard n.标准
capital n.首都
antastic adj.巨大的
design v.设计
.except prep.除了
.complain v.抱怨
.continually adv.不断地
13.bitterly adv.刺骨地
14.sunshine n.阳光
15.operation n.手术
16.successful adj.成功的
17.following adj.下一个
18.patient n.病人
19.alone adj.独自的
20.exchange n.（电话的）交换台
21.inquire v.询问，打听
22.certain adj.某个
23.caller n.打电话的人
24.relative n.亲戚
25.country n.国家
26.special adj.特别的，特殊的
27.complete v.完成，完善
28.anxiously adv.忧虑地，不安地
29.return v.返回
30.dream v.做梦
31.retire v.退休
32.shock n.震动，打击

语造句

D；2.C；3.A；4.E；5.B

法精练

good, well；2. heavy, heavily；3. strongly,

ng；4. bright, brightly；5. carefully, careful

gree to, suitable

upport, education

rovide, with

9. used, discarded, recycled

10. Though, bring, should be cared

11. fewer, fewer habitats

12. used to be, was discovered, endangered

13. ten feet long, weighs, pounds

阅读理解

1.C；2.B；3.B；4.A；5.B

6.B；7.D；8.B；9.A；10.A；11.D；12.A；

13.C；14.A；15.C；16.B；17.D

同步拓展训练 14

听写检测

1.hostess *n.*女主人
2.unsmiling *adj.*不笑的，严肃的
3.tight *adj.*紧身的
4.fix *v.*凝视
5.globe *n.*地球
6.despair *n.*绝望
7.rude *adj.*无礼的
8.mirror *n.*镜子
9.hole *n.*孔
10.remark *v.*评说
11.remind *v.*提醒
12.lighthouse *n.*灯塔
13.musical *adj.*精通音乐的
14.market *n.*市场，集市
15.snake charmer 玩蛇者
16.pipe *n.*（吹奏的）管乐器
17.tune *n.*曲调
18.glimpse *n.*一瞥
19.snake *n.*蛇
20.movement *n.*动作
21.continue *v.*继续
22.dance *v.*跳舞
23.obviously *adv.*显然地
24.difference *n.*差别
25.Indian *adj.*印度的
26.beside *prep.*在旁边
27.conversation *n.*会话，交谈
28.abroad *adv.*往国外，海外
29.modern *adj.*现代的
30.suddenly *adv.*突然地
31.regret *v.*后悔，遗憾
32.terrible *adj.*可怕的，糟糕的

口语造句

3；6；7；4；1；5；2

语法精练

1. most beautiful；2. living；3.drop；4. depends；5. used；
6. are made from；7. is made up of；8. will fly；9. are sure；10. lying
11. C（listening 改为 listening to）
12. D（health 改为 healthy）
13. A（real 改为 really）
14. D（improve 改为 improving）（或 Is 改为 Does）
15. A（Eat 改为 Eating）

阅读理解

1.B；2.A；3.C；4.B；5.A；6.B；7.C；8.C；9.D；10.C；11.B；12. C；13.D；14.D

同步拓展训练 15

听写检测

1.pole *n.*（地球的）极
2.fight *v.*打仗
3.explorer *n.*探险家
4.lie *v.*处于
5.serious *adj.*严重的
6.point *n.*地点
7.seem *v.*似乎，好像
8.crash *v.*坠毁
9.sack *n.*袋子
10.exciting *adj.*令人兴奋的
11.aircraft *n.*飞机
12.endless *adj.*无尽的
13.plain *n.*平原
14.forest *n.*森林
15.risk *n.*危险，冒险
16.picnic *n.*野餐
17.edge *n.*边缘
18.strap *n.*带，皮带

19.possession *n.*所有
20.breath *n.*呼吸
21.content *n.*（常用复数）内有的物品
22.mend *v.*修理
23.clear *adj.*无罪的，不亏心的
24.conscience *n.*良心，道德心
25.wallet *n.*皮夹，钱夹
26.savings *n.*存款
27.villager *n.*村民
28.per cent 百分之……
29.successfully *adv.*顺利地
30.mountain *n.*山，山脉
31.order *v.*命令
32.rush up 催促

口语造句

1. This；2. speak；3. hold；4. take；5. that；6. will；7. soon；8. would

语法精练

1.so…that；2. So；3. had better；4. sure；5. keep; 6. the others; 7. in time; 8. by the end of;
9.doesn't like；10.has worked
11. don't feel well,have a cold.
12. has, headache, sore throat, see, doctor
13. stressed out, doesn't improve(isn't improving)
14. glad, hear, healthy
15. Eating, is ,for, health
16. too tired, make, ill(sick)
17. don't, healthy, hardly ever exercises
18. help us, study more, better
19. to drink milk, good for, health
20. every forty minutes

阅读理解

1.F；2.T；3.F；4.T；5.F
6.D；7.A；8.C；9.B；10.B；11.D；12.C；13.A；14.D；15.A

同步拓展训练 16

听写检测

1.unload *v.*卸（货）
2.wooden *adj.*木制的
3.extremely *adv.*非常，极其
4.occur *v.*发生
5.astonish *v.*使惊讶
6.pipe *n.*堆
7.woollen *adj.*羊毛的
8.goods *n.*货物，商品
9.discover *v.*发现
10.admit *v.*承认
11.confine *v.*关在（狭小的空间里）
12.normal *adj.*正常的，通常的
13.thirsty *adj.*贪杯的
14.ghost *n.*鬼魂
15.haunt *v.*（鬼）来访，闹鬼
16.block *v.*堵
17.furniture *n.*家具
18.whisky *n.*威士忌酒
19.suggest *v.*暗示
20.shake *v.*摇动
21.accept *v.*接受
22.pull *v.*拔
23.cotton wool 药棉
24.collect *v.*收集
25.collection *n.*收藏品，收集品
26.nod *v.*点头
27.meanwhile *adv.*同时
28.contain *v.*包含
29.account for 说明，解决
30.expensive *adj.*昂贵的
31.question *n.*问题
32.impossible *adj.*不可能的

口语造句

1. book；2. many；3. From；4. single；5. What's；6. per；7. full

语法精练

1. leaving；2.to go sightseeing；3. relaxed；4. singer；5. babysits；6. going away；
7. soon, comes；8. late for；9. either, or；10.as, as；11. It, to

12. who used, should be；13. that made us successful；14. realized, had left

阅读理解

1.B；2.A；3.C；4.B；5.D；6.D；7.C；8.A；9.C；10.D；

11.T；12.T；13.F；14.F；15.F

同步拓展训练 17

听写检测

1.tired *adj.*厌烦的

2.real *adj.*真正的

3.owner *n.*主人

4.spring *n.*弹簧

5.mattress *n.*床垫

6.gust *n.*一阵风

7.sweep *v.*扫，刮

8.courtyard *n.*院子

9.smash *v.*碰碎，摔碎

10.miraculously *adv.*奇迹般地

11.unhurt *adj.*没有受伤的

12.glance *v.*扫视

13.promptly *adv.*迅速地

14.ride *n.*旅行

15.excursion *n.*远足

16.conductor *n.*售票员

17.view *n.*景色

18.reward *n.*报偿

19.virtue *n.*美德

20.diet *n.*节食

21.forbid *v.*禁止

22.hurriedly *adv.*匆忙地

23.embarrass *v.*使尴尬

24.guilty *adj.*内疚的

25.strict *adj.*严格的

26.reward *v.*给奖赏

27.occasionally *adv.*偶尔地

28.save *v.*节省，节约

29.proud *adj.*骄傲的

30.blow *v.*风吹

31.countryside *n.*乡下地方

32.recently *adv.*最近

口语造句

1.F；2.B；3.A；4.C；5.D

语法精练

1. collect water；2. is sure；3. haven't heard；

4. has watered

5. has, taken, away；6.grows up；7. was given；

8. chating

9.has written；10. has won

11. What are you doing for vacation?

12. When are they going?

13. Who is he going with?

14. How long are you staying there?

15. How is the weather there?

16. What is it like there?

阅读理解

1.C；2.B；3.A；4.A；5.C；6.D；7.C；8.B；

9.D；10.A

11.B；12.A；13.B；14.C

同步拓展训练 18

听写检测

1.temporarily *adv.*暂时地

2.inch *n.*英寸

3.space *n.*空间

4.actually *adv.*实际上

5.hot *adj.*带电的，充电的

6.fireman *n.*消防队员

7.cause *v.*引起；*n.*原因

8.examine *v.*检查

9.accidentally *adv.*意外地，偶然地

10.remains *n.*尸体，残骸

11.wire *n.*电线

12.volt *n.*伏特（电压单位）

13.power line 电力线

14.solve *v.*解决

15.mystery *n.*谜

16.snatch *v.*抓住

17.spark *n.*电火花

18.sticky *adj.*粘的

19.finger *n.*手指

20.pie *n.*馅饼

21.mix v.混合，搅拌
22.pastry n.面糊
23.annoying adj.恼人的
24.receiver n.电话的话筒
25.dismay v.失望，泄气
26.recognize v.认出，听出
27.persuade v.说服，劝说
28.mess n.乱七八糟
29.doorknob n.门把手
30.sign v.签字
31.register v.挂号邮寄
32.bookcase n.书架

口语造句

1. help；2. see；3. here；4. keep；5. longer；6. renew；7. in；8. bring；9. lend；10. Certainly

语法精练

1. friendly；2.kind of lazy；3.an exciting job；4.goes shopping, went to the movie；5.went swimming, studied；6.medium, mushurooms and cheese；7.Her favorite singer；8.are afraid of
9. B（to 改为 for）；10.B（rides 改为 ride）
11. D（take a train 改为 taking 改为 taking a train）
12. C（get 改为 to get）；13. C（take 改为 will take）

阅读理解

1.D；2.C；3.A；4.D；5.C；6.B；7.A；8.C

同步拓展训练 19

听写检测

1.mine n.矿
2.treasure n.财宝
3.revealer n.探测器
4.invent v.发明
5.detect v.探测
6.bury v.埋藏
7.seashore n.海岸
8.pirate n.海盗
9.soil n.泥土
10.entrance n.入口
11.finally adv.最后
12.worthless adj.毫无价值的
13.thoroughly adv.彻底地
14.trunk n.行李箱
15.confident adj.有信心的
16.value n.价值
17.excitement n.激动，兴奋
18.handsome adj.漂亮的，美观的
19.wheel n.轮子
20.explosion n.爆炸，轰响
21.course n.跑道；行程
22.rival n.对手
23.speed v.疾驶
24.downhill adv.下坡
25.madam n.太太，夫人
26.jeans n.牛仔裤
27.hesitate v.犹豫，迟疑
28.serve n.接待（顾客）
29.scornfully adv.轻蔑地
30.punish v.惩罚
31.fur n.裘皮
32.eager adj.热切的，热情的

口语造句

1. been；2. when；3. built；4. What；5. used；6. protecting
7. Why；8. one；9. the；10. all

语法精练

1. to buy；2. drinking；3. results；4. healthy；5. ourselves；6. have；7. although；8. exercises；9. wants；10. keep；11. get, tickets, for；12.used, be；13. hobby, collect；14. been, abroad, once；15. has borrowed, on；16. out, has taken

阅读理解

1.C；2.D；3.B；4.A；5.A；6.D；7.D；8.C；9.A；10.C；11.A；12.D；13.B；14.C；15.A

同步拓展训练 20

听写检测

1.blessing *n.*福份，福气
2.disguise *n.*伪装
3.tiny *adj.*极小的
4.possess *v.*拥有
5.cursed *adj.*可恨的
6.increase *v.*增加
7.plant *v.*种植
8.church *n.*教堂
9.evil *adj.*坏的
10.reputation *n.*名声
11.claim *v.*以……为其后果
12.victim *n.*受害者，牺牲品
13.vicar *n.*教区牧师
14.source *n.*来源
15.income *n.*收入
16.trunk *n.*树干
17.bark *v.*狗叫
18.press *v.*按，压
19.paw *n.*脚爪
20.latch *n.*门闩
21.expert *n.*专家
22.develop *v.*养成
23.habit *n.*习惯
24.remove *v.*拆掉，取下
25.future *n.*未来，前途
26.fair *n.*集市
27.fortune-teller *n.*算命人
28.crystal *n.*水晶
29.relation *n.*亲属
30.impatiently *adv.*不耐烦地
31.mention *v.*提及，提到
32.complain *v.*抱怨

口语造句

1. Where；2. What；3. Dig；4. dig；5. knock；6. enough；7. straight；8. back；9. tie；10. Keep

语法精练

1. are listening to；2. really；3. babysits；；4. science test；5. helped；6. to discuss
7. can, go, concert with me
8. for telling me
9. who are different from me
10. funny, makes us laugh
11. Who, more intelligent, or
12. important to, more important to her
13. the most outgoing
14. should make me feel

阅读理解

1.C；2.C；3.B；4.D；5.C

同步拓展训练 21

听写检测

1.telescope *n.*望远镜
2.launch *v.*发射
3.space *n.*空间
4.billion *n.*10 亿
5.faulty *adj.*有错误的
6.astronaut *n.*宇航员
7.shuttle *n.*航天飞机
8.grab *v.*抓
9.atmosphere *n.*大气层
10.distant *adj.*遥远的
11.galaxy *n.*星系
12.universe *n.*宇宙
13.control *n.*控制
14.desolate *adj.*荒凉的
15.threaten *v.*威胁
16.surrounding *adj.*周围的
17.destruction *n.*破坏，毁灭
18.flood *n.*洪水，水灾
19.authority *n.*当局（常用复数）
20.grass-seed *n.*草籽
21.spray *v.*喷撒
22.quantity *n.*量
23.root *n.*根
24.century *n.*世纪
25.patch *n.*小片
26.blacken *v.*变黑，发暗
27.circle *n.*圈子
28.admire *v.*赞美，钦佩
29.close *adj.*亲密的
30.wedding *n.*婚礼
31.reception *n.*招待会
32.sort *n.*种类

口语造句

1. help；2. looking；3. What；4. size；5. in；6. much
7. cost；8. expensive(dear)；9. money；10.

Anything

语法精练

1. because；2. raining；3. laugh；4. helped；5.smart

6. inviting；7. serious；8. show

9. been, been, twice

10. haven't, seen, have, been

11. Surfing, favourite

12. No, matter, doesn't, believe

13. speaks, highly, of

14. Has, given up smoking

阅读理解

1.C；2.A；3.D；4.B；5.D

同步拓展训练 22

听写检测

1.tunnel *n.*隧道
2.port *n.*港口
3.ventilate *v.*通风
4.chimney *n.*烟囱
5.double *adj.*双的
6.ventilation *n.*通风
7.invasion *n.*入侵，侵略
8.officially *adv.*正式地
9.connect *v.*连接
10.European *adj.*欧洲的
11.continent *n.*大陆
12.versus *prep.*对
13.circus *n.*马戏团
14.accompany *v.*陪伴，随行
15.approach *v.*走近
16.weigh *v.*重
17.fortunate *adj.*幸运的
18.Lancaster *n.*兰开斯特
19.bomber *n.*轰炸机
20.remote *adj.*偏僻的
21.rediscover *v.*重新发现
22.aerial *adj.*航空的
23.survey *n.*调查
24.package *v.*把……打包
25.enthusiast *n.*热心人
26.restore *v.*修复
27.imagine *v.*想像
28.packing case 包装箱
29.colony *n.*群
30.hive *n.*蜂房
31.preserve *v.*保护
32.beeswax *n.*蜂蜡

口语造句

1. like；2. much；3. long；4. been；5. Since；6. swam

7. learnt；8. fail；9. up；10.true

语法精练

1. held；2. France；3. surfing；4. show；5. difference

6. sports；7. theirs；8. practice；9. highly；10. pride

11. Kate is taller than her brother.

12. He is more outgoing than me.

13. Who is calmer, Lily or Lucy?

14. What do you like about Maria?

15. My best friend is more popular than me.

16. Sam likes watching soccer games on TV on weekends.

阅读理解

1.C；2.B；3.D；4.B；5.A

同步拓展训练 23

听写检测

1.volcano *n.*火山
2.active *adj.*活动的
3.erupt *v.*（火山）喷发
4.violently *adv.*猛烈地，剧烈地
5.manage *v.*设法
6.brilliant *adj.*精彩的
7.liquid *adj.*液态的
8.escape *v.*逃脱
9.alive *adj.*活着的

10.persistent *adj.*坚持的，固执的
11.avoid *v.*避开
12.insist *v.*坚持做
13.murder *n.*谋杀
14.instruct *v.*命令，指示
15.acquire *v.*取得，获得
16.confidence *n.*信心
17.examiner *n.*主考人
18.suppose *v.*假设
19.tap *v.*轻敲
20.react *v.*反映
21.brake *n.*刹车
22.pedal *n.*踏板
23.mournful *adj.*悲哀的
24.fear *v.*害怕
25.present *n.*礼物
26.ought 应该
27.damage *v.*毁坏
28.wreck *n.*残骸
29.rescue *v.*营救
30.lifetime *n.*一生
31.cave *n.*洞穴
32.licence *n.*执照，许可证

口语造句

2 5 1 6 8 3 7 4 9

语法精练

1. since；2. for；3. throw；4. Taking care of；
5. used to
6. picked；7. spat；8. doing well in
9. Can you come to my birthday party?
10. I have to help my mom.
11. He has to study for English test.
12. Thanks a lot for invitation.
13. I am going to the movie with my cousins.

阅读理解

1.C；2.B；3.D；4.C；5.A
6.A；7.D；8.C；9.D；10.B

同步拓展训练 24

听写检测

1.bullfight *n.*斗牛
2.drunk *n.*醉汉
3.wander *v.*溜达，乱走
4.ring *n.*圆形竞技场地
5.unaware *adj.*不知道的，未觉察的
6.bull *n.*公牛
7.matador *n.*斗牛士
8.remark *n.*评论，言语
9.apparently *adv.*明显地
10.sensitive *adj.*敏感地
11.criticism *n.*批评
12.charge *v.*冲上去
13.clumsily *adv.*笨拙地
14.bow *v.*鞠躬
15.safety *n.*安全地带
16.sympathetically *adv.*同情地
17.parliament *n.*议会，国会
18.erect *v.*建起
19.accurate *adj.*准确的
20.official *n.*官员，行政人员
21.observatory *n.*天文台
22.check *v.*检查
23.microphone *n.*扩音器，麦克风
24.tower *n.*塔
25.racing *n.*竞赛
26.horsepower *n.*马力
27.burst *v.*爆裂
28.average *adj.*平均的
29.footstep *n.*足迹
30.famous *adj.*著名的
31.immense *adj.*极广大的
32.length *n.*长度

口语造句

1. trouble；2. feel；3. have；4. temperature；5. Open；6. got(caught)；7. long；8. anything；9. like；10. Take

语法精练

1. has too much；2. play tennis with me
3. will be free；4. go fishing, whole day

5. have, study for, geography test
6. because of；7. as soon as possible；8. least expensive
9. woke up；10. enjoyable；11. slowest；12. playing；13. fell asleep

阅读理解

1.B；2.A；3.C；4.B；5.C；6.B；7.A；8.D；9.C；10.B
11.A；12.B；13.D；14.A；15.B

同步拓展训练 25

听写检测

1.record-holder 记录保持者
2.truant *n.*逃学的孩子
3.unimaginative *adj.*缺乏想象力的
4.shame *n.*惭愧，羞耻
5.hitchhike *v.*搭便车旅行
6.meantime *n.*期间
7.lorry *n.*卡车
8.border *n.*边界
9.evade *v.*逃避，逃离
10.limelight *n.*舞台灯光
11.precaution *n.*预防措施
12.fan *n.*狂热者，迷
13.shady *adj.*避阴的
14.sheriff *n.*司法长官
15.notice *n.*告示
16.sneer *n.*冷笑
17.travel *v.*旅行
18.discover *v.*发现
19.meantime *n.*其间，同时
20.creep off 蹑手蹑脚地走
21.biscuit *n.*饼干，小点心
22.pick up 看到
23.authority *n.*权威，当局
24.actor *n.*男演员
25.ancient *adj.*远古的，旧的
26.recognize *v.*认出，承认
27.disguise *v.*假装，伪装
28.perfect *adj.*完美的
29.wonderful *adj.*奇妙的，极好的
30.spot *v.*认出，发现
31.comfortable *adj.*舒适的
32.appear *v.*出现

口语造句

1. that; 2. one; 3. shopping; 4. when; 5. where; 6. take
7. on；8. on；9. Which；10. bus

语法精练

1. B（much too 改为 too much）
2. C（call 改为 calling）
3. C（in 改为 on）
4. C（for 改为 to）
5. B（goes 改为 go）

6. None of, have been
7. or, be late for
8. cheaper, more enjoyable
9. it difficult, understand
10. didn't begin until, stopped
11. never seen such an
12. rushed trip, air(plane)

阅读理解

1.T；2.T；3.T；4.F；5.T
6.C；7.A；8.B；9.D；10.B

同步拓展训练 26

听写检测

1.thick *adj.*厚的
2.signal *n.*信号
3.stamp *v.*踩，跺
4.helicopter *n.*直升飞机
5.scene *n.*现场
6.survivor *n.*幸存者
7.fool *n.*傻瓜
8.bulletin *n.*新闻简报
9.announcer *n.*播音员

10.macaroni n.通心面，空心面条
11.leading adj.主要的
12.grower n.种植者
13.splendid adj.极好的
14.stalk n.梗
15.gather v.收庄稼
16.thresh v.打（庄稼）
17.process v.加工
18.present adj.目前的
19.champion n.冠军
20.studio n.播音室
21.passenger n.旅客，乘客
22.crash v.碰撞，坠毁
23.suitcase n.手提箱
24.terribly adj.可怕的
25.overhead adj.在头上的
26.signal n.信号
27.harvest v.收割，收获
28.expect v.期待，期望
29.cartload n.一满车
30.local adj.当地的
31.increase v.增加
32.competition n.竞赛，竞争

口语造句

1. Excuse；2. tell；3. way；4. along/down；5. take；
6. right/left；7. until；8. see/find；9. east；10. Thanks

语法精练

1. How much；2. How many；3. How many；4. How much
5. How much；6. How many；7. How many；8. How much

阅读理解

1.A；2.D；3.B；4.C；5.D；6.B；7.C；8.B；9.D；10.D
11.C；12.D；13.B；14.C；15.D

同步拓展训练 27

听写检测

1.mummy n.木乃伊
2.temple n.庙
3.mark n.斑点
4.plate n.（照相）底片
5.disease n.疾病
6.last v.持续
7.prove v.显示出
8.resin n.树脂
9.skin n.皮，皮肤
10.section n.切片
11.figure n.体形，人像
12.normally adv.通常地
13.survive v.幸免于
14.entitle v.以……为名
15.calm v.使镇定
16.nerve n.神经
17.concentration n.集中，专心
18.suffer v.受苦，受害
19.symptom n.症状
20.temper n.脾气
21.appetite n.胃口，食欲
22.produce v.拿出
23.urge v.力劝，怂恿
24.satisfaction n.满意，满足
25.delighted adj.欣喜的
26.successful adj.成功的
27.operation n.手术
28.singer n.歌手
29.rare adj.罕见的，杰出的
30.cigarette n.香烟
31.pleasure n.愉快，快乐
32.enormous adj.巨大的，庞大的

口语造句

1. been；2. up；3. threw；4. protecting；5. keep；6. onto
7. duty；8. on；9. much；10. more

语法精练

1. champion; 2. grows up; 3. studied; 4. record; 5. write articles； 6. admire; 7. learning; 8. practice

9. Could I watch TV?
10. Could I stay out late?
11. Could I use your bike?
12. Thanks for taking care of my dog.
13. Please take out the trash.
14. Don't forget to clean your room.

阅读理解

1.A；2.C；3.D；4.B；5.A
6.C；7.B；8.D；9.C；10.A

同步拓展训练 28

听写检测

1.parent *n.*父（母）亲
2.flight attendant 空中乘务员
3.frightened *adj.*害怕，担惊
4.curious *adj.*急于了解，好奇的
5.bomb *n.*炸弹
6.plant *v.*安放
7.palace *n.*宫殿
8.extraordinary *adj.*不平常的
9.exhibition *n.*展览
10.iron *n.*铁
11.various *adj.*各种各样的
12.machinery *n.*机器
13.display *n.*展览
14.steam *n.*蒸汽
15.profit *n.*利润
16.college *n.*学院
17.holiday *n.*假期
18.take charge of 负责，看管
19.unpleasant *adj.*不高兴的
20.experience *n.*经验，体验
21.occasion *n.*机会，场合
22.gain *v.*获得
23.height *n.*高度
24.keep calm 保持冷静
25.enormous *adj.*巨大的，庞大的
26.thoroughly *adv.*十分地，彻底地
27.fortunately *adv.*幸运地
28.wonderful *adj.*奇妙的，极好的
29.million *num.*百万
30.museum *n.*博物馆
31.remain *v.*保持
32.burn down *v.*烧为平地

口语造句

5；1；8；3；4；2；6；7

语法精练

1. was busy with, met, yesterday evening
2. borrow your dictionary, Mine
3. Thanks, taking care of
4. is going to invite, to the party
5. hates sweeping, floor, doing the laundry
6. get a ride, have to go to the meeting
7. help make dinner, come over

阅读理解

1.A；2.C；3.B；4.A；5.C
6.C；7.D；8.A；9.B；10.C

同步拓展训练 29

听写检测

1.prisoner *n.*囚犯
2.bush *n.*灌木丛
3.rapidly *adv.*迅速地
4.uniform *n.*制服
5.rifle *n.*来复枪，步枪
6.sodier *n.*士兵
7.march *v.*行进
8.boldly *adv.*大胆地
9.blaze *v.*闪耀
10.salute *v.*行礼
11.elderly *adj.*上了年纪的
12.grey *adj.*灰白的

13.sharp *adj.*猛烈的
14.blow *n.*打击
15.monster *n.*怪物
16.sailor *n.*海员
17.sight *v.*见到
18.creature *n.*动物，生物
19.peculiar *adj.*奇怪的，不寻常的
20.shining *adj.*闪闪发光的
21.oarfish *n.*桨鱼
22.drag *v.*拖
23.darkness *n.*黑暗
24.discover *v.*发现
25.escape *v.*逃跑
26.obviously *adv.*明显地
27.fisherman *n.*渔民，渔夫
28.seaman *n.*海员，水手
29.occasionally *adv.*有时候，偶尔
30.powerful *adj.*强大的，有力的
31.realize *v.*认识到，实现
32.eventually *adv.*最后，终于

口语造句

3；1；5；2；7；4；6

语法精练

1. most delicious；2. part；3. takes；4. walk；5. really；6. friendlier；7. friendliest；8.the biggest；9. but；10. never

11. I think Lily should tell her friends to do more speaking.
12. I want to be a lawyer like my father.
13. There are a lot of things you could do.
14. Last night I had an argument with my parents.
15. It seems that everything goes well.
16. He has the same haircut as I do.
17. My best friend is more popular than me.

阅读理解

1.B；2.B；3.C；4.D；5.D；6.B；7.A；8.C；9.A；10.C

同步拓展训练 30

听写检测

1.election *n.*选举
2.former *adj.*从前的
3.defeat *v.*打败
4.fanatical *adj.*狂热的
5.opponent *n.*反对者，对手
6.radical *adj.*激进的
7.progressive *adj.*进步的
8.suspicious *adj.*怀疑的
9.strike *n.*罢工
10.busman *n.*公共汽车司机
11.state *v.*正式提出，宣布
12.agreement *n.*协议
13.relieve *v.*减轻
14.pressure *n.*压力，麻烦
15.extent *n.*程度
16.volunteer *v.*自动提出，自愿
17.gratitude *n.*感激
18.press *n.*新闻界
19.object *v.*不赞成，反对
20.recent *adj.*新近的，近来的
21.retire *v.*退休，隐退
22.political *adj.*政治的
23.on duty 值班
24.entrance *n.*入口，门口
25.exactly *adv.*正确地，严密地
26.temper *n.*脾气，情绪
27.due to 由于，应归于
28.continue *v.*继续
29.general *adj.*普通的，全面的
30.condition *n.*条件，环境
31.private *adj.*私人的，私有的
32.university *n.*大学

口语造句

3；2；1；4；6；5；7

语法精练

1. an astronaut；2. gentleman；3. on computers；4. make time

5. to be；6. except；7. suffering；8. won；9. large；10. invited

11. was built；12. be planted；13. is sold；14. Neither, nor；

15. is spoken, them；16. are, used for；17. What is；18. What, used for

阅读理解

1.A；2.C；3.A；4.C；5.C；6.D；7.D；8.A；9.B

同步拓展训练 31

听写检测

1.inform *v.*告诉，通知
2.headmaster *n.*校长
3.contribute *v.*捐助，援助
4.gift *n.*礼物，赠品
5.album *n.*签名本，相册
6.patience *n.*耐心
7.encouragement *n.*鼓励
8.farewell *n.*告别
9.honour *n.*敬意
10.coincidence *n.*巧合
11.total *n.*总数
12.devote *v.*致力于
13.gardening *n.*园艺
14.hobby *n.*爱好，嗜好
15.swing *v.*转向
16.speedboat *n.*快艇
17.desperately *adv.*绝望地
18.companion *n.*同伙，伙伴
19.water ski 滑水
20.buoy *n.*浮标
21.dismay *n.*沮丧
22.tremendous *adj.*巨大的
23.petrol *n.*汽油
24.drift *v.*漂动，漂流
25.gently *adv.*缓慢地，轻轻地
26.mark *v.*标记
27.unwillingly *adv.*不情愿地
28.curious *adj.*好奇的
29.entirely *adv.*完全地，一概地
30.remark *v.*评论，谈及
31.steer *v.*驾驶
32.considerably *adv.*相当地

口语造句

2；1；4；6；3；5

语法精练

1. were, doing；2. was listening；3. were having；4. were dancing；

5. kidding；6. was studying；7. was having；8. was doing, was playing

9. outside；10. jumped；11. bedrooms；12. happened；13. surprised

14. anywhere；15. is wearing；16. around

阅读理解

1.A；2.B；3.C；4.B；5.C；6.D；7.D；8.D；9.B；10.D

同步拓展训练 32

听写检测

1.alibi *n.*不在犯罪现场
2.commit *v.*犯（罪）
3.inspector *n.*探长

4.employer *n.*雇主
5.confirm *v.*确认，证实
6.suggest *v.*提醒
7.truth *n.*真相
8.trap *v.*陷入，使陷入困境
9.surface *n.*地面，表面
10.explosive *n.*炸药
11.vibration *n.*震动
12.collapse *v.*坍塌
13.drill *v.*钻孔
14.capsule *n.*容器
15.layer *n.*层
16.beneath *prep.*在……之下
17.lower *v.*放下，降低
18.progress *v.*进展，进行
19.smoothly *adv.*顺利地
20.murder *n.*谋杀
21.travel *v.*旅行
22.later *adj.*更迟的
23.suppose *v.*推想，假设
24.unusual *adj.*不平常的
25.mine *n.*矿井
26.rescue *v.*救援，营救
27.prove *v.*证明，证实
28.cause *v.*引起，促成
29.therefore *adv.*因此，所以
30.intend *v.*想要，打算
31.meanwhile *n.*其间，其时
32.microphone *n.*麦克风

口语造句

7；1；4；2；5；3；6

语法精练

1. said；2. clearly；3. more interesting；4. his；5. runners；6. ourselves；7. health；8. diving
9. was washing；10. was；11. finished；12. watching；13. politely
14. are looking for；15. the cheapest；16. catch up with；17. by sea；18. never

阅读理解

1.C；2.A；3.C；4.D；5.D；6.C；7.A；8.C；9.A

同步拓展训练 33

听写检测

1.slip *n.*小错误
2.comedy *n.*喜剧
3.present *v.*演出
4.queue *v.*排队
5.dull *adj.*枯燥，无味
6.artiste *n.*艺人
7.advertiser *n.*报幕员
8.chip *n.*油煎土豆片
9.overfish *v.*过度捕捞
10.giant *adj.*巨大的
11.terrify *v.*吓，使恐怖
12.diver *n.*潜水员
13.oil rig 石油钻塔
14.wit *n.*理智，头脑
15.cage *n.*笼
16.shark *n.*鲨鱼
17.whale *n.*鲸
18.variety *n.*品种
19.cod *n.*鳕
20.skate *n.*鳐
21.factor *n.*因素
22.crew *n.*全体工作人员
23.local *adj.*地方的，当地的
24.unfortunately *adv.*不幸地
25.fail *v.*失败，不及格
26.disappointed *adj.*失望的
27.programme *n.*节目，程序
28.obviously *adv.*明显地
29.awkwardly *adv.*笨拙地
30.favourite *adj.*特别喜爱的
31.frequently *adv.*常常，频繁
32.frighten *v.*使惊吓

口语造句

5；1；6；3；2；4

语法精练

1. not to smoke；2. burning；3. have been；4. has gone；5. leaves；6. hasn’t heard；7. give；8. had；

9. traveling；10. best；11. No, is；12. give than, receive；13. without water；14. where, lives；15. how many, there are

阅读理解

1.T；2.F；3.T；4.T；5.F

同步拓展训练 34

听写检测

1.balloon *n.*气球
2.royal *adj.*皇家
3.spy *v.*侦察
4.track *n.*轨迹，踪迹
5.binoculars *n.*望远镜
6.fast *adv.*熟（睡）
7.ladder *n.*梯子
8.shed *n.*棚子
9.sarcastic *adj.*讽刺的，讥笑的
10.tone *n.*语气，腔调
11.pilot *n.*飞行员
12.inform *v.*通知，告诉
13.explain *v.*解释
14.mystery *n.*神秘
15.control *v.*支配，控制
16.aircraft *n.*飞行器
17.object *n.*物体，目标
18.afterwards *adv.*后来
19.photograph *n.*照片
20.descend *v.*下来，下降
21.contain *v.*包含
22.ring *v.*按铃
23.doorbell *n.*门铃
24.asleep *adj.*睡着的，睡熟的
25.towards *prep.*向，朝
26.bedroom *n.*卧室
27.fall off 下降，跌落
28.immediately *adv.*立刻，马上
29.interrupt *v.*打断，妨碍
30.prefer *v.*更喜欢，宁愿
31.forget *v.*忘记
32.wake up 醒来

口语造句

4；1；5；7；2；3；6

语法精练

1. Frenchmen；2. produced；3. cutting；4. locked；5. spoken
6. interesting；7. surprised；8. built；9. drinking；10.entrance
11. delicious；12. whether；13. farther(far)；14. diving；15. try our best
16. in a month；17. on the Internet；18. sight-seeing

阅读理解

1.C；2.A；3.B；4.C；5.A；6.A；7.C；8.D；9.B；10.C

同步拓展训练 35

听写检测

1.noble *adj.*高尚的，壮丽的
2.monument *n.*纪念碑
3.statue *n.*雕像
4.liberty *n.*自由
5.present *v.*赠送
6.sculptor *n.*雕刻家
7.actual *adj.*实际的，真实的
8.copper *n.*铜
9.support *v.*支持，支撑
10.framework *n.*构架，框架
11.transport *v.*运送
12.site *n.*场地
13.pedestal *n.*底座
14.instruct *v.*指导，传授
15.reluctant *adj.*勉强的，不愿意的
16.weight *n.*重物
17.underwater *adj.*水下的

18.tricycle *n.*三轮车
19.compete *v.*比赛，对抗
20.yard *n.*码
21.gasp *v.*喘气
22.design *v.*设计，计划
23.figure *n.*外形，轮廓
24.metal *n.*金属
25.especially *adv.*特别，尤其
26.construct *v.*建造，构造
27.entrance *n.*入口，门口
28.erect *v.*使竖立
29.officially *adv.*正式
30.symbol *n.*符号，象征
31.harbour *n.*港口
32.experiment *n.*试验

口语造句

2；1；5；7；3；8；4；6

语法精练

1. wide；2. times；3. Planting；4. millions；5. harder
6. third；7. biggest；8. often；9. more careful；10. me
11. Neither,nor；12. must, be, handed；13. What, is, used
14. was, bought；15. How, long；16. No, needn't
17. told, not, to,be；18. if, would,like；19. hasn't
20. aren't, any

阅读理解

1.A；2.D；3.C；4.C；5.D；6.D；7.A；8.B；9.C；10.D

同步拓展训练 36

听写检测

1.fantasy *n.*幻想故事
2.ambassador *n.*大使
3.frightful *adj.*可怕的，令人吃惊的
4.fire extinguisher 灭火器
5.drily *adv.*冷淡地，枯燥无味地
6.embassy *n.*大使馆
7.heaven *n.*天，天堂
8.basement *n.*地下室
9.definitely *adv.*肯定地
10.post *v.*派任
11.shot *n.*子弹
12.festival *n.*节日
13.lantern *n.*灯笼
14.spectacle *n.*景象，壮观，场面
15.shock *n.*打击
16.pale *adj.*苍白的，无力的
17.mess *n.*混乱，脏乱
18.exclaim *v.*呼喊，惊叫
19.notice *v.*注意到
20.hole *n.*洞，孔
21.accurate *adj.*正确的，精确的
22.cheerful *adj.*愉快的，高兴的
23.occasion *n.*机会，场合
24.welcome *v.*欢迎
25.journey *n.*旅行，旅程
26.throw *v.*投，掷
27.consider *v.*考虑，照顾
28.unlucky *adj.*不幸的
29.drift *v.*漂流
30.guide *v.*指导，带领
31.moving *adj.*感人的
32.crowd *n.*人群

口语造句

6；1；5；2；4；3

语法精练

1. I think yon should go to college.
2. He is going to travel around the world.

3. Mr. Li made a living by teaching three years ago.
4. If you take a bus to the party,you will be late.
5. Don't laugh at the people who are in trouble.
6. I have been practising the piano since 10:30.
7. Maria has been running for 15 minutes.
8. He has known Mary since last year.
9. Peter has been studying Chinese since he was six years old.
10. We have run out of our savings.
11. knocking at；12. be repaired；13. is singing；14. has taught
15. were written；16. Do, like；17. bought；18. had left；19. joined
20. was working

阅读理解

1. He was born.
2.He met John and formed a band together.
3. He helped to form the "Beatles".
4. He got married.
5. The band broke up.